EPIC

BESTSELLING AUTHOR
TRUDY STILES

SINS

EPIC FAIL SERIES

Cover Art by Sarah Hansen of Okay Creations
Editing by Murphy Rae of Indie Solutions
Interior Design and Formatting by Elaine York of Allusion Graphics, LLC/Publishing & Book Formatting

Content Warning: This book is not suitable for young readers. It is intended for mature adults only (18+). It contains strong language, adult/sexual situations and potential trigger subject matter.

To contact Trudy:
Email: authortrudystiles@gmail.com
Facebook: http://www.facebook.com/authortrudystiles
Instagram: https://instagram.com/trudystiles/
Website: www.trudystiles.com
Goodreads: http://www.goodreads.com/trudy_stiles
Twitter: @trudystiles
Amazon: http://www.amazon.com/Trudy-Stiles/e/
B00H3O0OJ8

Editorial Reviews

Trudy Stiles' first three novels, Dear Emily, Dear Tabitha, and Dear Juliet received stunning praise from the indie community. Read these books to enhance your reading experience with Epic Sins and see what these incredible bloggers, reviewers and authors all saw in Trudy's work.

Dear Emily Reviews:

Natasha Tomic, Natasha is a Book Junkie: "This book has the power of touching the reader so deeply by giving us unique and very precious insight into the world of child adoption, from both viewpoints of the birth mother as well as the adoptive parents. I walked away at the end of this book feeling like my heart had grown tenfold, overflowing with so many emotions, and desperately hoping that fiction, in this case, had found its roots in real life."

Mollie Kay Harper, Tough Critic Book Reviews: "I was blown away by the story's originality. I was blown away by the romance and passion. I was blown away by the heartache and pain. I was blown away that I whole heartedly invested my emotions into the lives of these two women."

Gitte & Jenny, Totally Booked: "What a truly breath-taking, compelling and beautifully stirring debut from Trudy Stiles. The writing was truly beautiful and the story which shows the past as well as the present was so raw and gripping my heart was so full of cracks by the time I'd finished."

Chris' Book Blog Emporium: "I love when a book can grip you right from the first few pages, pull you in and not let you go until the very last page. Trudy has written a page turner. Her debut novel knocked my socks off and she is definitely an author to check out."

Nic Farrell, Flirty and Dirty Book Blog: "I'm not sure what I expected when I started Dear Emily by Trudy Stiles but one thing is for sure, I had no idea how emotional of a read it would be. Not your fluffy and mushy love story, Dear Emily was so much more."

Becca Manuel, Becca the Bibliophile: "It's a love story that is so profound and yet it is hardly ever spoken of. It's the story of two women, torn apart by life that had left them scarred and a bond that they will forever share in a little girl neither have met yet – Emily."

Rebecca Shea, USA Today Bestselling Author: "When a book leaves you thinking about it days later – that's a good thing. This was a 4.5 star before because it was good, really good…as in amazing. It's now a 5 star because it did something to me…it left me wanting more – needing more. That is the sign of a 5-star amazing book."

Jen Skewes, Three Chicks and Their Books: "I am not even sure that I can begin to express just how much I loved this book and how truly amazing and touching it was. Dear Emily is by far one of my favorite books this year. It is one of those books that will stay with you."

Jesey Newman, Scmhexy Girls Book Blog: "Dear Emily is a beautiful story about love, lust, family and the tragedies endured by Carly and Tabitha, our leading ladies. Trudy Stiles has woven the lives of these women both past and present, in such an amazing way."

Amanda Maxlyn, author of "What's Left of Me": "There are books that will pull you along as you read, and then there are books that will literally pull you into the story as you read. Dear Emily is the book that will suck you in with the first sentence and not let you go until the last word. Trudy Stiles has a gift. She created a beautiful, yet pained world of two strangers that become connected in the most stunning way."

JJ Rossum, author of "Thou Shalt Not": "Well, Ms. Stiles, you really knocked this one out of the park. I loved it. Unique story line, characters you could root for and emotions you could really feel."

Kelly, Perusing Princesses Book Blog: "Trudy Stiles has entered the indie writers world with an impressive boo – get ready for the shockwaves to hit, because this is one debut you do not want to miss!"

Kathryn Perez, author of "Therapy": "With so many books out there today, it's hard to find one that isn't just a cookie cutter version of the next. I personally enjoy books that are more than a "surface" read. I like to walk away from it having gained a message. I like to feel the story and characters. Trudy Stiles does just that with this book. She conveys with her writing a beautiful story that grips you, touches you and stays with you."

Tiffany Marie, Everything Marie Book Blog: "The entire story will leave you in tears and provoke strong emotions from you. It is very touching and so personal, it's hard not to love this book. For a debut novel, this book really hit the mark."

Dee McGee, Booze, Bookz and Bad Boyz: "I absolutely loved Dear Emily. Trudy Stiles debut novel impresses the heck out of me. She took what could have been a straight forward dark, tragic plot and turned it into a beautiful story about coming to terms with adversity."

Virginia, Love N Books: "Trudy's writing is detailed, emotional and beautiful. She tugs at your emotions and makes you feel as if you know these characters. You can't help but feel for these broken women and wish their heartache would end and they would find happiness."

Dear Tabitha Reviews:

Natasha Tomic, Natasha is a Book Junkie: "Confession time. I was terrified of this book. Literally, breaking out in a cold sweat the moment I decided to read it. This is truly a book like no other. This story is told with honesty and heart, making the reader feel so many different emotions page after page, but most of all the author's reverence for her own characters. I walked away feeling like every half-empty glass in my life was suddenly full to the rim, thankful for this journey and determined to read every word this author ever decides to write.

Robin Segnitz, Hesperia Loves Books: "Dear Tabitha is a powerful story of healing, love an family. I felt a range of intense emotions while reading including anger, rage, sadness, love and joy. I found Dear Tabitha absolutely satisfying and the best work yet for Trudy Stiles. Five stars for Dear Tabitha!"

The Danish Bookaholic: "Ms. Stiles has a wonderful way with words, and I find it difficult to fully express how uch I love this book. Every single page moved me, sometimes to laughter, sometimes to tears. My heart was hurting so much for both Tabitha and Alex, and my romantic soul could not stop hoping and praying that, despite Tabitha's silence, they would somehow find their way back to each other again.

Annie Gabor, All is Read: "Trudy is an amazing storyteller who easily makes her characters become so realistic. You will feel every emotion they feel, the frustration that boils up and puts you on the edge of your seat, the heartbreak, forgiveness and love.

Beth, The Indie Bookshelf: "This is a great emotional read. Ms. Stiles makes you feel, laugh, cry and hope. Sometimes hope is the most dangerous emotion."

LL Collins, Bestselling Author: "Trudy Stiles is an amazing storyteller, reaching in a gripping your heart right from the get go. She's an author to watch, and I'll be sure to read anything she writes."

Jesey, Schmexy Girls Book Blog: "This is a journey that will tear your heart out. The past, the present, and the future all come together beautifully to bring this story to an end."

Sarah Griffin, Books to Breathe: "I will leave you with this: the emotions displayed between Alex and Tabitha, when they allowed their walls to crumble and their hearts to open, were enough to make the darkest of hearts smile. Just know this, it wrecked me, completely and utterly wrecked me, and I'm a better person for it."

Dee McGee: "Trudy Stiles writing continues to keep me enthralled. Dear Tabitha is a heart-wrenching, deeply emotional story about two people overcoming a turbulent past and trying to find themselves…and love."

Dear Juliet Reviews:

Amanda Maxlyn, Bestselling Author of What's Left of Me and What's Left of Us: "There's a difference with just simply writing a story and writing a story with real, powerful emotion that will stay with you forever. Trudy Stiles is one of those writers that has the ability to bring words to life. When you read a Trudy Stiles book you're not just reading a story about two characters and their path to finding peace and happiness in life, you're reading a story about raw heartache and the real struggles in life that shapes and molds characters into strong individuals who you'll connect and root for throughout the entire novel. She creates a world that will leave you speechless and content. It's a world that you'll fall in love with beyond your own control and won't want to let go."

Becca Manuel, Becca the Bibliophile: "This book encompasses love, friendship, heartache and fate. The ending totally blew me away and I never saw that coming at all. But it is a surprise that helps everyone finally find some peace. I adore this series and this author to bits and pieces. A must read and one that will forever have a little piece of my heart."

Virginia Carey: "Dear Juliet is beautiful. Just beautiful. I am seriously in love with this book, Trudy's writing and the entire series. Trudy writes about real life. And I love it. Life isn't always easy but we learn, we grow and we continue to live. And her characters and their experiences reflect all that. Dear Juliet is the perfect conclusion to an amazing series. All of the books tie so perfectly together. And I was disappointed to see it end."

Elizabeth, Perusing Princesses: "Trudy grabs a hold of your heart and soul and just wrings it out with every emotion to the very last drop with this beautifully heart wrenching story of Juliet and Seth.

She takes you on an incredible journey that starts on the very day that Juliet was born, and through her school years, young adult and grown adult. She includes heartwarming and soul crushing scenes that leave you breathless."

Juliana Cabrera: "Trudy's writing is always heartfelt, thought-provoking ride on your emotional rollercoaster. I love every second of it."

Kellie Montgomery, Eye Candy Bookstore: "I really loved this book. While Dear Emily will always be my favorite and hold the most special place in my heart, this one touched some deep emotional places and I adored the bond that Juliet and Seth had- it was timeless and once in a lifetime. Five stars as always. One of my favorite series of all time."

Jesey Newman, Schmexy Girl Book Blog: "Dear Juliet…another AMAZING book to add to the Forever Family Series by Trudy Stiles. It's no secret that this series is on my must reads list. It's also no secret that I am not (well…WAS not) a fan of Seth's. After reading this book I realize that it is so easy to judge one's character when you don't have all the facts. There is so much more to him than what we saw in Dear Emily and Dear Tabitha. I am now 100% #TeamSeth!!!"

Beth O'Gwynn Rustenhaven, The Indie Bookshelf: "So Many Feels. I am out of emotions. This last in the Forever Family Series will make you reevaluate how you felt about previous characters. Juliet should be a confident well adjusted young lady. She has a family that loves her. That wants her. But her self-confidence is in the dumpster thanks to overheard conversations and lingering doubt about her worth. Seth has every reason to be skeptical of families. His is the pits. It colors his relationships but not his hope. He is forever hopeful. Even if that hope is buried deep down."

I Heart Books: "How do I say this without sounding totally cheesy? Trudy Stiles has cemented herself as one of the big dogs in the world of indie authors with this one. Just amazing. Perfect ending to the series. Perfect way for things to come full circle. Fantastic."

Tabby, Tantalizing Reviews: "Trudy Stiles wrote a series where not one but all the characters involved will forever hold a special place in my heart. I so much enjoyed experiencing every heartbreak and triumph that these characters went through."

Robin Segnitz: "Dear Juliet is about lifelong friendship. Healing. Redemption. It's a story about best friends who become lovers. It's an emotional story. There were times the story was very sad, and I really struggled with what Seth and Juliet were experiencing. Please follow these characters through the years, and I promise you will be rewarded. I finished this novel with a huge smile on my face!"

T Tbird London: "I have always loved that Trudy's books are based on adoption. The beauty and miracle of adoption is shown at all angles with her series, but she also shows the heart break and emotion that comes along with such a choice. I was constantly reminded in Dear Juliet how our choices as parents will affect our children at some point. Our response to loss, be it death or abandonment will leave either a lasting scar or a positive message with our children. This is what Juliet found out. Being loved by her adoptive parents was vital, but feeling like the one person who was supposed to love and want you didn't, never let her freely be the woman she was meant to be."

Jade, Blushing Babes Up All Night: "Excellent Job Trudy! The writing of this beauty was completely worth it because you NAILED IT! You twisted my perceptions of characters I previously met and made me like them... love them even. BEAUTIFUL!"

Synopsis

This book is not suitable for young readers. It is intended for mature adults only (18+). It contains strong language, adult/ sexual situations and potential trigger subject matter.

Garrett Armstrong, the lead guitarist of Epic Fail, womanizer and not-so-nice guy, leaves a trail of women in his wake. A recent one-night stand wreaks havoc and turns his present completely upside down. He's faced with a reality that he never expected. Never wanted.

Samantha Weston can't escape the black cloud that follows her. She suffered an unspeakable loss as a teenager and has been climbing uphill ever since. As soon as her life starts to become manageable, she's slammed with another tragic event, forcing her to abandon the only thing in life that she cherishes.

A heartbreaking situation throws this unlikely pair together. They're forced to face things that seem impossible. Can Sam get past the demons that haunt her? Can Garrett accept a fate he swore to avoid at all costs?

Can they conquer the sins that are poised to destroy them, or will they become an Epic Fail?

Epic Sins is the first book of the Epic Fail series, a spinoff of The Forever Family series.

Reading The Forever Family series is not required as these are all spin-off/standalone novels, but it may enhance your experience.

Music Inspiration

Every book of mine plays out to a soundtrack in my head. This book was written while listening to Marilyn Manson and Royal Blood on constant repeat.

DEDICATION

For my son.
Your smile will always be my strength.
I will do anything to make sure it's always bright.
I love you.

PROLOGUE

Sam
Past
Villanova, Pennsylvania
Age 16

"SAMANTHA, HONEY, ARE YOU IN HERE?" Aunt Peggy's voice is muffled through the closed door. I pull the covers over my head and hold my breath, just like I did when I was a kid. The scent of dryer sheets fills my nose, bringing me back to reality. I'm in the guest room of my aunt's house, trying to hide from everyone, from everything. There are strangers all over her house, and I'm terrified to hear anything they have to say. The doorknob rattles and I sink deeper into the bed, hoping that I'm invisible to her. To the world.

"Sam?" Her voice is clearer, closer. The bed sinks beneath her weight and I feel her warm hand through the comforter. She rubs my leg and I whimper as I hear her voice shake. "I'm here for you. We're going to get through this."

I suck in all available air around me as my tears begin to soak through the sheets. "I can't—I just can't," I manage to say while turning onto my side, still covered completely.

"I know how hard this is for you. How senseless and difficult it is to understand." She pauses and allows her sobs to come freely. "It's wrong and I'm mad. Angry, goddammit." I tense as the curse word flies from her mouth. Aunt Peggy has never raised her voice around me, and I certainly have never heard her use profanity. "How that monster ever deserved to breathe the same air as us, as *them*, I will never comprehend." She inhales deeply and her voice becomes more controlled, calm. "We're going to get through this. *They* would want you to live. To be happy."

My heart races; sweat from my temples rolls down my cheeks and mixes with my tears. I'm teeming with anger. Hate. I bolt up, tossing the covers off of me. "Be happy? How the hell are we supposed to *ever* be happy again? They're gone! Gone! *He* took them from us." Aunt Peggy's eyes widen and her already pale face turns ashen. She looks confused, then scared. "He took away my parents. My home. *Everything*." I'm practically screaming as I clench the comforter in my fists.

Voices from the hallway come closer, and soon Detective Michaels' shadow fills the room. "Ms. Weston," he addresses my aunt. "I'm so sorry to interrupt. Do you have a minute? We have a few more questions for you." Despite his ominous presence, his eyes seem kind. "Is that alright?" I swallow the bile that has risen and feel it burn as I force it back down my throat. *What else could he possibly want to know?*

Aunt Peggy's eyes find mine and her face softens. "I'll be right outside, okay? I won't be far." I nod and look away, finding a smudge on the wall to hold my focus. The smudge begins to blur as tears once again fill my eyes, threatening to spill onto my cheeks. I want these people away from us. I can't bear to hear them repeat the events that happened this morning. The events that destroyed my family.

She reluctantly stands up and follows the detective into the hallway and down the stairs. Detective Michaels's voice is anything but quiet and discreet. "We're trying to understand how he was able to leave the treatment facility. There are no witnesses, and we're scouring through hours of surveillance footage."

"I don't understand. Wasn't there security? What kind of place was this?" Aunt Peggy asks, anger rising once again in her tone. "And what makes you think I could possibly have any information about this?"

"He admitted himself into the rehab center. He was there of his own accord. While there was security, it was light. What we're trying to figure out is what caused him to snap and why he chose to go to your brother's house. Are you sure you've never heard your brother or sister-in-law mention his name?"

"I'd like to know the same thing, Detective. I promise you, my brother and his wife did not know this man," she hisses.

I find myself standing in the open doorway, straining to listen to their conversation from downstairs. *I don't want to know. I don't want to know.* My feet pay no attention to the mantra I repeat in my head, and my legs shake as I follow their voices. I quietly walk down the stairs and peer into the living room, hoping I'm still invisible. *Let this be a dream. I don't want to know. I don't want to know.*

"Detective Michaels," a new voice echoes from the kitchen. "We have the nine-one-one call ready." *Oh no.*

No. No. No.

As much as I want to turn and run back up to the bedroom, I can't.

Papers rustle and several people move quickly through the living room into the kitchen, filling the space around the large center island where a laptop computer sits. My aunt stands behind them, frozen in place, grasping one of the stools at the counter, knuckles white.

No. No. NO.

"Nine-one-one, what's your emergency?"

"Help us! Help us, please! He's in the house!" A crushing pain tears through my chest as I listen to my mother's desperate screams.

"Hang up that phone. I just need some help." An unknown voice is heard in the background. It sounds shaky. Desperate. That's not my father. It must be him. Bile once again rises in my throat.

"Stay away from me!" my mother frantically yells.

"Ma'am, we're tracing your location now. We'll be sending help as soon as possible. Please stay on the line and try to get away from the intruder. Get into a room and lock the door." The operator sounds calm as I hear her talking on another line with a dispatcher, giving him directions.

"No! Please don't do anything else to him! He's already hurt. Please don't hurt him anymore!" She's pleading, begging with the stranger. The monster. Who is she talking about? Who's hurt?

"I didn't mean to hurt him." The man's voice is distressed. *"I didn't think I hit him that hard. Please, I just need some medication. Do you have anything here? Oxy? Vicodin? Benzos? Anything?"*

"I don't know what any of that is! No! I have none of that!"

"Ma'am, tell him that you'll check your medicine cabinet upstairs. Go quickly and lock yourself in. Help is on the way. Is there anyone else in the house with you?" The operator gives her clear instructions and I hear my mother's breathing hitch.

"Just my husband. My daughter is at school." She pauses and says calmly, *"I'm four months pregnant."* I close my eyes as tears stream down my cheeks.

"*Hang up the phone!*" the lunatic screams at my mother and I hold my breath.

"*Wait!*" she says desperately and I hear the lie form in her voice before the words come out of her mouth. "*I-I think I have some of those pills upstairs…in my medicine cabinet.*"

"*Don't lie to me!*" he yells.

"*What are you doing?*" My mother's voice becomes frantic and it sounds like the phone fumbles in her hand. "*Why are you doing that?*" Her voice is strained. "*Stop that!*"

"*Insurance,*" he says calmly, sounding crazy and sadistic at the same time. "*If you do anything stupid, we all go up in flames. You don't want that—do you?*"

"*You're crazy!*" She's yelling at him, and it sounds like she's trying to get away. "*Ben, wake up! Wake up!*" She screams my father's name in a desperate attempt to get him to respond to her.

"*Make it stop,*" the man yells and pleads. "*Make it stop.*" He's moaning and my mother holds her breath.

"*Turn off the gas, please. You don't want to hurt anyone,*" my mother begs him as the man moans louder.

"*Ma'am, get out of the room now. Do you hear me? Run,*" the operator calmly but firmly says to my mother.

"*Ben! Wake up, please!*" Her voice sounds farther away, like she dropped the phone on the floor. Her cries become incoherent. She's screaming and sobbing. "*Ben!*"

"*Stop. I told you to stop. Make it stop!*" the man yells again, and I suddenly hear my mother gasp.

Then nothing.

Nothing.

"*Ma'am?*" the operator asks. I then hear her say to someone off in the distance, "*The line has been cut off.*"

A few moments later.

"Explosion reported in a subdivision off of Route Three-Thirty-Two. All units in the area, respond immediately."

I sink to the floor, holding my breath, hoping to hear my mother's voice one more time.

Nothing.

When my legs give out, I hit the floor with a thud and all six heads in the kitchen turn to look at me, eyes wide and worried. Sad and full of pity.

"Sam!" My aunt gasps as she rushes toward me.

"Somebody get some water." Detective Michaels' voice is distorted, and his face blurs as I try to focus.

"Sam, stay with us, okay?" Aunt Peggy's voice is soothing, and I feel her cradling my head in her lap. I throw up all over her as I close my eyes.

I don't want to know.

I didn't want to know.

Please let this be a dream.

It has to be a dream.

I try to picture the day as any other day. If I try hard enough, maybe I'll wake up from this awful nightmare. I close my eyes and see my mom in the kitchen, planning a quiet dinner at home after a hectic day. She's smiling and doing what she loves. My father is at her side, helping prepare my birthday meal. They're in love. Happy. Perfect.

And then they are gone.

Boom.

"GARRETT, DINNER'S READY," my mother calls from downstairs. I kick over the Lego tower that I was almost done building, watching the pieces fly all around my room. Hundreds of colorful Lego bricks spread across my floor and get stuck in places I know I won't be able to reach.

"Stupid Legos," I say and stomp down the stairs.

I climb up onto a stool and rest my elbows on the center island while my mother fills the dinner plate in front of me. Roasted chicken, mashed potatoes and cauliflower. The only thing I like on this plate is the chicken, and I pick at the skin before she's finished putting the rest of the food on my plate.

"Garrett, can you be patient?" my mother scolds me, but gently.

"Yes, Mom."

When she's finished, she fills her own plate with food and covers everything else with tin foil. I don't know why she's doing this; Dad never comes home for dinner. In fact, I haven't seen him in over a week.

She smiles at me and takes a clean plate and utensils out of the cabinet and drawer, setting them neatly next to the warming leftovers.

She pulls her stool around the other side of the island and sits across from me.

"How was school today?" she asks. The same question she asks every single night.

"It was fine."

I pull the remaining skin off the chicken and drag it through the pile of ketchup on my plate, tossing it into my mouth. "Chicken's good, Mom."

"Thank you, sweetie, I know it's your favorite."

I finish the chicken and swirl the cauliflower into the mashed potatoes. She's watching me mess with my food, so she knows I'm not eating it. "Can I be done?" I ask.

"You didn't eat any of your vegetables. Have at least two pieces of cauliflower and four spoonfuls of potatoes."

Every night she tries to get me to eat more, especially things that I don't like. She's trying to make a deal with me. "How about one and three?" I say.

"No, Garrett, eat what you're told."

"Okay, Mom," I whine.

We both jump when the laundry room door flies open. My father comes in, throwing his briefcase on the floor in the corner of the kitchen.

"Dad!" I say excitedly. I can't believe he's home.

He says something I can't hear and my mother pushes her plate away. She quickly grabs his clean plate and covered meal. "John, thank goodness you're home."

He shoots her a look that makes me move around in my seat. He doesn't look like my dad. He's a mess and his shirt is untucked.

"I'll eat later, Claire," he responds and walks past us through the kitchen and into the den. He smells like smoke.

My mother moves his food back to the top of the stove so it can stay warm. Her lips are tight and her eyes look sad.

I finish everything on my plate, hoping to bring a smile to my mother's face. She doesn't notice and takes my empty plate, putting it directly into the dishwasher.

Behind us, in the den, drawers are opening and closing loudly. I hear my father saying bad words beneath his breath.

"Claire, where's the box I had under the entertainment center?" he calls out angrily.

"I—I don't know what you're talking about," my mother responds. She looks worried.

"Goddammit, Claire!" he screams and tears through magazines and books, throwing everything to the floor. "Where are my things?" He's making a giant mess.

"John, I don't know!" my mother yells back.

She reaches for my hand and leads me to the stairs. "Garrett, go to your room. Close your door and watch some television." She kisses my cheek and turns toward the den.

Worried, I walk up the stairs. Loud banging comes from downstairs and my father sounds really angry. I close my door like my mom told me.

I suddenly hear loud noises coming from outside my door. It sounds like my father is running up the stairs. "John, where are you going?" My mother's voice trails behind him and now they're in the hallway.

His voice becomes calmer and almost sweeter. "Where's my money? Please tell me you have that box."

"How much do you owe this time?" she asks nervously.

"It doesn't matter," he says, and I wonder what they're talking about.

"John, we can't keep living like this. The last time you owed them money, they took our car." *Who took our car? I don't remember that.*

"I owe them thirty-five thousand," he says, and my mother lets out a loud gasp.

"How?" she asks.

"The Rutgers game. I thought they would cover the spread. I had so much riding on that game. It would have paid off our debts. We would have had money in the bank for the first time in years." He sounds upset and my mother starts to cry.

"Thirty-five thousand dollars. John, what the hell were you thinking? We could get help. My parents can help us out. Why are you throwing away our future?"

"If I don't find that box, we may not have a future, Claire. They threatened to do some major damage this time if I can't come up with the money."

"What do you mean?" she asks, and she sounds really upset. I think she's scared. My heart jumps into my throat and is beating wildly.

"They said that you and Garrett would pay if I couldn't."

"Oh my God." I hear her rush down the hall, into their bedroom, and my father follows. *What could happen to us? What would we pay with?*

"Daddy? It's Claire." She must be on the phone. *What's going on?*

I can barely hear her voice now, like she's far away. About ten minutes later, the door flies open and my father's voice is strained. "Don't do this, Claire. Please. It's all getting taken care of. Your parents are helping. Our lives can go back to normal now." He's pleading with her.

"My father will meet you at the diner in thirty minutes with a check to pay off these thugs. After that, I never want to see you in our home again. You will not put our lives in danger, and I refuse to allow our son to be used as a pawn. It's over, John. Get out of my house."

"Claire." His voice begins to shake. "I'm sorry," he says, and I hear my mom start to cry.

"No you're not. This is the third time we've been in this same situation except now you've brought our family into it. Never again. Leave now. Daddy's expecting you soon. Take what you want because the rest of your things will be in the trash tomorrow."

She opens my door and I see my father standing in the hallway. I raise my hand slowly and wave goodbye.

She shuts the door and pulls me against her chest. "I'm sorry you heard that, honey. Everything's going to be okay. I promise."

I hear the front door close and his car start. My father's gone and I don't think he's ever coming home.

"What were you building?" she asks. She's happy now and she's smiling. Her eyes look puffy, though.

"A big tower, but it was crooked. I didn't like it."

"I can see that." She laughs and sits down on the floor next to me. "You know, I played with Legos when I was your age and I built some of the greatest towers ever." She takes a large base piece and begins building a solid foundation. "Pass those red ones over to me."

She quickly starts to add layer after colorful layer. The tower is almost as tall as I am before I know it. It's wider at the bottom and smaller at the top. "That's pretty cool, Mom."

"It's perfectly balanced, see?" She leans back. I think she likes her tower.

I take one of the Lego guys and stand him on the top. "Look! A super hero," I say, and I can hear her taking deep, calming breaths.

"Mom, am I going to see Daddy again?" I ask, afraid of the answer.

"I don't know, Garrett. I hope so. Now, where's that Lego Millennium Falcon you got for your birthday?" She looks around the room, trying to find it.

"In my closet," I say and jump up, excited. I find it on the shelf and bring it back to her. I almost knock over the tower, but she grabs it before it can fall over. She moves it against my bookcase and it looks like it will be okay.

"I've always wanted to do this one. They didn't have it when I was your age. Legos back then were a bit simpler."

"I guess I'm lucky then, huh?" I say and shrug my shoulders. I wonder what it was like back when my mom was a little girl. I can't imagine her playing Legos. I only picture dolls and flowers. "Didn't you have tea parties and stuff back then?"

She says softly, "I was a bit of a tomboy. I played sports with my brothers and didn't have too much time for dolls." She has four brothers who are my uncles. They're all cool, but I barely see them because they live in North Carolina. I have like ten cousins too that I hardly ever see.

"Can I be Darth Vader?" I ask her when we dump the contents of the box onto my rug.

"You can be anything you want, Garrett." She rubs the back of my head and pulls me against her for a hug. "And I mean that for the rest of your life. You know I'll support you in anything you want to do," she says.

"I want to be a garbage man. It's so cool that they get to drive a big truck!" I exclaim, and Mom laughs.

"That sounds like it would be a lot of fun." She smiles and begins to separate the bags of Legos. She lines them up in number order.

"Why don't we try to put together the first two bags tonight, and we'll work on the rest of it throughout the week."

I nod. "Yeah, this could take a while and it's already dark outside."

She rips open the first bag and dumps out the pieces. I immediately find the figures and assemble Darth Vader, Princess Leia, and Han Solo. There are a few Storm Troopers too.

Mom smiles as she begins to put together the pieces that will make up the Millennium Falcon. I play-fight with the figures. Darth Vader tries to beat up Han Solo, but Princess Leia kicks his butt.

I really enjoy these times with my mom. I just wish my dad could be here too.

Hopefully once those people get their money, he can come home, just like he said.

CHAPTER 2

Sam
Past
Villanova, Pennsylvania
Age 7

"DADDY, LOOK!" I SCREAM as I'm about to jump into the deep end of the pool. He waves and his smile is huge. I know I'm going to make him so proud by finally being brave.

My feet hit the cool water first and I feel it rush through my toes and up my legs. I squeeze my nose closed as tight as I can, suck in lots of air and hold my breath. My heart is pounding as the rest of my body sinks below the surface. I kick my legs as fast as I can, trying to reach the sunlight through the water. The muffled sound of clapping hands becomes louder as my head pops out of the water and I take huge gulps of air.

"Great pencil dive, Sam!" Daddy yells from the porch. He's surrounded by his friends from work. We're having a party to celebrate his secretary's retirement, and everyone loves her so much, they wanted to come and share this special day with her. Lucy is super sweet and she says she's going to travel the world with her husband. She's old, like fifty or sixty. I don't know why she waited so long to follow her dream of seeing things like the

Eiffel Tower and the Tower of London. Lots of towers. Kind of seems boring.

Her granddaughter, Cassie, is my age and she's here too. She's a really good swimmer and taught me how to jump into the deep end. Today's the first day that I'm not wearing my swimmies.

"Woo-hoo!" Cassie says from the diving board. "It's my turn now!"

My heart is beating fast as I try to paddle to the shallow end. My arms feel really heavy and it's hard to keep my head above the water. My toes scrape along the bottom of the pool that is the slope leading to shallower water. *I'm almost there.*

"Sam, please stay in the shallow end when you don't have your swimmies on," my mother calls from the stairs. As soon as my feet are firmly planted on the flat surface of the shallow end, I turn and smile. "I'm okay, Mommy. See!" I throw my hands up in the air, splashing water around me. She smiles as she shakes her head and turns to pass a tray of food to one of Daddy's friends from work.

"Cannonball!" Cassie yells from the diving board, pulling her knees to her chest. She lands in the water and doesn't even have to hold her nose. Her eyes are open huge and she's laughing as her face disappears beneath the waves that she just made. She doesn't come up right away and I'm suddenly worried. Before I can say another word, I feel a cool hand wrap around my ankle and I'm underwater again, flailing and laughing.

We both surface while I cough out the water I just swallowed. "Hey! No fair. And no playing rough or your grandma will be down here before you know it," I say to her as she pulls herself onto a large raft. It's Mommy's raft and is usually off limits to kids, but she's busy with Daddy's friends and probably won't notice. Cassie paddles over toward me and I climb on next to her.

Our shoulders are touching on the raft. It's really hot.

"I like your pool," she says, covering her eyes with her arm.

"Thanks," I say, doing the same with my own arm.

Cassie giggles and kicks her foot in the water, spraying it all over us.

"My dad is sad that your grandma isn't going to work for him anymore. He keeps saying he doesn't know what he's going to do without Lucy," I say and see Lucy and Mommy looking out from the deck.

"I know, Grammy is pretty sad, but she and Grampy have been planning their retirement for a long time. They said I can come on a road trip with them in their RV. I think they're going to take me to Florida next summer and maybe to Maine."

"I'm going to Disney World next month for my birthday," I say and think about all of the fun things we're going to do there.

"Really? Oh, I wish I could come!" Cassie whines and splashes me again. I laugh and try to shield my face from the cold water from the pool.

"I bet you'll go there when your grandparents take you next summer."

"Yeah, maybe." She sighs.

We float quietly around the pool for a while. I shiver when a breeze tickles my feet. "Goosebumps!" Cassie screeches and rolls off the raft with a splash. I'm about to do the same when I notice we've floated into the deep end. "C'mon in, it's so much warmer than the air." She dives and disappears under the water.

I look up at the deck and my parents aren't there. I see a lot of people that Daddy works with. I lean a little on the raft and see the deep water below me. Shadows from the trees make it look deeper than it really is. Cassie is now sitting all the way across the pool on the stairs and tosses her head back to sun her face. *I can do this.*

I lean a little further so I can easily slide off the raft when suddenly I'm under and water fills my mouth and nose. Panic sets in and I kick my feet hard, but I'm not moving. I try to yell when my head pops out of the water, but I can't, and I go under again. My screams are muffled by the water and my arms are flailing around me. I feel like I'm attached to something—my bathing suit is tight around my back, almost choking me.

I'm kicking and pushing and nothing is happening! I can't scream anymore because I can't breathe. I hear noises outside the water and Cassie's voice yelling something. I keep kicking my feet, but I'm being pulled with a weight on my back. I'm stuck!

There's a rush of water next to me and I feel the warmth from the air on my face again. I cough up lots of water. "Samantha! Are you okay?" My father's worried voice is booming around me as my body hits the pavement next to the pool. Pain shoots up my back and I feel something tugging at me. I feel the raft tear at my bathing suit. Coughing takes over and I roll to my side, gasping for air.

His strong arms are wrapped around me, drying me off with a towel. "Sam, talk to me."

"I can't—" I choke again and cough for what seems like another five minutes. My mother's voice comes from behind me and she says, "Sam, what happened?"

I'm still trying to catch my breath when Cassie chimes in, "I didn't see it, Mrs. Weston. One minute we were floating together on the raft, and after I jumped off and swam to the other end of the pool she was in the water. I swear I didn't see anything!" She starts to cry, worried that she's going to get blamed for my accident.

Tears are flowing from my cheeks now and my chest hurts really bad. "It's okay, honey," my mother says as I'm pulled against her chest. "You're okay. If you can cough, you can breathe. Take it easy and try to calm down."

Cassie's cries mix with my own and we're both sobbing like babies. My father's warm voice begins to overpower our tears and I rub my cheeks.

"You're both okay. Let's stop the crying and figure out what happened. Sam, it looks like the raft somehow became attached to the back of your bathing suit. When you jumped off, the raft flipped and must have pinned you beneath it." He's rubbing my back as my sobs begin to subside.

"I told you girls that the raft was off limits," my mother scolds us.

"It's my fault, Mrs. Weston. I took the raft. I didn't think it was a big deal. I'm really, really sorry." She bursts into tears again and throws herself into her grandmother's arms.

"Girls, take it easy. Everyone is fine. And it's a good thing there were adults around to help you," Lucy says, and she looks over at my father. I turn to put my face into his chest and he's soaking wet.

"Daddy, I'm sorry. You ruined your outfit." I tighten my arms around his neck and he pulls me close.

"It's okay, sweetheart. I have plenty more clothes and these will certainly dry."

"Ben, why don't we get the girls inside so they can change into dry clothes too," my mother says, and I'm lifted into the air.

Within minutes, Cassie and I are dried off and in the house. "Samantha has plenty of clothes in her room, Cassie, if you don't have any to change into." We follow my mother upstairs, and soon we're in my room. The thick pink carpet beneath my toes feels so good.

"Oooh, you have the Barbie Townhouse!" Cassie exclaims as my mother quickly pulls a sundress over my shoulders. She unties my bathing suit and hands me a clean pair of Barbie underwear.

"Go finish getting changed and you and Cassie can play all you want *inside* for the rest of the night." I grab my undies from her hand and march into the bathroom.

"Cassie, here is a dress for you too."

"It's okay, Mrs. Weston, my Grammy has my clean clothes downstairs. I'll go get them. Be right back!" I hear Cassie run down the stairs, calling for her grandmother.

"Sam, are you okay in there?" my mom asks through the bathroom door.

"Yes." I slowly open the door and step back into my room. "I'm sorry for not being careful, Mommy." Tears fill my eyes again and she pulls me into a huge bear hug.

"You're okay. That's all that matters." She pushes me away from her gently and places her hands on my shoulders. "Promise me something?" she says, her eyes soft but stern.

"Yes, Mommy?" I look up and feel bad that I let her down.

"Promise me that you won't take chances like that without me or your father around. I mean, until you can swim strongly without your swimmies, you need to be supervised. Okay?"

"Okay, I promise Mommy. I'm sorry." I throw my arms around her waist as warm tears flow down my cheeks once again.

"Hey, hey. No tears, okay? I'm proud of you for trying your best and being brave, but we want to make sure that you're strong enough to swim on your own."

I wipe my tears on the back of my hand and sniffle back the boogies that are about to fall out of my nose. She puts a tissue in my hand and hugs me again.

"Cassie's a nice girl, isn't she?" Mommy asks and leads me over to sit on my bed while I finish cleaning up my messy face.

"She sure is. I wonder how she learned to swim so good. I wish I was as strong as her."

"I bet she started swim lessons much sooner than you. Mommy and Daddy didn't think to get you swim lessons when you were younger and before we put in the pool. I'm going to call someone tomorrow to make sure you get stronger throughout the rest of the summer."

I hear Cassie's footsteps in our hallway and she's back in my room before I know it.

"Let's play summer vacation! How many Barbies do you have?" she asks as she pulls out the canvas storage boxes from underneath the hutch in my room.

"I don't know. Maybe twenty or thirty?"

"I'll leave you girls to play. I'll come get you when dinner is ready. Have fun." My mother kisses my forehead as she lets go of my hand.

Cassie pulls out all of my Barbie dolls and pets. "I also have the Barbie Beach House. Let me get that out of my closet." I open my closet door and pull out the house along with a Jeep.

"This is going to be awesome!" Cassie exclaims. "Our girls will live in the city and head out to the beach on the weekends. Just like my parents."

"Cassie, we don't live in the city."

"I know that, silly, but my parents are always out at our beach house in New Jersey. That's where they are this weekend. Maybe you and I can go with them one weekend. Would you like that?"

"Oh yeah!" I say, excited.

"Cool. I love the beach. Especially the boardwalk and the rides. My favorite ride is the rollercoaster!" She stands up with one of my Barbie dolls in her hand and pretends to have her ride an imaginary rollercoaster in the middle of my room.

"I'm not sure about rollercoasters, but I do love the beach," I say hesitantly.

"Hey, if you could jump into the deep end today, you can ride a rollercoaster."

I smile as I begin to set up the furniture in the townhouse. The plush sectional couch barely fits on the second floor, but I make it work.

"We'll see, Cassie."

She leaps through the air with the doll and gives me a huge hug. "I'm so glad you're okay, Sam! I don't know what I'd do if something happened to you."

"I was scared, but I'm okay now."

"You almost drowned! You were coughing up so much water I didn't know what to do. Thank God for your Daddy. He was in the water and pulled you out so fast. He saved your life."

"Yeah, I guess he did." I smile.

Thank God for my Daddy.

CHAPTER 3

Garrett
Present
Philadelphia, Pennsylvania
Age 26

"YOU CAN'T GO BACK THERE!" Our driver, and sometimes security guard, Mick's voice booms from the front of the tour bus. The fog begins to lift as the naked body next to me shifts. "Garrett?" she asks quietly. I open my eyes and try to identify where the soft voice came from. A mess of blonde hair is draped over my chest.

Shit.

I hate when they spend the night. Her warm hand moves slowly up my thigh and I quickly push that regret aside. She could be of use one more time…

The voices in the hallway echo as my head remains glued to the pillow. Footsteps quicken, and I hear another voice coming from the front of the bus.

Heath.

"Hey, can I help you with something?" he asks the nameless stranger who seems to still be barreling toward the back of the bus. It's a rare event anyone can get past him. He's six foot five and easily fills the cramped hallway of the tour bus. It's also a rare event that anyone *wants* to get past him, especially girls. He's the new lead singer of Epic Fail and is also the newest obsession for the endless groupies. He's also my biggest competition for those groupies. *Dick.*

I never thought I'd say or think this, but I miss Alex. *He* would step aside and push the girls my way. There was never any competition with Alex for the girls. His heart only ever belonged to one person. And that one person is the reason why Alex is no longer on the road with us. Well, her and the family that they've built together.

I groan as loud banging echoes throughout the small cabin. I groan louder as the nameless blonde wraps her hand around my—

The door flies open as a gasping Heath is pushed into the room, and another blonde falls through the door. The light blinds me, causing me to momentarily forget about the soft hand that's vigorously pumping my shaft. *Another blonde. Jackpot!*

I stretch my arms over my head, feeling victorious for what's about to happen. *Take that, Heath.*

Cool air breezes over me as the pumping suddenly stops. The girl in bed with me scrambles to cover herself, partially tearing the covers from me. She's hidden under the blanket now, turned away from me, and my erection deflates. I watch Heath struggle to grab the other flailing form in the room. "Mick, I could use your help back here!" he bellows. *Wimp.*

"Get your fucking hands off of me," the intruder slurs and stumbles away from him. Her glazed eyes catch mine, and she squints trying to focus on me. She looks crazy. She *is* crazy. But, she also looks familiar. *How do I know her?*

She's unsteady, swaying in place, and I immediately notice how dirty she is. And not the kind of dirty that I like. She's *filthy.*

Her clothes are torn in strange places, and there is a coating of dirt and grime on her arms, causing her intricate tattoos to seem veiled and blurred. Her fingernails are misshapen and dirt is caked underneath them. I remain fixated on her atrocious appearance and immediately get itchy just looking at her.

Mick's hulking frame fills the small doorway, causing me to divert my eyes to him. "Venue security has already been called," he says calmly as he pushes past Heath and lifts the drunken blonde off of her wobbly feet. *How did she get past them both?* She can barely stand, but her arms are windmilling through the air, trying to make contact with anything. A flask and baggie filled with what seems to be drug paraphernalia flies from her open backpack.

"Calm down," Mick says as he grabs both of her wrists with his left hand, making it look easy.

"Dude." I chuckle, mocking Heath's attempts to stop her. "Way to get this under control."

Heath ignores my jab and turns to leave the room. "You got this now?" he asks Mick, who lifts his chin to acknowledge that he does indeed 'got this.' He continues to maintain his control over the crazy drunk chick.

"Garrett, you need to come with me," Drunk Girl slurs. Blondie whimpers from beneath the sheets.

"Go with you? Where?" I ask, almost mocking her. I glance toward the heap of blonde hair poking out from the covers. *I'm not going anywhere. I have unfinished business here.*

"I'm Sadie…" A piece of paper falls from one of her clasped hands, and I watch it fall to the floor. Suddenly, her eyes roll back into her head and her body starts convulsing. She's limp in Mick's arms.

"Fuck," Mick exhales and then calls out, "Heath, get me my phone. Now." He grabs her chin, holding her head up as drool falls from her mouth. She gags as foam begins to drip from her lips, and I wonder what the hell this girl is on.

Sadie?

"What the hell?" I ask, sitting up in bed as Blondie rolls over, tucking the covers around her body. She gasps and turns to hide her face against my chest. *Drama.*

Heath emerges from the doorway and hands Mick a cell phone. He stares helplessly at the convulsing heap of a girl as Mick hits his speed dial. "It's Mick. I need medical on *Epic Three*. Overdose." He disconnects the call and slides his phone into his back pocket without dropping the girl. *Sadie?*

"What did she say her name was?" I ask Mick, even though I know I heard her correctly.

Ignoring me, he rolls his eyes as he continues to support her head. She gags and coughs up foam, like a rabid dog. "Can you get her out of here?" As the words leave my mouth, I realize I sound like a douche, but she's frothing all over the place.

Heath looks at me with his typical disgust and bends down to help support her.

Mick's phone rings from his back pocket, and somehow he swipes it quickly without dropping the girl on the floor. "Yeah," he says abruptly. "No, not *Two*, we're on *Three*." He hangs up abruptly. This is the first time we've had three buses on tour. Heath and I share *Epic Three*, Tristan and Dax share *Epic One*, and *Epic Two* is for our crew. We don't have a name for the rig that carries all of our gear.

Within minutes, the cabin is swarming with paramedics and security officers, and I hear sirens in the distance, quickly approaching. They work on the girl, and as quickly as they enter the bus, they're gone with their new patient. Heath, Mick and I stare in awkward silence as sobs come from underneath the blanket next to me. Mick rolls his eyes once again and grabs her skimpy clothes from the floor. He extracts her from the bed, expertly keeping her naked body shielded while leaving me partially covered with the remaining blanket. Her matted hair falls to the side, and her face is swollen and streaked with tears and black makeup. "Is she dead?" she asks.

"No, honey, she's not dead," Mick says as he ushers her into the hallway. "You can get dressed in the bathroom," he instructs.

"But…" She looks at me longingly, and she's suddenly not as attractive to me as she was last night.

Mick shakes his head, silently telling her this is the end of the road for this tryst. He closes the door before either of them can judge me for being the complete tool that I already know I am.

Heath leans against the closed door, scowling at me as the girl's sobs can be heard through the wall while she's getting dressed.

"What?" I ask as I attempt to discreetly pull my boxer briefs on.

"Are you serious?" he asks. "Do you really need me to tell you 'what'?"

I toss the covers off of me, get out of bed and grab my jeans from the floor. I ignore his judgment and finish getting dressed.

"Garrett, do you even see what just happened here?"

"Of course I do," I snap.

"You let your latest conquest leave here in tears, but not before another one stormed in and practically died from a drug overdose in front of us. Get your fucking shit together."

"Oh, and you're so fucking innocent. Stop acting like this crazy shit doesn't happen with you too." My response is weak and sophomoric. *I'm an asshole.*

Yet I still feel the need to defend myself in this ridiculous situation.

"And by the way, the girl who OD'd isn't a conquest. I don't think I even know her."

"You don't *think*?" he yells. "Seriously, dude, there is something very wrong with you."

"Whatever," I respond defensively. *But there is something very wrong with me.*

He bends down near the bed and picks up the paper that slipped from the girl's hand. I watch as he scans it, wondering why he's staring at it so intently.

"Who's Sadie?" he asks.

"I have no fucking clue."

"Well, this piece of paper says that you absolutely do know her." An amused, yet disgusted grin spreads across his face. He reads the paper again and nods his head.

"Congratulations, Garrett. It's a boy!" He tosses the paper my way, and I watch it float slowly to the floor.

I'm confused and scared and I can't move.

Sadie?

Who the fuck is Sa—

"Well, Daddy, now do you remember who your baby mama is?" Heath no longer looks amused, and his voice now sounds angry, accusing.

"What the fuck are you saying?" My voice cracks and I sink onto the bed. A vague memory, an image of Sadie, enters my head, and I now realize who she is. *Baby?*

"Do you know her?" Heath asks, confused.

"I don't know—" More memories flood into my head, and I remember a wild night a while ago when Sadie and a friend followed me back to the bus. I remember wanting to bang the both of them, but the only one who was interested in me was Sadie. Her friend was too busy snorting coke and popping pills. Sadie and I spent a few hours in this exact room while the other

41

girl got so high, she passed out snoring in the lounge area. The friend was a hot mess and Sadie was just… hot… I think.

Baby?

He bends down to pick up the piece of paper from the floor. "Stop," I say as he's about to pick it up. "Just get rid of it."

"What?" he says.

"Leave it. I'm sure it isn't real." I don't even know why I'm saying this. I'm not even sure what it is or why there's a baby involved.

He ignores me and pushes the paper into my hands. "Looks real to me, ass. And it has your name right here." He slams his index finger into the paper and my eyes try to focus on what he's pointing at.

"It says right here that you're a father."

I'm looking at what appears to be a birth certificate.

Name: Kai David Armstrong-Moore
Date of Birth: August 10, 2014
Mother: Sadie Leilani Moore
Father: Garrett David Armstrong

"Bullshit," I snap and push the paper along with his jabbing finger away. I suddenly feel clammy, and I'm sweating profusely. "This is just a fucking piece of paper. It means nothing, and I barely remember this girl."

But I *do* remember. I remember *a lot*. Looking around the room, I remember fucking Sadie on almost any clear surface for hours. I was drunk and she was wildly stoned. It was like she was on speed or something crazier. She was an animal and I loved it.

Heath's revulsion is tangible as he tries to remain calm. "Man, stop being a fucking prick for one second and think. Did you fuck her?"

I stumble to the bed and sit down. "I'm sure I did, Heath. She's a bimbo groupie. You know there's a decent likelihood that I did." *I know I did. Many times.*

"So think about it. This could really be your kid." He raises his eyebrows, and for a moment I see a twinge of worry in his eyes, as if he's trying to imagine himself in my shoes right now. "She must know you pretty well if she has your full name." His tone becomes accusing again.

"You can get my damn name off of Wikipedia, you fuck."

"Whatever, G. You need to address this now before it gets out of control. The baby was born a few weeks ago, and this birth certificate looks legit to me."

"I have no intention of doing a single thing." Except puking. My stomach churns and sweat starts dripping from my brow.

"You don't look too good." He grabs a bottle of water from the table near the door and tosses it onto the bed in front of me. My fingers are tingling as I reach for the cool bottle.

There's a loud knock at the door, and Mick doesn't wait for either of us to answer before he comes in. "This situation is not good." He folds his arms across his chest and walks closer to the bed. "That girl OD'd. She's dead."

"Holy shit," Heath says immediately.

"What?" I ask, my mouth suddenly dry.

"She coded as soon as they put her in the ambulance. One of the paramedics just called to tell me that she was D.O.A." Mick shakes his head then looks back to me. "You okay?" he asks.

"No, I'm not." I don't want to tell him about the birth certificate she had dropped on the floor before she passed out.

His eyes sweep the room quickly. "The police are asking us to clear the bus while they collect her belongings." He nods toward the flask and the other items that fell from her bag.

"Grab what you need. I booked a suite for you at the Marriott for the rest of the day."

Heath picks up the birth certificate, folds it and shoves it into his back pocket. *Why would he do that?*

I try to ignore his act and address Mick. "I'm going home. Can you get me a ride back to my house?" I have a home just west of Philadelphia that I rarely spend any time at. My housekeeper, Peggy, is there more than I am.

He nods and leaves the room.

I grab a tee shirt from the floor and put it on, walking past Heath. I pat my back pocket to make sure my phone and wallet are still there and walk off the bus barefoot, steamy August air filling my lungs. I begin sweating immediately, and my shirt is already stuck to my back. A dozen or so police officers are waiting to board the bus, and I slide into the back of the black car parked in front it. Before the door closes, Heath is in the car with me.

"I'm not going to the hotel," I remind him, annoyed.

"I know," he says.

"I don't remember inviting you to my house."

"You didn't," he responds.

He looks out the window as we pull away from the concert venue. There is yellow tape spanning a large area around the bus, and people are gathering with their phones extended in the air, taking pictures of everything unfolding in front of them. There are girls screaming, and a few touch the window as we drive slowly through the crowd.

Heath takes out his phone and his thumbs fly over his keyboard. "I'm letting Dax and Tristan know what happened and where we're going."

"Do you expect me to have a fucking party back at my

house?" I lash out at him and he huffs.

"I'm letting them know that we're okay, *asshole*. Their bus is on the other side of the lot, and I'm sure they would want to know that it wasn't one of us taken away in that ambulance."

"Fine. But my house isn't open for everyone. You're not even invited."

I slouch down in the seat and close my eyes. I want to burn the image of that birth certificate from my brain, but it's all I see.

Kai David Armstrong-Moore

Fuck.

CHAPTER 4

Sam
Present
Philadelphia, Pennsylvania
Age 23

"HEY," CASSIE SAYS, pulling me out of my haze. I've been in a fog all morning, unable to shake the cobwebs from my head. I haven't slept in what seems like days. This time of year is especially difficult. My parents' birthdays are this week, and it's an unwelcome reminder that they aren't here with me.

I shake my head and force a smile. "Sorry, it's been a rough week."

Cassie knows all too well how hard it is on me. She's dried my tears on more than one occasion. "I'm so glad you have your aunt. She's awesome and can help in any situation." Her words of encouragement do anything but that. They only remind me of everything I have lost.

"Aunt Peggy's the best," I respond, thankful that I have her support.

Cassie pulls me against her firmly and squeezes. "You're amazing, Sam. You know that?" I let her pull me tighter. "I say this all of the time, but I'm so proud of you. You went to college, got a nursing degree and now you're here, in one of the best neonatal intensive care units in the state. You did this all yourself." She hugs me tighter and then releases me to look into my eyes. "And you brought me along for the ride."

"I'm not doing it alone," I say humbly. "I'm still living in my Aunt's house." My aunt took me in right after my parents were killed. She has a large home in Villanova and I have my own space there.

Aunt Peggy's a personal assistant and housekeeper to some guy who moved to the area when I was in nursing school. I think she said he's a musician or something like that. He's barely ever home, and she basically takes care of everything while he's away. She's been doing this type of work her entire life. The last family she worked for moved out to California when their daughter landed a role in a television sitcom. She worked for them for almost twenty years, and they were devastated when she told them she couldn't move with them. We argued about it, actually. She insisted that she stay with me, and I feel tremendous guilt over this. I wish she was able to go out to California; it would force me to finally do things for myself and on my own.

I wish I wasn't her obligation. Her burden. I absolutely hate it. Which is exactly why I'm saving every dime that I earn, so I can get my own place and let Aunt Peggy finally live her own life, instead of feeling the need to take care of me.

"Well, you're doing a fantastic job. Someday you'll get to do this for a husband and kids." Today, we're wearing our pink teddy bear scrubs. Our unit coordinates our scrubs each day of the week, and today is pink teddy bears.

"Right," I say sarcastically. "And don't forget the little detail of a husband. Or lack thereof."

"There are dozens of men patiently waiting for you to wake up and dive into the dating pool."

"Dozens?" I say, raising my eyebrow and giving her my best smirk possible. "Now that's a bit of an exaggeration, don't you think?"

"You don't even know how stunning you are, do you?"

I laugh heartily. "Seriously, these teddy bear scrubs are super hot. Step aside and let me break all of the hearts of the countless men waiting for me outside." I giggle, laughing harder than I have in a long time. Cassie is kind and my best friend, but she's seriously delusional. I haven't been out with a guy in ages. I honestly can't remember when someone has even shown interest in me. My last boyfriend broke up with me almost two years ago, when it became apparent to him that my career was an important part of my life. He wanted me to himself, all of the time. I was working nights and weekends and barely had time to sleep. I was exhausted. He was exhausting.

"Just wait, Sam. He's out there, waiting. Ready to sweep you off your feet and give you the life you deserve."

"You're drunk," I say to her. "What guy is out there, ready to fall in love with a hot mess of a nurse? I've got too much baggage, Cassie. It'll never happen for me."

"I promise you that it will. You're too special to not have that kind of love in your life. You've got a great head on your shoulders, and as much as you don't want to admit it, you're a beautiful person." She grabs my hand, pulling me toward the door of the on-call room. "Break is over. Dr. Hagan will be doing her rounds in a few minutes." My adrenaline kicks in, and I realize we have a long, trying day ahead of us.

This week has been exceptionally difficult here at work. The neonatal intensive care unit is at capacity. The last baby admitted to our unit is a baby boy, born eleven weeks premature.

He's barely three pounds and it's been touch and go for the past several days.

I hop on alternating feet as I cover my Dansko clogs with blue sterile booties. We take turns scrubbing our hands in the sink in the outer room of the NICU and slip into sterile gowns. The change of shift is always hectic, and we ask that the families vacate the room while we discuss with the doctors and nurses their medical updates. I see the young mother of the eleven-week-old preemie, Olivia, looking pale and drawn. She's curled up in a chair next to her son's incubator, her hand pressed up against the clear casing.

I nod toward her and raise my eyebrow to Becky, the overnight nurse. "Rough night?" I ask softly, not wanting Olivia to hear us.

"She won't leave him. And for once, I can't force her to. His neuro scans came back a little while ago and he has two brain bleeds. One is a grade two, but the other is grade three. Dr. Hagan wants to run a new scan in a few hours, but she's very concerned. To top it off, his bradycardia episodes are getting worse and they are going to intubate him again." Seeing babies with breathing tubes is very scary, but so vital for their long-term prognosis. Every time he stops breathing or his heart rate slows, he could be doing more damage to his organs and brain.

My heart drops for this tiny little life. Olivia is only twenty years old, just married last year. Her husband is deployed and has been in Afghanistan for the past five months. She moved up to Pennsylvania to live with her mother so she wouldn't have to be alone. The baby wasn't due for several more months, and her husband would have been home for his birth. Now he's here, way too early, and desperately struggling to live.

We see babies like this every day. Premature, not ready for

this world. We do everything we can to make sure they get the care that they need so they can thrive and grow and go home.

"She named him today," Becky whispers as her eyes glisten. "Benjamin."

I suck in my breath and grab my chest. *My father's name.* "Ben," I say softly and hear my mother's voice screaming his name. *"What did you do to him? Ben? Can you hear me?"*

"Are you okay?" Cassie asks, concern sweeping over her face.

"I'm—I'm okay," I stammer and reach for the charts we're about to review with Dr. Hagan.

"You sure? You don't look so good," she says and places her hand on my arm.

"Yup," I force out my breath, regaining my composure.

"Are you ladies ready?" Dr. Hagan enters the room. The overnight nurses, Becky and Marcie follow close behind her, detailing the stats for the five babies in the NICU. Cassie and I listen intently, quietly cataloguing the precious details. I watch Olivia closely when we near baby Benjamin's incubator. She stares at him with fear in her eyes. She's too young to be dealing with the hardships in front of her and what may lie ahead with her son. A grade two bleed is bad, but a grade three bleed is worse. Ben could have permanent damage or worse.

Dr. Hagan makes arrangements for another scan for Ben and signs discharge papers for little Hope. Her family is going to be thrilled, and I'm happy that I get to tell them during my shift.

Becky and Marcie stop and say goodbye to Olivia, Marcie's hand lingering on her shoulder. My heart grabs again as Ben's monitors sound loudly. Marcie opens the incubator and softly presses his chest with her gloved hand. It takes a few moments, but his heart rhythm begins to normalize. Dr. Hagan nods toward the ventilator and Becky moves away to scrub her hands again. They're going to put him back on the vent. "Mrs. Gibson, can you move out to the hallway for a few minutes? We're going to examine Ben." Dr. Hagan doesn't tell her what we're about to do, and I'm glad. Intubating an infant looks scary, but under her delicate hands, it will be effortless.

"Okay," Olivia says feebly. She stands up, and her sterile gown practically slides off of her slight frame. Her dark, hollow eyes are sad and scared.

Once she leaves the room, Dr. Hagan gently places her stethoscope on Ben's fragile chest. He's so tiny; you can see his heart beating underneath his frail ribcage. Becky moves to her side, and soon he's on the ventilator, the breathing tube safely inserted. My pulse races as I watch his chest move up and down mechanically. He's sedated now but doesn't look peaceful. My heart is breaking for this little guy.

"I'm going to get Hope ready to go." I turn away and grab her chart. I don't know why, but watching Ben struggle is excruciating. I've seen so much worse. Watched babies take their last breath and their families' lives shattered. But Ben...

I attempt to smile at the little girl I'm washing up. Her tiny legs are kicking and her arms are flailing in the air. She moved into a bassinet last week and was able to drink from a bottle yesterday. She graduated from 'feed and grow' to 'feed and thrive,' and her parents were ecstatic. I hear Cassie on the phone with them right now, telling them to bring her car seat. Before they leave the NICU, they have to watch a video, explaining all that they need to look out for. Baby Hope is going home with a heart and lung monitor, so her parents have to meet with the vendor and get a tutorial on how to operate it and transmit the daily readings. She's so tiny, only four pounds. But she's eating on her own and has consistently gained weight every day this week. She's the perfect NICU graduate.

"Yes, you are? Aren't you?" I say through my smile. I rub lotion into her soft skin and say, "Our little graduate. You're going to grow up to be a beautiful girl." I hold her tiny feet in the palm of my hand, massaging the lotion gently. "These little feet are going to run along the beach and dance up a storm." Her eyes search for me as her tongue peeks out of her mouth. I place a pink rubber pacifier against her lips, and she eagerly takes it, sucking on it like her life depends on it. Her eyes roll into her head and she falls asleep. All of this excitement tuckered her out. I swaddle her tight in her blanket and place my hand over the crown of her head. "I'm going to miss you, Hope. Grow big and grow strong." I say this to all of our graduates—a private moment just for me and my patients.

I turn and look over at Ben. Olivia is back and curled up in her familiar position in the chair. Eyes glazed over, worry set in. She's nodding her head as Dr. Hagan explains why Ben is back on the ventilator, and I wonder if she's grasping the dire situation. He isn't able to breathe on his own, and his heart rate has been dangerously erratic. With a significant brain bleed on top of this, I'm terrified that this is going to end very badly. This *can't* end badly.

We can't lose Ben.

Garrett
Past
Villanova, Pennsylvania
Age 15

I JAM THE PIECE OF PAPER into my pocket and quietly close my mother's top dresser drawer. I can't believe I'm invading her privacy like this, but I really have to take care of something, and she's the only one who has the answers I need. I tip-toe out of her room and close the door behind me. I pass my room and go down the stairs, two at a time. Before I run out the front door, her voice comes from the den.

"Garrett?"

"Yeah, Mom?"

"Where are you off to?"

"I have a school project that I need to work on with…" My mind goes blank. There is no school project, and I can't come up with a name to save this lie I'm about to tell.

"Who?" she asks, sensing my tension.

"Rob. You know, Rob Shultz. He has everything we need and he's expecting me. So I better go." Rob and I have been friends since third grade. He lives on the other end of our neighborhood, about a ten-minute bike ride away.

"Okay, Bill should be home by six. Will you be home in time for dinner?"

Bill Armstrong married my mother almost six years ago. We moved from Newtown to Villanova, leaving my childhood home behind. He officially adopted me last year after my father's parental rights were finally terminated. Bill's a cool dude, and he's really good to my mother. She's been happier with him than she ever was with my father, and that makes me feel good.

"I don't think so. He's ordering pizza for us." I lie again.

She places a bookmark into the book that she's reading on her lap and pulls off her glasses. Shit is about to get serious.

"Is everything okay?" she asks, and I shift back and forth, a bit jittery.

"Everything's cool." I wrap my hand around the doorknob and she speaks up again.

"Because you just don't seem yourself."

I let go of the handle and run my hand through my hair. "Mom, it's all good."

She puts her glasses back on, and the tension eases from my shoulders. She's going to let me out without grilling me any more.

"Okay, if you say so." She picks up her book again and opens it to the place where she shoved the bookmark. Her eyes drop to the pages and she says, "Tell Mrs. Shultz I said hi."

Shit. I didn't think this through. What happens when she sees Rob's mom next week at the P.T.O. meeting?

I can't worry about that now.

I pull the door open and ride my bike down the street. I look at my watch and see I only have ten minutes to make the next train on the Main Line. I increase my speed and turn the corner.

I lock up my bike on the bike rack and jog toward the train station. I'm panting as I reach the ticket booth and slide my money through the window. "Upper Darby." I inhale deeply so I can regulate my breathing.

A ticket pops up, and my change is pushed back through the small opening. I swipe both and jog over to the track as the train pulls up.

If my mother knew I was getting on the train by myself, she'd flip. We've had long talks about me going into the city, and I'm not allowed to be doing this. *I'm not really going into the city,* I tell myself as if it's okay to be going as far as I am.

I hop onto the train as soon as the doors open, pushing past the people trying to get off. I find the first empty seat and slide into it. As the doors close, I pull the crumpled piece of paper from my pocket. The address is written in my mother's elegant handwriting. There's a phone number under the address, but it's been scratched out, barely legible.

I watch the stops speed by and soon it's time to get off the train. After a quick cab ride, I'm on the street scrawled on the piece of paper that I'm holding. My heart starts to pound as I find the house with the number eighteen. The numbers are on a moldy post by the front door. They're lopsided, and the number one is barely hanging on a bent rusty nail.

I force myself to walk up the overgrown sidewalk leading to the front door. All of the shades are drawn, and there's no car in the driveway.

I wonder if he's even home.

I press the cracked doorbell and don't hear any chimes coming from inside the house. *Broken.*

I knock loudly on the storm door, and it rattles like it's about to fall off the hinges. It pops open, revealing it wasn't even latched or locked. I wait a few minutes for someone to respond to my knock on the outer door and then open it to bang louder on the front door.

Still no answer.

I hear the melodic beat of drums and try to determine where the sound is coming from. It's not coming from inside *this* house, but it's nearby. I bang again on the front door, this time with as much force as I can. My knuckles sting after the eleventh knock.

I back up and listen for sounds coming from inside the house.

Still nothing.

The drums get louder, and I hear the screeching sound of an electric guitar.

Where is that music coming from?

I flip open the black mailbox hanging next to the front door. It almost falls off the wall, but I notice that it's stuffed to the brim. I pull out a couple pieces of mail, and there's a notice from the post office stating they are holding all mail until they hear from the resident. It's dated three months ago.

He's not here.

I quickly turn and walk back toward the street, wondering how I'm going to find another cab to take me to the train. This was a complete waste of time, and if Mom finds out about this trip, she's going to kill me.

The music is louder now, and I finally see where it's coming from. Maybe they know where he is.

I walk up the driveway, and as soon as they see me, the music comes to a screeching halt. "Hey," I say when they all lay their eyes on me.

The guy behind the microphone with the electric guitar says, "What's up?" He nods his head, and the rest of the band watches me intently.

"Uh. I'm looking for the guy next door. Have you seen him?"

The drummer quickly responds, "What do you want him for?" He raises his eyebrows and is suddenly suspicious.

I look to the rest of the group and shove my hands into the pockets of my hoodie. "No reason. It just looks like he hasn't been there in a while, and I was wondering if you knew where I could find him?" *I wonder if he's dead.*

"No man. That dude is sketchy. He moved in, like, seven years ago. I think I've only seen him maybe three or four times." The bass guitar player shifts back and forth and looks around to the other guys. There's three of them in all, and they seem to be about my age. They all nod their heads in agreement.

"My mom said he went to jail," the drummer says.

"Oh," I say, and I can only imagine why. The last time I saw my father, he was rifling through my childhood house looking for money to pay off gambling debts. Years later, my mother explained that she got a restraining order filed the next day. Apparently the people he owed money to threatened to hurt me and her. She says it was to protect us from him. I believed her, but I've always had this need to find out why he never came back. Why he never tried to make things right.

"Yeah, he's a weird dude. I don't know why you'd want to see him," the guy in front of the microphone says, and his voice echoes throughout the street. "Damn, I forgot to turn off the mic." He smirks and steps on a pedal in front of him.

"You guys have a pretty cool setup," I observe. Rob and I have only tinkered with our instruments and have nothing close to what these dudes have. There are at least six amplifiers, and their instruments are high end. I look around the neighborhood and see that it's pretty run down. These guys don't seem like they can afford some of the instruments that they're holding in their hands. The bass player is playing a Rickenbacker that I know for a fact is over twelve hundred dollars. The guitarist, and I presume the lead singer, is playing a Fender American Telecaster—a majorly expensive model. The drums are a seven-piece Gretsch kit that reminds me of the setup of Taylor Hawkins from the Foo Fighters.

Who are these guys?

"I'm Tristan," the bassist says. "This is my house."

I nod toward Tristan as I ogle the extra guitars lined up in front of the lead singer.

"Do you play?" the drummer asks.

"A little," I say, and I walk toward one of the Fender Stratocasters.

"What's your name?" he asks.

"Garrett."

"You already met Tristan. I'm Dax, and this is our fearless leader, Alex."

I pull my left hand out of my pocket and wave. "Nice to meet you."

"We're Epic Fail," Tristan says.

"Cool name," I say and realize my hand is on the neck of the Strat.

"Play with us," Alex says as he steps on one of the pedals in front of him and strums his American Telecaster. The sound fills the garage and Dax slaps his sticks together. They burst into a familiar song and within seconds I'm caught up in the perfect rhythm they have.

Before I know it, the Strat is around my neck and I'm taking over lead from the singer. He switches to rhythm guitar almost immediately, and the transition is seamless.

After playing a half-dozen cover songs together, I place the guitar back on its stand. I'm in a bit of a daze, and their whispers are caught on the still open microphones.

"He's amazing," Tristan says, and both Dax and Alex nod their heads in agreement.

I suddenly feel out of place as I look toward my father's vacant home. "I need to leave," I say and back out of the garage, pivoting on my feet.

"Wait!" Alex's voice booms through the amplifiers.

Chuckles reverberate behind me and I turn around.

"Come back next Saturday. We'll be rehearsing for a local gig and it would be cool if you came." Alex has his hand over the mic and is talking in a normal volume.

"Really?" I ask. My mother will never let me come out here. This is going to be impossible to explain.

"Yeah, dude. Your hands were like magic!" Tristan says. "The way you and Alex played off each other was like, really amazing."

I stuff my hands back into my hoodie and almost trip walking backwards.

"Thanks, but, um…I don't live around here."

"Who cares!" Dax says. "You need to get back here next week."

I nod and try to figure out what lie I'm going to tell my mother.

Hanging with these dudes was the most comfortable I've been in a long time. Playing music with them felt so natural. Melodic.

I look over at my father's house again.

"How do you know that dude?" Alex asks.

"I had the wrong address. I don't know him at all," I lie and crumble the paper that's in my pocket with my father's name and address, tossing it into the trashcan at the curb.

Alex raises his eyebrow but seems to accept my fib.

Dax walks toward me and hands me a business card. The words 'Epic Fail' pop from the front. They look like they were spray-painted onto the card over a deep gray background. These look professional, and I can't believe these guys are about my age.

"Call me on Friday to confirm. I'll add you to the gig for Saturday night. We'll be playing all of the songs we covered today, so you're good."

I swipe the card from his hands and nod. "Yeah, I guess I'm good."

"Later," Tristan says, putting his bass back on its stand.

"Later," I respond and look up the street past the corner. I see a few cabs passing on the main road about a quarter of a mile away. Hopefully, I'll be able to catch one of them and jump on the Main Line before it gets dark.

"Epic Fail!" they yell in unison behind me as I jog toward the intersection.

I throw up my right hand in a backwards wave.

I like the sound of that.

CHAPTER 6

Sam
Present
Philadelphia, Pennsylvania
Age 23

ROUNDS ARE OVER, and Cassie and I settle into our daily routine. Today's scrubs are baby monkeys. Monkeys swinging from vines. Monkeys eating bananas. Monkeys hugging each other. Cassie hates these particular scrubs because the background color is beige. And she hates beige.

"Ugh, I can't do anything right today," she exclaims as she tosses a feeding tube into the garbage. Beige also makes her pissy. I look around the room and it's filled with babies. Very sick babies. Two monitors go off at the same time, and we both rush to opposite ends of the room to check the vitals of the babies causing the alarms.

Suddenly, the door flies open and yet another baby is brought into the already crowded room. "Suction," Dr. Hagan directs Becky as they work on this new baby. Cassie closes Baby Grace's incubator.

She walks back over to Ben to begin his feeding tube again and gets flustered. "There are too many babies in here," she says, dropping the tube onto the floor. Her reaction is surprising to me since she usually remains so calm under pressure.

"Here, let me." I grab a new, sterile tube and begin prepping it for Ben. "Cassie!" Dr. Hagan calls as she's working on the new baby. "Get Terry on the phone, please. We need to make sure transport is ready to send this little guy over to CHOP once he's stable." Children's Hospital of Philadelphia is another level 4 NICU in the city, and since ours is now beyond capacity, we need to make sure space is available elsewhere. This happens from time to time, and we do the same when other hospitals are over capacity. Baby Grace's monitor alarms again while Cassie is quickly talking to the NICU at CHOP. Becky details the new baby's situation. "Baby boy, full term. Hypertonic, exposed to various drugs. Mother tested positive for benzodiazepine, anti-depressants, and marijuana. Infant tox screen is pending. Mother is refusing transport."

Great. A drug addict mom who doesn't want to be with her sick baby. It never ceases to amaze me what some mothers will do to themselves, *knowingly.* I look around the room at all of the sick babies whose mothers did everything right, but they were all dealt a challenging hand. Two more monitors sound and I look down at Ben, who we've been trying to feed for the past hour. He's miraculously off the breathing tube, for now, but this guy needs to eat.

Cassie makes the arrangements for transport while Dr. Hagan continues to work on the new baby boy. His screams are sharp and shallow and tear through my heart. The cries of drug-exposed infants are unique and heart wrenching. "Becky, we'll need a tox screen on him. Cassie, please let social services know what's happening. They're going to want to speak with the mother."

Cassie relays information to Heather, the hospital social worker, and quickly hangs up the phone, rushing to another monitor alarm. When it rains, it pours in here.

I get Ben's feeding tube in place and turn on the drip. Dr. Hagan is finished examining the baby boy, and Becky wipes his foot clean of blood from the tests she just administered. Dr. Hagan leaves the room and sinks into a chair in the outer office. She looks exhausted.

Finally, the monitors have silenced, and Cassie, Becky and I all return to our standard routines.

"Where's Olivia?" I ask, looking at the empty chair next to Ben's incubator.

Cassie is pale and seems really off now. "I'm not sure. Her mother came to get her about ten minutes ago. There are some other people here to see her." Cassie walks over to Mikey and turns on the lights above him. He's here because he has severe jaundice and the lights help lower his bilirubin counts. Mikey's large belly spills over his infant diaper. He's huge. Well, huge for a baby in the NICU. Weighing in at almost eleven pounds, he's the largest baby I've ever seen in this hospital. He's perfect and fat and already has thighs that any mother would brag about. But since he has jaundice, he needs our help. He sleeps peacefully, full, content and looking so out of place here in the NICU. He's been doing well, and if that continues, he should be going home by tomorrow. She adjusts the light above him and looks over at Ben.

"The bleed on the left side remains a grade three. Not good," Cassie mumbles and sits on the stool in front of her computer.

"No, not good at all," I say quietly, looking away from Mikey. It's amazing how this room can go from frantic to quiet in a matter of minutes. "Cassie, are you okay?" I ask, concerned as to why she's so off today.

"Yeah, it's just…"

She stops talking as we hear a woman scream from the hallway, "No! No! No!"

Cassie and I turn our heads and see Olivia outside the NICU window, throwing herself into a large man, punching his chest. My heart grabs in my chest when I see another man next to him wearing similar clothes. *Military.*

"Oh no," Cassie exhales and stands up.

Olivia's wails turn to sobs, and her mother pulls her off of the Marine. She holds her daughter tight against her chest as the two Marines stand quiet and respectful.

"That can't be good," Cassie says. "When my cousin was visited by two Marines, she found out her husband was killed in Iraq. It's never good when there are two of them. Never." Her voice trails off as she moves to the window and peers out at them.

Olivia is shaking her head and then collapses onto the floor. One of the Marines bends down to a knee and scoops her into his arms, carrying her over to the couch in the lounge area. She doesn't look conscious, and I call out to Dr. Hagan, who lifts her head from the desk. "Can you help? Olivia just passed out in the hallway." She grabs smelling salt taped to the cabinet door and rushes out.

As soon as Dr. Hagan swipes the salts under Olivia's nose, she opens her eyes and immediately begins to sob and wail. Her mother slides on the couch next to her, cradling her head in her lap. I can't bear to watch this any longer.

"I hope to God she didn't just hear what I think she did, but my instinct tells me she just found out her husband is gone." Cassie pulls the blinds shut, giving Olivia privacy from our curious eyes. My chest tightens, and I try to fight the grief I feel for this young mother and her new family.

I look over at Ben and close my eyes. "God, please let this boy grow up strong and healthy," I whisper quietly.

His monitor suddenly starts beeping wildly, jolting me from my silent prayer. Cassie and I both rush to the incubator and open it. His color is grayish and his heart rate is dangerously low. The monitors go off again, indicating something is wrong with his tube. *The brand new tube that I just inserted.* I feel faint and desperate.

Cassie puts her stethoscope to his chest and gasps. "His lungs are filled with fluid." She begins working on him as Becky runs into the hallway to alert Dr. Hagan.

Several other nurses rush in with the doctor and I back away into the corner. I'm frozen as I watch them work on Ben. Cassie looks over at me, shaking her head. Her eyes are frantic and questioning. I look out of the blinds and see Olivia sitting up, drinking juice that one of the nurses brought to her. The Marines are still there, trying to give her space but also to comfort her. I look back toward Ben and I can't see him. He's surrounded by doctors and nurses.

Cassie's eyes meet mine and I know.

We're losing him.

I'M SEATED NEXT TO CASSIE inside the hospital administrator's office.

I'm numb.

"Miss Weston, can you answer me?" Jim Burke, Chief of the NICU, asks again.

"I don't know how it happened," I say quietly. *It's my fault.*

"You don't know how the feeding tube was placed in his *lungs* instead of his *stomach*?" he asks accusingly.

"No, sir. I listened to his chest. I heard it in his stomach. I didn't think it was in his lungs." Cassie grabs my hand and squeezes. *Did I actually listen to his chest? I don't even remember. Holy fuck.*

I've inserted hundreds of feeding tubes in babies tinier than Ben. Hundreds of tubes placed in the exact spot they were supposed to be placed. All the right way, never in their precious lungs. Lungs so tiny and desperate for air. Lungs trying to work hard to keep Ben alive.

Ben.

"Miss Weston, we're placing you on administrative leave until we can conduct a full investigation into this situation."

I inhale as Jim stands up behind his desk.

"But…" I say and break down. "I didn't mean to, Jim. I did everything right. I don't know what happened. Oh my God."

It begins to sink in exactly what I've done. Cassie grabs me by my shoulders and guides me out of the room.

"Cassie." I sob and fall to my knees in the hallway.

It's my fault.

It's my fault.

IT'S MY FAULT.

"Hush, Sam." She sinks to the floor next to me and throws her arms around me. "Don't say anything, okay?" She begs me not to confess. Not to tell her what I did.

"Whatever happened was an accident. Do you understand? The NICU was a zoo today. So much was going on. Too much was going on." She rubs my arms, pulling me against her. I can hear the regret in her voice. She was assigned to Ben today, and it was her feeding tube that I inserted wrong. Her guilt is tangible, but not as thick as mine.

An accident? It was neglectful. Sloppy. Wrong.

"I killed him," I whisper into her shoulder. "I killed Ben."

CHAPTER 7

Garrett
Present
Philadelphia, Pennsylvania
Age 26

HEATH MOVES THROUGH MY HOUSE like he's been here before. He finds the whiskey and two glasses and quickly pours heaping servings for the both of us. He slides one across the large island in the kitchen that I'm propped against. I drink it down in one gulp, feeling the burn of the brown liquid in my throat and into my chest. I wince as a delayed burn attacks my nose. My eyes water as I push the glass toward him. He refills it without thinking and his eyes meet mine.

"Dude, you have a kid."

The words hang in the air between us, and I swig the second shot of whiskey.

"You don't know that," I say, trying to convince myself that the birth certificate isn't real.

"And his mother is dead." He drops his eyes and swirls his drink before sucking it back.

I slide onto the barstool and place my forehead on the cool granite. *This can't be happening.*

Heath's cell phone chimes loudly and he answers it after the first ring. "Mick," he says, and I close my eyes, keeping my head pressed to the counter. "Right. Okay. Thanks." He drops the phone on the counter next to my head.

"The police are finished. They gathered everything they could find. They want to talk to you, and Mick gave them your home address."

What could they want to talk to me about?

"I don't understand," I mutter and slowly lift my head. "What could they want with me?"

Heath shrugs his shoulders and pours me another shot of whiskey. "That girl died. I'm sure they want to tie up any loose ends. Maybe try to figure out how you knew her and how she OD'd."

Sadie was completely wasted. More than when I fucked her a while back. *Was it nine months ago?* I try to remember where we were when I met her. It was cold. And snowing. We were in Philadelphia for the first leg of our tour, and it was right after Thanksgiving last year. Holiday lights were everywhere, so it was definitely before Christmas.

Exactly nine months ago.

"Oh my God," I murmur.

Heath stiffens in front of me, and his eyes focus over my right shoulder. "Ma'am?" he says, addressing whoever is behind me.

Peggy.

I rub my hands over my face and inhale deeply.

"Garrett?" Without turning, I can picture her confused and worried face. She and I are rarely here at the same time, but when we are, she's like a second mother to me. She takes care of everything and adds her extra-special motherly touch. Fresh meals, clean sheets and warm smiles. I never tell her this, but being around her completely grounds me when I'm home. Something I don't get with anyone.

"Hey, Peggy," I say and push the empty glass from me. I'm suddenly embarrassed that I'm a little buzzed and ashamed about the birth certificate she knows nothing about.

"Is everything okay?" she asks hesitantly, and she moves to the end of the island, transferring her gaze between Heath and me.

"I should go—somewhere," Heath says and backs away.

"No!" I say, startling all of us. His eyes widen and he shakes his head slowly. "You don't know your way around the house." He looks confused at my feeble attempt to keep him in the room with me and Peggy.

She tenses and reaches for my arm. Her cool hand grabs my wrist and I stiffen. "Garrett, what's going on?" Her tone feels accusatory, and I pull my wrist from her grip.

"Nothing," I snap. "We had some free time today, and Heath wanted to see my place." I glare at Heath and expect him to corroborate my lies.

He turns to look out the window. "Hey, is that a pool house?" He quickly makes his way to the back door that leads to the backyard and the indoor pool at the back of my property. The door closes before I can stop him.

Peggy moves to fill the space where Heath was before. Her worried eyes find mine. "Garrett, I'll ask you again, is everything okay?" she asks and reaches across the granite to cover my hand with hers.

"Not exactly."

She raises her brow and squeezes my hand tightly as the front door chimes.

"I'll get the door." She walks toward the front of the house and turns to address me. "Are you here?" she asks, knowing that I frequently tell her to send people away.

"Yes," I answer reluctantly. I know who's outside my door.

I hear the door open and several voices outside. "We're here to see Garrett Armstrong."

Peggy gets flustered and escorts them toward the kitchen. Her eyes are now wide with worry. "Um, Garrett, the police are here to see you."

Two uniformed police officers enter, followed by a woman dressed in plain clothes. *Is she a detective?* My heart jumps in my chest as the situation begins to feel more suspicious.

"Mr. Armstrong?" One of the police officers walks toward me, and I instinctively back up, defensive.

"Yes, how can I help you?"

"We were told that your friend, Heath Strickland, is also here. We'd like to question both of you regarding the death of Sadie Moore."

Peggy quickly walks to the back door. "He's out back. I'll get him." The look on her face indicates alarm and fear.

"I'm Officer Andrews and this is Officer Newman." I nod toward the police officers and look at the woman behind them. "This is Nicole Thomas. She's the social worker assigned to the case."

Social worker?

Peggy and Heath return and introductions commence again.

"How did you gentlemen know Ms. Moore?" Andrews addresses both of us.

"Heath didn't know her. I mean, he just met her today when she came to see me on our tour bus."

"Okay, so how did *you* know her, Mr. Armstrong?" I don't like his tone.

"She was a groupie. We met last year, and I hadn't seen her since then until today." I snap back at him.

"How did she know where to find you?" he asks.

"We're on tour. It's not hard to know where we are." This guy is pissing me off. Peggy moves through the kitchen and gets my attention. Her eyes tell me all I need to see. She wants me to hold it together.

"Did you have a relationship with her?"

"No. Like I said, we met *once* last year. I never heard from her again until today."

Newman steps forward. "We're trying to understand what happened today. Ms. Moore entered your bus and then died of a drug overdose within minutes. We'd like to know how this happened and where she got her drugs from."

"How can I possibly know that?" I practically shout. "I haven't seen her since last year. We didn't even know each other. It was a one-time hook-up." I run my hand through my hair and try to regulate my breathing.

"So you never saw the drugs that she took? You didn't share any with her? Are you willing to submit a urine and saliva sample for drug testing?"

What the fuck?

Suddenly Heath speaks up. "I don't see the need for Garrett to submit any samples to you for drug testing. He wasn't hanging out with her. When she barged onto our bus, she was already wasted." He pauses. "Do we need to get a lawyer here? My father is the District Attorney, and I'm sure he'll have some recommendations."

What?

Andrews and Newman back down for the first time and relief floods my chest. "No. No need to call the D.A., I mean, your father," Newman says. "I think we have what we need regarding Ms. Moore."

"Can I speak to Mr. Armstrong now?"

I turn toward the voice behind me and the social worker, Nicole Thomas, walks past us into the kitchen.

"We'll be outside," Andrews huffs, and the officers leave through the front door.

"Is there someplace more comfortable we can go?" Her tone is much softer than the two police officers, but somehow more serious.

"The den is in here." I lead her through the kitchen into an open space toward the back of the house. She sits in one of the oversized chairs and I sit on the large sectional couch.

"Are you aware that Sadie gave birth to a baby boy about two weeks ago?" she asks.

I want to lie to her. Tell her that I have no idea what she's talking about. Tell her to leave my house immediately and never come back. But I see Peggy standing in the kitchen with her arms crossed over her chest. She can hear everything we're saying, and I don't want to lie in front of her. I can't.

"Yes," I say reluctantly and pull the crumpled birth certificate from my pocket.

"Sadie showed me this right before she…"

Nicole reaches out and looks at the birth certificate and nods. Her expression changes and she looks upset. Her eyes glisten, and she places the paper on the table in front of her. "I've been working with Sadie for a long time. She was a drug addict. As soon as she tested positive for drug use after she gave birth to Kai, I was called to intervene. She refused care and left the hospital shortly after he was born. He was very sick as you can imagine. He also tested positive for drugs and has been in the neonatal intensive care unit for the past two weeks." She pauses and wrings her hands together.

"Why are you telling me all of this?" I stand up and begin pacing back and forth. I feel every fiber from the rich rug beneath my still-bare feet. I imagine the carpet pulling me in, hiding me away. *I need to escape.*

"Kai has no one. He's alone now."

"What the hell do you want me to do about it?" I spit back at her. She can't be thinking what I think she is.

"Please sit down. You're making me nervous."

I stop pacing and see that Peggy and Heath are huddled in the kitchen. I sink back onto the couch and throw my head back, exhaling deeply. I don't want to hear what she has to say. I don't want to know anything more about Sadie or Kai.

"Mr. Armstrong?" Nicole implores. "You need to hear me out."

I lean forward, placing my elbows on my knees so my hands can support my head. "Fine."

"Sadie Moore is a product of the foster system. I've been her social worker since she was nine years old. Her biological mother was a drug addict and was incarcerated for possession with the intent to distribute. While she served a five-year sentence in prison, Sadie was placed in foster care. Her mother was released when Sadie was fourteen and wanted nothing to do with her. Her mom disappeared shortly after her prison stay, and we never heard from her again. Sadie remained in the foster system until she was eighteen and then was placed in a group home." Nicole pauses and tears fill her eyes.

"I failed Sadie. I was supposed to help her and I failed. She followed in the footsteps of her mother and became an addict. That can't happen to Kai. *We* can't let that happen."

I look up at her as she brushes tears from her cheeks. I feel the couch sink next to me and realize Peggy has joined us.

"What can we do?" Peggy asks.

Nicole looks surprised and focuses her gaze on Peggy. "I'm sorry, who are you?" she asks.

"Margaret Weston. I'm Garrett's aunt. Everyone calls me Peggy."

What? What is she doing? Why is she lying about being my aunt?

"I'm sorry," I interrupt. "I don't know what's going on, but I don't think *my aunt* has anything to add here."

"I disagree," Peggy states sternly. "Please continue with your story, Ms. Thomas." She grabs my forearm and holds tight, her nails digging dangerously into my skin.

Nicole takes a deep breath and her eyes lock onto mine. "Sadie was a troubled girl, as you can imagine. She was in and out of juvenile detention centers throughout her teen years. It was hard keeping her in a good foster environment. She was very violent toward her caregivers and the state had a difficult time finding a foster home without any other children. Because of her violent disposition, they needed to place her alone. We tried everything and finally we thought we found the perfect home for her. This was just before her seventeenth birthday and she wanted nothing to do with it. She took off, and we lost track of her for close to a year. By the time we found her again, she was arrested for prescription drug fraud and placed again in a juvenile detention center. She was released a few weeks after her eighteenth birthday and put into a group home."

"Why are you telling me all of this?" I ask. "This has nothing to do with me."

Peggy's nails threaten to pierce my skin, and I try to pull my arm away from her grasp.

"This has everything to do with you, Mr. Armstrong. You're Kai's father, and he needs a good and stable home." She looks around my house, taking it all in.

"Then find him one. Just not here." As soon as the words leave my mouth, Peggy gasps and practically draws blood from me.

"We're trying." Nicole's tears are back, and her face begins to blur. The room seems to be tilting or spinning or something.

"Garrett? Are you okay?" Peggy releases her death grip on my arm and calls out to the kitchen. "Heath, can you bring some water?"

He tosses a bottle my way, and I open it up right away. I take a sip then gulp the rest down. I feel like I'm on another planet right now or in a dream. *Please let this be a dream.*

"We're trying to find Kai a home. As I mentioned before, I had been working with Sadie again recently, helping her form an adoption plan. She realized she couldn't take care of her son and was supportive of the plan. She even went as far as selecting a family to potentially adopt him. We had begun working with an attorney who specializes in private adoptions. The day that Kai was born, Sadie tested positive for multiple drugs. We had to disclose this to the adoption attorney, who informed us that the family that he had been working with declined to adopt Kai. Sadie was devastated and left the hospital. That was the last time I saw her—alive."

"Jesus," Heath and I say at the same time.

"I don't know what I can do," I respond honestly. I'm not equipped to bring a baby into this house. I'm not equipped to take care of anyone. *I'm not equipped to be a father.*

"Just try to work with me, *please*. My goal is to place Kai with family. You're his only family now."

"This isn't right. You can't just come in here and try to throw this major guilt trip my way about a sick little boy who needs a father!" I'm angry at how unfair this situation is and I want her out of my house.

"Garrett!" Peggy's voice booms throughout the den. "Hear her out. There's a solution here, and we need to do what's best for this little boy."

What the fuck is going on?

"Please listen to me. I'm begging you," Nicole pleads once again.

"Please, Garrett," Peggy says calmly.

"Here's how I can help. I have plenty of money. Let me hire a private investigator and see if we can find some real blood relatives out there. They have to exist." The possibility of the alternative is terrifying.

"There is nobody else. We've tried to find Sadie's family before. I've been trying since she was nine years old. She had no one. She died alone."

"But there must be a foster home willing to take him, right?" I'm grasping, desperate.

All three sets of eyes in the room turn to me, and I feel them burn through my skull. *Judging.*

"I'm in a band. Constantly on the road. I can't commit to this," I say weakly, suddenly embarrassed.

"Really?" Heath interrupts. "Our tour is over after tomorrow night's show. Then we have time off before we begin writing our next album. I expect we'll be here for at least twelve to eighteen months before we're back on the road again."

"Exactly! Until we're back on the road *again*. Like we are for six to eight months every year. Sleeping on tour buses. Partying like the rock stars that we are. Dude, what are you trying to do?" My fists are clenched, and I'm doing everything I can to not jump up and strangle Heath.

"Why don't we call your parents?" Peggy quietly interjects. "I know that between me and them, we can help raise this baby in a loving environment and give him the home he deserves."

Holy shit.

"Leave my parents out of this, *Aunt Peggy*. They're in North Carolina and are too far to be involved in this decision."

"Yes, but they still have a home in town and can be here at a moment's notice. They're retired, and I'm sure they would be thrilled to know they have a grandson."

Is she threatening me? What is she trying to do?

"I don't know. This is all so crazy. I can't do this." The room begins to spin again and this time I think I'm going to throw up.

Nicole fidgets in her seat and looks uncomfortable. She crosses her legs, her eyes sad and pleading.

"Mr. Armstrong, I have to tell you that this is a highly unusual situation, even for me. I shouldn't even be here, begging you like this. But I feel—I feel responsible for this child's life more than I can express. If I could take him myself, I would. I have four of my own children at home and a husband who works the night shift. We live in a tiny three-bedroom home and have no room for our own family much less adding another. I wish I could take him. Oh my God, I need to leave. This is wrong…"

Nicole bolts out of the chair and runs toward the front door. My emotions are all over the place and I'm suddenly worried for this baby who everyone keeps telling me is mine. I'm worried that he'll wind up in some dark alley like Sadie. Alone. Forgotten.

"Wait!" Peggy and I call out in unison. Nicole stops and slowly turns around, and Peggy grabs my hand.

"What were you going to say?" I ask Peggy.

"I was going to tell her that we'll take him," she responds quickly. "Isn't that what you were going to say?"

I swallow heavily and shake my head. "No, Peggy, I plan to offer her money." The look of disgust on her face chokes me, and I want to hide. Nicole comes back into the room with hope in her eyes, and I'm about to crush her yet again.

Peggy pulls me into a tight hug and says sternly in my ear, "You'll take your son, and I am going to help. You need to trust me."

How can this woman have so much control over me? She's my housekeeper. Someone I barely spend time with. Yet she's become ingrained in my family. My parents keep tabs on me through her. She's a fixture here, and now she's offering to help raise a child I just learned about today.

"Peggy, I don't—" I can't seem to say the words that are stuck in my throat, choking the life out of me.

"Nicole, what do we need to do to make this happen?" Peggy interrupts and Nicole lets out a relieved breath.

She fumbles with her cell phone and says, "Let me call the hospital now and make all of the arrangements."

"Hospital?" I ask hesitantly.

Nicole responds with sadness in her eyes, "Mr. Armstrong, your son is a very sick little boy."

Peggy grabs my hand and squeezes tight. I look at her with dread.

"We got this," she says confidently.

CHAPTER 8

Sam
Past
Villanova, Pennsylvania
Age 10

"SAMANTHA, ARE YOU READY?" Mom's voice echoes through the house as I pull together what I need from my desk.

"Coming, Mom!" I call as I run down the stairs.

"Dad's waiting outside. He's already loaded the car." She kisses me on my cheek and we rush out the door together.

He's outside, closing the back of our SUV. "We're all set!" he says cheerfully and rushes to get into the driver's seat. I slide into the back and look over my shoulder.

My science project is perfectly positioned in the back—our universe literally hanging by a thread.

"Dad, do you think we have the planets balanced okay? Jupiter looks like it's a little droopy," I say, reaching back trying to touch the Styrofoam planet and position it properly.

"Don't touch it, Sam. I had to creatively position it so it would fit. We'll assemble it as soon as we get there," Dad says confidently.

Now I'm worried. What if all of our hard work gets crushed in the back of our SUV? This is the science fair. THE science fair.

"Dad, why can't I just—" I stretch as far as I can, but Jupiter is still out of my reach.

"Breathe, Sam. *Breathe.*" His voice is soothing, and I relax my arm until it drops into my lap.

"It just needs to be perfect, Dad. This is like ninety percent of my grade this marking period."

"Stop exaggerating. It's not ninety percent. It's not even twenty percent of your grade. Your teacher said it was extra credit, and you already have an *A* so calm down." He smiles and says, "You know, you remind me of myself when I was your age. In fact, I seem to remember doing something very similar. I was obsessed with math and science and won first place in my science fair that year with a very similar-looking solar system."

"No pressure or anything, Dad!" *First place? Ugh!*

We pull up to the school, and I see all of the familiar faces from my science class. Cassie's here with her grandparents. She didn't do a project; she's just here to support me.

"Oooh! Look at the planets." She stares into the back of our SUV. My mother disappeared as soon as we got here and quickly emerges from the building with a rolling cart.

"It should fit nicely on this," she exclaims, very proud of herself with the assist.

"That's perfect, honey," my dad says, and they smile at each other. I swear, I never see them upset, sad or arguing.

With my help, we slide the solar system onto the cart and carefully roll it into our gymnasium that's been converted to a science fair.

I look around and don't see any other solar systems. *Phew!*

"Let's get this to your table." Dad maneuvers through the crowds of people and expertly transfers the solar system onto my table.

I circle the display, making sure every pin is in place, every planet is in proper alignment. After confirming the labels are in the correct places, I take a deep breath. "It looks good, Dad."

"It sure does. You've got yourself a winner here," he says proudly and pulls me into his chest for one of his famous hugs.

I scan the other displays and try to find my steepest competition. Eddie Boyle is testing his volcano, and it doesn't seem to be working. Trisha O'Toole has a greenhouse-like contraption with a lopsided tomato plant as its focal point. Piper Greenstein is watering a sunflower, and there may or may not be a bumble bee buzzing over her head. *Nice touch, Piper.*

There are at least fifteen other students fussing with their displays and worry begins to set in.

"You've got this," my dad whispers in my ear. "Don't let them see you sweat."

"I don't know, Dad. Piper has a live bumble bee." We both look over toward her table when Mr. Fahey swats at the bee, knocking it to the floor, and then stomps on it.

"Not anymore." My dad laughs.

"Ew," I say as Mr. Fahey grinds his foot into the floor even harder. I think it's officially mushed.

Good, Piper no longer has a chance now that her bee is dead.

"Boys and Girls. Moms and Dads." Mr. Fahey's voice is barely audible over the speaker system.

"Thank you for coming today to the Fifth Grade Science Fair. I know the students who chose to participate worked really hard on their projects." His eyes scan the room and find Cassie. She refused to do a project and didn't care if she missed out on the opportunity to get a boost in her grade. I know he was disappointed that she decided not to participate.

"For the next sixty minutes, science teachers from other schools in our district and I, will make our way to each display. We will rate it on several factors, including accuracy, size and scale, functionality and overall merit. Good luck to all of you and we'll announce winners when we're finished."

"What does merit mean?" I ask my father.

"It means it has to be good overall. They'll take it all under consideration and base their judgment on that. Don't worry, Sam. Your solar system is perfect."

"You mean *our* solar system." I smile and give him a kiss.

The next hour is stressful. I watch the judges move from table to table with scowls on their faces. They don't seem to like any of the projects, and I'm sure mine will not impress them in the least.

Mr. Fahey leads the group to my table and stops, quietly observing. I see them bending and measuring the distance between planets. They keep referring to the scale that I placed at the corner of my table. One of the other judges takes a plastic ruler from her pocket, and places it over the scale and nods her head. I have no idea what is going on, but they are all mumbling amongst themselves.

"Ms. Weston, can you tell us the size of our solar system?" My chest clenches and I look over at my dad, who just smiles and nods his head.

"Well, I don't think anyone has been able to come up with an exact size, but many astronomers say if you drove your car from the Sun to Pluto, it would take six thousand years."

"And our entire solar system?" Mr. Fahey presses.

"That could take a car almost nineteen million years to drive, Mr. Fahey. It's really, really big."

I take a deep breath and try to think of other things they could possibly quiz me on.

"This solar system is constructed remarkably, Ms. Weston. Your attention to detail is quite stunning," one of the judges says with a smile. My dad nudges me and I swat his hand away.

"Thank you."

The group moves on to Eddie's table, and he's practically in tears. His volcano hasn't worked properly all day, and I suddenly feel sorry for him.

"See?" Dad's voice booms with pride. "I told you it was going to be a piece of cake!"

"That was wonderful, honey," my mother says as she kisses me on the cheek. "You make us so very proud."

"Thanks, Mom and Dad, but I didn't win yet. They still have to visit a few more tables and who knows what they thought of everyone else. I'm not holding my breath."

Cassie comes running over. "Did you see Piper's project? The sunflower is practically dead! I don't know what she's trying to prove with hers, but she's going to lose." It's no secret that Cassie doesn't like Piper, but you have to give the girl credit for trying.

"Be nice," I state, and Cassie giggles.

"You, on the other hand, definitely put in the work. You can light it up like a Christmas tree."

She grabs my hand when she sees Mr. Fahey and the other judges deliberating in the corner. "This is it!" she squeals.

My father places his hands on my shoulders and squeezes. "We got this," he says confidently.

HOURS LATER, I'M STANDING in front of my bedroom mirror, and I can't wipe the smile from my face.

They were all right.

The First Prize blue ribbon is hanging on my bedroom mirror. I touch it and feel victory with every stroke.

"We're so proud of you, Sam." Mom's voice is soft behind me.

I see my parents' reflection in the mirror as they enter the room. Dad's arm is draped around Mom's waist.

"Thanks. I couldn't have done it without you *both*."

"That's the first of many prizes for your hard work," Dad says.

"Let's go celebrate!" Mom grabs my hand and leads us both out the door.

As we head out to our favorite restaurant, my smile remains huge. I watch my parents hold hands in the front seat of the SUV, and I can feel their love all around me.

They make me so happy, and I never want this feeling to go away.

They're everything to me.

CHAPTER 9

Garrett
Past
Philadelphia, Pennsylvania
Age 18

"GARRETT, WE'RE SO PROUD OF YOU." My mother's face shines through the haze of the smoky bar.

"Son, we couldn't be prouder," Bill says, squeezing my shoulder.

Son.

It still feels weird and a little uncomfortable, but I called Bill 'Dad' accidentally a few weeks ago, and he's been calling me 'Son' ever since. He's a great guy and loves Mom so much. He's given us both a wonderful life and hasn't ever looked down on the profession that I've chosen.

Of course, it wasn't so easy the night that my mom found out that I hadn't really gone to Rob Shultz's house almost three years ago. She called Mrs. Shultz the second I walked out the door, confirming her immediate suspicions that I was lying to her. As soon as I got home, she grilled me about where I'd gone and why I felt like I couldn't tell her the truth. So I stopped lying and told her everything.

I told her that I'd gone to find my father. She was crushed, like I had kicked her in the stomach. I told her that he hadn't been there, and I had been strangely relieved. I honestly don't know what I would have done if I'd seen him that day. The last time I saw him was when I was seven. That wasn't a pleasant day, nor was it a great memory to have of your father who abandoned the only family he had. Mom told me it was for the best. I told her that the guys next door said he was in jail, and she nodded like she already knew that.

Who knows if he's still in jail. I don't really care. Even before he left us, my mother had taken over all of the parental responsibilities. She was *both* my mother *and* my father for so long. That is until Bill came along. He moved into our lives effortlessly.

I'm thankful for him and so happy that my mother ended up with the type of man she was meant to be with.

"Thanks," I say to my parents as Bill gives me the best bro-hug he can imitate.

Tristan catches my eye, and he's being followed by no less than a dozen girls. I smile and kiss my mom on the cheek. "Thanks for coming, but I—uh—I have to be somewhere."

"Be careful, Garrett." My mother looks disapprovingly toward Tristan and our first-ever groupies. "Those girls don't look like they have your best interests in mind."

Bill laughs out loud and squeezes my shoulder. "Claire, let him have fun. He's a good kid." He pats the back of my neck and pushes me toward Tristan. "Let's go home." He pulls my mother close and kisses her on the cheek.

"Dude!" Tristan yells after my parents leave the bar.

"Stop," I say. "No need to make fun. They had a great time and now they're gone."

"I didn't say anything. Them coming was nice and all, but it's about time they left so we can have fun with the *ladies*."

Several squeals come from his entourage, and I walk toward them. A short blonde catches my eye, and she flips her hair. "Hey," she says, her voice soft.

"Hey." Suddenly, I'm pulled backwards toward a booth in the corner. Dax says, "She's off limits."

"What?" I ask and slide into the booth across from him. "What do you mean she's off limits? Since when do you have dibs?" I ask jokingly.

"No dude, she's Bob's niece."

Bob is the bartender here at The High Note and, if I remember correctly, she's only fifteen.

"What the fuck is she doing in here—looking like *that*?" She's wearing the shortest shorts I've ever seen with half of her ass hanging out. Her tank top is way too small and her tits are practically spilling out the sides.

"Bob's on vacation with her parents. She snuck out tonight with her *very* underage friends. Stay here while I grab Tristan before he gets arrested for what he's about to do with the redhead." Dax bolts out of the booth and sprints toward the girls surrounding Tristan.

Alex walks over and slides into Dax's spot. "What's with all of that?" he asks and gestures toward the group.

"Something about Bob's niece and her friends. Whatever," I say and toss some popcorn from the bowl in between us into my mouth.

"Shit, Bob is going to kill him." He looks over at Tristan, who's now flanked by both Bob's niece *and* the redhead. We watch as Dax whispers into Tristan's ear and his face suddenly turns white.

I practically choke on the popcorn just watching his expression. I can read his lips perfectly as he says, "No shit."

They desert the girls quickly and join us in our booth.

"Jailbait." I smirk and punch Tristan in the shoulder.

"Not funny, you fuckers. That girl looks at least twenty, if not older."

"You almost went for Bob's niece, douche-face," Dax says to me and throws a handful of popcorn into my face.

Tristan punches me back and declares, "We're even. Now don't punch me again."

I shake my head and wince.

Girls are easy to find, especially here, but hooking up with Bob's niece would have been a major problem—on so many levels.

"We should start asking these chicks for I.D.," I say. "It would suck if one of us got nabbed for sex with a minor." I look to my right and Tristan is twirling a straw in his fingers.

"Whatever, man," he says. "I'm no trolling pervert, but there is *no way* you can tell those girls are only fifteen and sixteen years old. Their parents should seriously lock them up."

Alex is silent, and he's totally out of sorts today. He rubs his ribs and winces. Dax witnesses his discomfort and asks, "How's the new tat?"

"What did you get this time?" I ask. Alex has been getting ink for as long as I've known him. He's always been able to pass for a little older, and the tattoo parlors he's gone to have never questioned his age. Now that he's eighteen, he can get anything he wants.

"Nothing," he says, dismissing my question.

"It's dark. That's all you need to know," Dax says, protecting Alex as usual. Those two have a pretty strong bond, and at first

I thought they were brothers. Alex has lived with Dax for a few years, and I only recently found out why.

Alex's father killed himself four years ago after he tried to kill Alex.

Totally fucked up.

I can't even imagine his situation. My dad was never abusive toward my mom or me. He put us in harm's way when he owed tens of thousands of dollars in gambling debts, but he would never raise a hand to hurt either of us.

Thank God Alex was taken in by Dax's family. I think he would have self-destructed otherwise.

"What's next?" Tristan asks, addressing Dax. "When's our next gig?"

Dax pulls a folded piece of paper from his pocket and smooths it out on the table in front of him.

"Next Thursday, Friday and Saturday we're back here. We play one gig on Thursday night, two on Friday and one on Saturday."

Tristan groans. "Does that mean we're playing Happy Hour on Friday, because the last time we did that, we were singing to fifty-year-old dudes."

"Suck it up, asshole. Do you want to be able to pay your rent this month?" Dax says, annoyed.

Tristan pipes down and Dax runs through the next several weeks' worth of shows. Apparently, there's a record label interested in seeing us. Alex is skeptical, but the rest of us think it's a major deal.

"We'll use these next few weeks to get ready for the label rep to come see us next month. He's coming here on the eighteenth."

"My birthday," I say, smiling.

"It's going to be an epic night."

CHAPTER 10

Sam
Present
Villanova, Pennsylvania
Age 23

"ABSOLUTELY NOT!" I yell at Aunt Peggy. I'm disgusted by what she just asked me, *practically begged me*, to do. "There is no way in hell I'm going to do this, so just back off."

"Hear me out, Samantha." Her tone is firm. There have only been two times she's spoken to me like this and neither time was good. "I need you to listen to everything I have to say before you say no again."

I flop onto the couch and yell again. "Do you have any idea what I've just been through? *What I've done?* I can't possibly consider what you're suggesting."

I'm hanging on by a thread right now after the incident with baby Ben. I haven't left my room for days. My guilt consumes me, and all I can think about is what I did wrong. How I killed a defenseless baby.

"Sam, if there is a child that needs you more than this one does, tell me and I'll leave you alone." She glares at me and I glare back.

"No child needs me! No child should be around me right now. I fucked up and I killed a *baby*! Do you hear me?" I'm screaming and shaking at the same time. She rushes to my side and throws her arms around me.

"Shhh, Sam. Calm down." Her hands get caught in my tangled curls.

"You can't ask me to do this," I plead with her. Tears are freely flowing down my face, and she looks at me with pity. *I hate that look.* I don't deserve her pity, or anyone's, for that matter.

She starts talking over my sobs and I know she won't stop until I hear her out. I wipe the dampness from my cheeks. I hate feeling sorry for myself. It makes me feel weak and useless. I nod once and she quickly jumps back into her request.

"Kai is a very sick little boy. His mother was addicted to some pretty bad drugs. She died of an apparent overdose, leaving him alone. She has no family at all. Now he's suffering and about to be discharged to his father, who only just found out about him yesterday. The social worker has done everything within her power to find Kai a stable and loving home, but everything has fallen through. This baby *needs* you, Sam. Please. I'm begging you."

Her stern voice turns soft and I see the worry and sadness in her eyes.

"Why are you asking *me*?" I ask.

"Because you're the only one who can do it. I've seen you with the babies you care for. You save their lives every moment you're with them. You're the first line of defense should something go wrong and you help some through their last breaths on this earth." I suck in a breath and open my mouth to correct her. I want to tell her that she's wrong. I'm a killer. She ignores me and continues, "You're the reason why ninety-nine-point-nine percent of the severely sick babies born in your hospital survive. You, Samantha."

My self-doubt creeps in and more tears flow. "But I'm also the reason why one very special little boy is dead. Don't you see? I'm not ready for this. I may never be ready for this ever again."

Her look is stern once more. "Stop. I won't listen to you talk like this. You'll come to accept that what happened with baby Ben was an accident. It will take time, but you'll accept it." She squeezes my hand and she knows I'm resisting. I don't want to believe her. I can never accept the damage that I've caused. I don't understand why she doesn't see that.

"I won't take no for an answer. You can't refuse to help this poor baby. You took an oath as a nurse. You can't turn your back on this child. I won't let you."

She's not going to back down.

"His social worker described what's wrong with him with some technical term." She pauses, trying to remember.

"Neonatal Abstinence Syndrome," I answer for her.

"That's it," she says, nodding her head. "So you know all about what it is and how to care for this child." *She baited me and is reeling me in.*

"Of course I do." She knows this already. She's heard me tell countless stories of babies just like Kai.

"That's what I thought. So tell me what we need to have on hand. He's being discharged from the hospital the day after tomorrow." She pulls out the pocket notebook that she carries with her everywhere. It contains her lists that help her run her daily life.

After I tell her the supplies I'm going to need, I suddenly realize what I've committed to and I feel sick.

"I don't even know your boss, Aunt Peggy. How can you expect me to move in there? This is absurd!"

She started working there when I went to nursing school and we never talk about it. She also does other personal assistant work for several families in our area, and I can never keep straight who she's working for when.

"His name is Garrett Armstrong and he's a musician."

Garrett Armstrong.

Garrett Armstrong.

I repeat the name over and over silently in my head, knowing it sounds familiar, but I can't quite place it.

I hear Cassie's high-pitched voice behind me, "GARRETT ARMSTRONG?" she screeches.

She runs around the couch and jumps up and down in front of me. "Do you know who he is?" Her voice goes up another octave and pierces my ears. I shake my head.

Aunt Peggy is finishing up her list and she clicks her pen after closing her notebook.

"Uh, Epic Fail?" Cassie says and the recognition sets in. I saw a tabloid article on the Internet this morning about Garrett Armstrong and some groupie OD'ing on his tour bus.

Cassie's eyes light up. "Aunt Peggy, if Sam doesn't want the job, I'll take it." She clasps her hands together and is nearly bursting at the seams.

"Fine, the job's yours," I say and stand up to leave the room. I can't be a part of any of this. My head is pounding, and I just want to curl up and go to sleep.

"Samantha Katherine Weston." My Aunt's voice booms through the living room.

Dammit.

"Oh shit," I hear Cassie say under her breath. "I was only

kidding, Aunt Peggy." Her voice turns sweet and she rushes past me up the stairs.

"Talk to your aunt. I don't think you have a choice," she says as she disappears down the hall and into my room.

I stop in my tracks and turn back to face my aunt.

"Do you care how I feel?" I try to expose her guilt.

"No. Not in this case. You've always trusted me, Samantha. You've always trusted that I know what's best. You *must* trust me now. *You* are what's best for Kai. You're going to help turn what could be a very troubled young life around. Give this baby a chance. Please."

I raise my eyes to meet hers again and they're filled with worry.

"I saw him this morning." She covers her mouth with her hand and chokes back a sob. "He's at your hospital."

My heart sinks.

"Dr. Hagan said he came into your NICU the day Ben died. He was supposed to be transferred to CHOP, but well, after what happened, there was a bed available at your hospital. She's spent quite a good deal of time with him, and she knows he has a good chance at a good life, as long as he has the proper care. I told her that I was going to ask you. She agreed it would be a good idea."

"You know I'm on administrative leave, right? I could possibly lose my nursing license. I may not be qualified for this job," I say, and she shakes her head.

"I spoke with Jim and confirmed that you can do anything you want while you're on administrative leave."

"Why would you speak with my boss? Aunt Peggy, you've gone too far." I'm angry now. She's never meddled in my career before, and it makes me uncomfortable that she's speaking with my co-workers and boss.

"When you meet Kai, you'll understand why I've done what I've done." She turns to leave the room. "I'm going to the pharmacy to buy everything on the list."

And with that, she's gone.

I hear her car back out of the garage and Cassie comes bounding down the stairs.

"Holy shit!" she exclaims.

Yeah, holy shit.

CHAPTER 11

Garrett
Present
Villanova, Pennsylvania
Age 26

I PULL INTO MY LONG DRIVEWAY and watch through the rearview mirror as the privacy gate closes behind me. I'm trapped in a cage now, and I'm dreading what's inside waiting for me.

I press the button above me and the garage opens slowly. I pass Peggy's parked car as I maneuver my way next to the Land Cruiser. Bile rises in my throat and I slowly open the door.

What am I doing?

Three days ago, Peggy talked me into taking in a sick baby. *My sick baby.* I've regretted even giving her the power to force that decision on me. *How did I let this happen?*

Before I can turn and flee, the door between the garage and the house opens and Peggy emerges.

"We picked up Kai a few hours ago, and Sam is getting him settled. I wanted to talk to you before you came inside, so you know exactly what to expect." Her worried expression tells me I shouldn't have allowed this to transpire.

I open my mouth to tell her to get them out of my house, but she ignores my movement and speaks again.

"Kai is sick. You already know this. He has Neonatal Abstinence Syndrome."

"I know," I state.

"He cries. A lot. And his cries aren't *normal* baby cries. They are high-pitched and will cut right through to your heart."

I don't know what she *thinks* she's preparing me for, but I turn back to my car and unlock it.

"Garrett! Where do you think you're going?" Her tone reminds me of my mother and I stop in my tracks. She grabs my arm, turning me around and leads me to the door of the house. She stops just before we enter.

"Sam has calmed him down, and he's sleeping for now. I just wanted to warn you in case he wakes up. I don't want you to be alarmed."

"Peggy, this whole situation is fucked up." I walk past her into the house, hoping I'm walking out of a bad dream.

The house is so quiet you can hear a pin drop. I walk through the kitchen looking for Peggy's niece. The counters are filled with bags from the pharmacy and Babies R Us. Open boxes line the floor and baby things are everywhere. Swings and diapers and blankets. I feel like I'm going to pass out.

Peggy quickly places a cold bottle of water in my hand and says quietly, "Drink."

"Whiskey," I say, and my voice is hoarse. My lips feel like they're cracking, and all I can think about is the double barrel whiskey that's in the liquor cabinet. I place the bottle of water on the counter and keep walking into the den. The cabinet is on the far end of the room, and I need to get there now. I reach for the door and it won't open. I tug again and it's jammed.

"Safety locks." Peggy's voice startles me. She walks past me and pulls something out of her pocket and swipes it along the door. I hear a click as the cabinet lock disengages and she hands me what appears to be a magnet.

"What the hell?" I say as she pours me two fingers of whiskey.

"Drink."

I swig it back and pass the glass back to her, indicating that I want more. She shakes her head and closes the cabinet.

"Are you relaxed yet?" she asks.

"No, and I don't see myself getting there anytime soon."

"Stop being so damn selfish and get yourself together," Peggy snaps at me and I stiffen.

The past three days have been a whirlwind. After *we* agreed to take Kai in, I flew to Charlotte so I could explain what was going on to my parents. I didn't want them to hear about this from the tabloids. Needless to say, my mother was shocked. Bill told me that he would help in any way that he could. They had already seen the news story about the 'groupie' dying from a drug overdose on our tour bus. Now they know the true story and not what the media is spreading. My return flight landed just under an hour ago, and I don't even recognize the home I left yesterday. Peggy has completely transformed my bachelor pad into a nursery. I feel sick.

She turns me around, and we head toward the back set of stairs that leads to the guest rooms. I hear soft music coming from the room farthest down the hall. It sounds so familiar, but it's an instrumental lullaby.

"Epic Fail Rock-a-Bye-Baby," Peggy whispers, and I stop in my tracks.

"What?"

"I wanted Kai to hear his father's music, but he isn't ready for rock and roll just yet, so I got him the softer, lullaby versions of your songs."

What the fuck?

I shake my head and look at her. "Is there anything else that you need to tell me?"

The soft pings of music I hear through the door are a complete bastardization of one of our chart-topping singles. It makes me want to vomit.

She opens the door slowly, and the first thing I see is a crib. The blinds are drawn in the room, but the ceiling is glowing with hundreds of stars and constellations. There's a person in the rocking chair at the far end of the room, holding a baby close to her chest. I only see her silhouette, outlined by long, flowing curls.

Peggy approaches her and whispers something inaudible in her ear. She nods and stands up slowly. Peggy takes her seat and they expertly transfer the baby from her arms to Peggy's.

She walks toward me, and her wide, blue eyes are the first thing I see. They pierce into my own and I feel a rush through my body. I don't move as she approaches me, and she suddenly looks confused. Her lips move, but I can't hear what she's saying.

"What?" I ask, too loudly, and I'm immediately shushed by Peggy.

"Hallway," she says and walks past me.

I follow her and stop outside the door. She brushes against me as she reaches to pull the door closed. Her shirt shifts and I see cleavage. My pants stir and my fight-or-flight response takes over. She's stunning. Tall. Athletic. Fucking hot. She can't be the baby nurse.

She can't be the fucking baby nurse.

"Hi," she says in barely a whisper. "I'm Sam."

She extends her right hand and I grab hold of it. Her cool, soft hand closes slowly around mine and she pumps up and down.

"Hi, Sam. I'm Garrett." I'm lost in her eyes and I can't stop shaking her hand. She blinks hard as if trying to snap me out of my temporary paralysis, and she snatches her hand away from mine.

"Let's go someplace where we can talk," she says as she brushes past me again. Her vanilla scent leads me. The only thing I want to do right now is pull her into my bedroom down the hall. *Completely inappropriate response.*

She walks past my room and down the front staircase. I suddenly forget about Peggy and the baby, and I pick up speed, bounding down the stairs two at a time.

She disappears into the library where I join her. She closes the door behind me and sits on the large leather sectional.

"I'm sure you have a lot of questions for me. Now is your chance before things get really—hectic," she says and crosses her legs. I notice she's wearing tight yoga pants that are rolled at her hips. She has tiger-striped ankle socks on and a loose fitting V-neck tee-shirt. Her brown hair is long, past her shoulders and curly. Very curly.

"What?" I ask.

A look of disgust snaps me out of the fantasy I'm about to let play out in my mind.

"Questions. Now's the time to ask because he won't be asleep much longer."

"I don't think I have any," I say and smile.

"Okay, so I guess I'll start."

She shifts on the couch, moving her legs so she's sitting cross-legged.

"I'm Samantha Weston, Peggy's niece. I'm a neonatal intensive care nurse, and I've seen all kinds of sick babies in my career. I've only been a practicing nurse for about two and a half years, but I've gained a ton of experience in that time. Your son, Kai, has Neonatal Abstinence Syndrome. As you know, he was exposed to a variety of illegal drugs and narcotic substances. The withdrawal from these drugs is causing him great distress." She looks into my eyes and nods.

I nod back, letting her know that I'm listening. Reality is setting in as this gorgeous woman tells me all about my very sick son. I hear all of the words she's saying very crisply, but her lips seem to move in slow motion. A weight begins to pull in my chest, and I lean back in the wing chair that I'm currently sitting in.

"Stop," I say, and she looks confused. "I don't think I can hear any more of this."

"Mr. Armstrong, you have to hear it. Because you're about to live it."

She tells me all about his feeding and other issues that he has. His high-pitched crying is mentioned again, and I don't understand why this is so important that both she and Peggy have mentioned it multiple times. She explains that the best care for him right now is tactile care. We need to be very hands-on and let him know that someone is always close. Swaddling him tight is also important so he feels safe. *What's swaddling?*

When Peggy talked me into this *situation*, I didn't expect that I'd need to be hands-on. Why did I hire Sam to begin with if she's going to expect me to be involved?

"I think there's some mistake," I interrupt her again, and she shoots me the same disgusted look she did just minutes ago.

"I'm sorry?" she asks.

"When I agreed to do this, Peggy assured me that you would have everything under control. I wasn't expecting to be too involved."

I'm glad I got that off my chest. I hope this clears the air.

She stands up and walks toward me. "Are you kidding me?" She scowls and now I can see the resemblance to Peggy. She smirks and says, "Let me get this straight. You *thought* that Peggy agreed to let me do everything while you ignored the fact that you have a *son* upstairs who needs his father?" Her arms are folded across her chest.

"Well, the way *you* say it makes me sound like an ass. But yeah, I didn't expect that I'd be involved in Kai's rehabilitation. I just found out about him the other day. I'm no more of a father than you are a mother."

Wow, now I sound like a complete asshole.

Her face contorts and her cheeks turn bright red. "Mr. Armstrong, I swear to God, you're lucky that I love my aunt more than life itself because—"

A piercing scream comes from behind her, and she turns quickly to grab what looks like a walkie-talkie from the couch. She turns the volume down, but the screams are high-pitched, sharp and shallow.

"What the hell is that?" I ask as dread sets in.

"That's your son, Kai." She opens the library door and darts up the stairs.

I remain glued to my seat as his cries travel down the stairs and pierce through my heart. He sounds like he's in so much pain, like he's being stabbed over and over again. It's the most awful sound I've ever heard. Worse than hearing my own mother cry.

My son is crying and I'm powerless.

CHAPTER 12

Sam
Past
Villanova, Pennsylvania
Age 15

"SAM, WHERE THE HELL ARE YOU?" Cassie's voice rattles through my head as I pull the phone away from my ear.

"My Dad is going to take me to the party after dinner." I pause and wonder what the important discussion they need to have with me is all about. When I got home from school today, there was a note on the board from my mother.

> *Don't go anywhere tonight until your father and I*
> *have had the chance to talk to you.*
> *No worries – it's all good! See you for dinner!*
> *X's & O's*
> *~ Mom~*

"What time will you be done?" she whines, and I know she's excited about tonight. Brad Mitchell is going to be there and Cassie has a huge crush on him. "What are you wearing?"

"Dinner should be ready in about five minutes, and I'm wearing a bathing suit, you dope. It's a pool party." I shake my head as I hold up the striped bikini that my mother says reminds her of some chewing gum she loved when she was younger. Fruit Stripes, I think.

"What are you wearing *over* your bathing suit? I need help accessorizing! Ugh!" She's frantic, and I know what my closet would look like if she were actually here getting ready with me.

"My white pullover and platform Steve Maddens."

"No! Absolutely not! The last time you wore those shoes, you wound up falling flat on your face in the mall. I cannot let you take your life into your hands like this. *Please* just wear flip-flops, or better yet, sneakers. You're a klutz, Sam."

I giggle and dismiss her worry. "Just stop. You know I only wear sneakers for gym."

"It's your funeral, sister. Now hurry up and eat and I'll meet you there by eight!" She hangs up and I rush to get dressed. After putting on my bikini, I slip the white cover-up-dress over my head. It falls about mid-thigh, and once I step into my Steve Maddens, I'm almost as tall as my father. I arrange my curls to cascade around my face and grab my Chapstick. It drives Cassie nuts that I never wear makeup. I usually only use Chapstick and sometimes mascara for a special occasion.

"Sam, dinner's ready!" Mom calls from the bottom of the stairs. I start to move toward the door when I slip and almost turn my ankle. I chuckle out loud and slide out of my shoes, bending down to swipe them from the floor.

"I think I'll carry you guys downstairs instead of walking, okay?" I say out loud to my favorite shoes.

By the time I reach the kitchen table, my parents are already seated and have our meals dished out. It's my favorite. My father's 'special' chicken, steamed veggies and fresh berries. My parents have always insisted on a colorful plate full of food, no matter what meal it is. He's been making this chicken for me ever since I was a little girl. I've always called it Daddy's Special Chicken when I know that it's really just breaded chicken cutlet. He loves making it for me, and I ate it practically every night for dinner for several years. I will never tire of it.

"Wow, dinner smells great," I say and slide into my chair.

Mom and Dad have smiles ear-to-ear and I can't imagine what has them so excited tonight.

"Okay, you guys look weird. What's going on?" I ask as I cut into the first piece of chicken and chew it. *It's so good.* It begins to melt in my mouth, and I savor the flavor from the breadcrumbs. "Can you pass the barbecue sauce?" Another one of my favorites.

My mother slides it across the table, and she drops her fork next to her plate.

"Your father and I have some really exciting news," she says and can't contain herself.

I look back and forth between them and my father's eyes light up even brighter.

"You do?" I ask. "Don't leave me hanging! What is it?"

Mom takes a deep breath and her eyes glisten a little.

"We haven't said anything at all because at first, we weren't sure. But it happened, and now we're thrilled and we just can't believe it!" She's all over the place, and I have no idea what she's talking about.

"What happened?" I ask and dunk a piece of chicken into the barbecue sauce and pop it in my mouth.

"Sam, we're going to have a baby," my father interrupts, and I practically choke.

"What?" I ask as I gulp down my chicken.

"Yes! I'm pregnant," my mother exclaims, and I stare between the two of them and wonder how this is even possible.

"A few years after you were born, we tried for another and were told that I couldn't have any more children. The doctors did everything they could, and we even went through fertility treatments. Nothing worked, so we decided we were happy with the family we had."

I never realized any of this, and I suddenly feel sorry for my parents for what they went through when I was little.

"So about two months ago, I wasn't feeling well, and I didn't think anything of it. I thought it was the flu or something like that."

I remember her being sick for a few weeks and she was constantly in the bathroom throwing up. I was thankful for not catching it. Now I know why I didn't.

"Mom, Dad, this is so cool." *I think?*

"Oh Sam, this is amazing! When I finally went to the doctor, he told me I was pregnant. We couldn't believe it. We'd suffered from secondary infertility for so many years and we just never thought it would happen. We never expected this, but we're so happy!"

"It's going to be an adjustment for us," my father pipes in. "We realize we aren't in our twenties or thirties anymore. With your mom turning forty this year, we're going to have to watch her closely and make sure everything is progressing along normally and healthily."

"Wow," I say and take another bite of chicken. "Do you know if it's a boy or a girl?"

"It's too early to tell yet. We'll know in ten or twelve more weeks," my mom replies and takes a sip of water.

"Wow," I say again. *A baby?*

"Cassie's going to freak out when I tell her." I laugh through chewing my food.

"Let's wait a little longer before we tell anyone else, okay?" my father asks.

"Why?"

"Because we want to make sure your mom and the baby are doing alright. We have an appointment with the doctor again next week. Why don't we see how that goes before we start sharing the news? We haven't even told Aunt Peggy yet."

"Okay." Aunt Peggy is going to be so happy. She's never been married nor has she had children of her own. She treats me like a daughter, and I know she's going to love my little brother or sister just as much. I swish water in my mouth and look down at my plate. I've eaten all of the chicken and veggies without even realizing it. The fresh berries are left, and I scarf them down without saying another word.

"Are you okay, Sam?" my mother asks hesitantly.

"Yeah. Of course I am. I'm just—just a little surprised?" *A lot surprised.*

"So are we. Oh my God you have no idea!" Mom says.

"It certainly took us by surprise, but we've realized this is a gift, just like you were. We're the luckiest parents alive." My father reaches out and grabs my hand. "We were blessed with you, and now we're all going to be blessed with this miracle."

Tears well in my eyes unexpectedly. I squeeze his hand and look over at my mother, who is outright crying now.

"I can't wait," I say honestly. The joy in my parents' eyes is infectious, and I can't help but feel like this baby is going to bring so much more love into our house.

I finish my meal, listening to my parents talk about the renovations they are going to make to the guest room upstairs.

"I hope Aunt Peggy is going to be okay with giving up her space when she stays here." I smirk, knowing how much she enjoys staying in the room next door to mine when she's here.

"We're going to renovate the first-floor library to add a daybed for guests. Since there's a bathroom off of that room, it will be like her own suite when she's here," my father says.

Aunt Peggy only lives about forty-five minutes from us as it is. She's so busy with the family that she works for, she barely spends any time in her own home.

I look at the clock, and my dad says, "We can be ready to leave in about twenty minutes. Is that good for you?"

"Yes. Cassie was very specific that I should meet her at the party by eight. Her mom is picking us up by midnight and we're sleeping at her house."

"You're not wearing those shoes, are you?" my mother asks, looking toward my Steve Maddens that I dropped next to my duffle bag near the center island in the kitchen.

"Yes I am. And I *promise* I'll be careful."

My father chuckles and says to my mom, "We've heard that before, Klutzy-McGee."

My mother chuckles and I roll my eyes.

TWENTY MINUTES LATER, we pull up in front of Trisha O'Toole's sprawling estate. There are cars parked along the circular driveway, and the backyard is lit up like a baseball stadium, music blaring.

"Her parents are home, right?" my father asks, skeptical.

"Yes, Dad."

"I think I'll come in and say hi to Mr. O'Toole. We're supposed to be playing golf at the club tomorrow, and I want to confirm the time with him."

"Ugh, Dad!" I know this is useless and he's going to come inside with me anyway. He's done this as long as I can remember, and I secretly like it. But since I'm a *teenager,* I need to give him a hard time whenever I can.

We get out of the car and walk into the grand foyer of the O'Toole's house.

"Benjamin! So great to see you," Mr. O'Toole's voice booms. "Are you ready for the tournament tomorrow?"

"Of course I am. But if I remember correctly, you weren't quite up to par the last time we played."

Mr. O'Toole laughs at my dad's pun and they walk toward his den.

"Have fun tonight, Sam." Dad pulls me in for a hug. "Watch yourself in those shoes, please."

"Don't worry." I smile confidently and walk, very deliberately, toward the back of the house. I certainly don't need to fall flat on my face, proving my father right. "Love you, Dad!" I call out before he's out of sight.

I step onto the vast patio and see the party in full swing down by the pool house.

"Sammy!" Cassie shrieks and comes running up the lawn. "You're here!"

I laugh as I walk slowly to meet her. "Take those shoes off this instant," she scolds me and grabs my hand. "You look *ah-mazing!*"

"Thanks, Cass."

"Your hair is so perfect tonight. What did you do to it?"

"I just added a little bit more shaping cream and let it air-dry longer than usual."

"Brad better notice me tonight. You better not catch his eye!" She giggles and I know she's totally kidding. I've seen Brad ogling her more than once, so I know she's on his radar.

We reach the pool house and Trish runs to greet us. "Sam! So great you could come. My dad has been talking about playing golf with your dad *all* week."

"Yeah, they're up at the house right now strategizing." I smirk and she hands me a drink.

"Shhh," she says. "It's just lemonade with a *teeny tiny* splash of citrus vodka." She winks and I take the cup hesitantly.

"Your parents are here, Trish. You better not let this party get out of hand," I say to her sternly, and she giggles out loud.

"Seriously, Sam. Lighten up." She turns to the crowd around the pool and signals to the DJ to crank up the music. The three of us dance our way across the patio and I kick off my shoes. *Just in case.*

I take a sip of the drink Trish gave me and practically gag. I drop the cup in the first trash bin I can find. I'm no prude, but I know better than to drink something Trish O'Toole has made for me. *Teeny tiny* equals *mostly* vodka.

The night flies by and most of it I'm consoling Cassie. "I can't believe he didn't come," she slurs and attempts to take another drink of Trish's electric lemonade.

"That's enough, my love." I laugh and replace the cup with a bottle of water.

She squints and peers across the lawn. "Brad! Over here!" she says and waves her hands in the air. I look toward the patio and see Brad and his older brother.

"Ugh," she says. "What the hell is Todd doing with him? Isn't he like a senior in college or something? What a *perv* coming to a high school party." She smiles through her teeth as Brad and Todd join us near the pool.

"Hey," Brad says to Cassie. He smiles quickly at me but then fixes his gaze back on her.

"Hi, Brad. I didn't know you were coming tonight," she says unconvincingly.

"Yeah."

Todd Mitchell strolls toward me and drapes his heavy arm over my shoulder.

"I'm Todd. You're hot."

My skin burns from his touch, and I squirm out from underneath him. Everything about Todd screams *run*. He's so creepy, and I've heard stories about him from Cassie's older cousin. He's rarely home from school, but when he is, he's constantly trolling for hookups. It's funny, but Brad is nothing like him. He's actually the exact opposite.

"Cassie, let's go swimming," I say, hoping to get away from this ogre of a guy. I notice Brad and Todd aren't wearing their bathing suits, so we should be safe in the water for a while.

"Okay, that sounds like fun." She giggles and shimmies out of her cover-up. Todd's eyes turn dark and Brad pushes him toward the pool house.

"Todd, thanks for the ride. You can go now," Brad says. I can see the embarrassment on his face that he's even related to this asshole.

"I think I'll hang out for a bit." He walks away, leering at other girls.

Cassie and I run toward the pool and we jump in holding hands. As soon as we hit the water, we each grab for our own bikini tops to make sure they're still in place. I hope the cool water sobers her up a little bit.

"Oh, this feels amazing!" she cries. Everything is amazing tonight to Cassie.

We slowly float toward the cozy corner of the pool where Trish and some other girls from our class are lounging.

"Trish, hey!" Cassie says.

"Girls." Trish smiles and takes a sip of her electric lemonade. "I see Brad finally made it, Cassie."

Cassie giggles and looks back toward the pool house. Brad and Todd aren't in sight, and I know she regrets leaving his side.

"Have you guys had sex yet?" Trish asks, loud enough for all of the other girls to hear. Their heads all turn inquisitively.

"What?" Cassie responds, embarrassed.

"Seriously, Cassie. Don't you think it's about time?" Piper chimes in.

Now I regret coming into the pool and subjecting Cassie to this inquisition. I know we both have a pact to wait to have sex until we're at least eighteen. That's a little more than two years away. I'm not worried, because I have no prospects on the horizon, but the way Cassie has been flirting with Brad lately, she could be jeopardizing our virgin pact.

"Ladies." Brad's voice is behind me, and Cassie immediately turns bright red.

He steps past the girls and wades into the pool toward Cassie. "You have a bathing suit?" she practically stammers.

"Of course. It's a pool party, isn't it?" He splashes her playfully and pulls her further into the water, away from us. Her eyes widen with delight and she flashes a smile just for the girls to see and be jealous.

"Well, I guess that answers our question," Piper says. "If it hasn't happened yet, it sure will tonight!" Her entourage laughs along with her, and I duck under the water, muffling their chuckles and voices. Trish's pool is huge and seems to weave through her backyard like at a sprawling resort. I swim toward the shadows of the pool so I can hide from them all and relax. I see Cassie and Brad flirting over by the waterfall, so I turn around and follow the pool toward the quiet end, giving them a little privacy.

I lean back and float, closing my eyes. I remember the conversation I had earlier tonight with my parents and smile thinking about how happy they were. I can't believe they're having a baby. *We're* having a baby. I can't imagine what it's going to be like, but I know that seeing my parents that happy makes me happy. My ears are filled with water, and I can only hear muted giggles through the water. I let the water guide me through the curves of the gigantic pool. It's almost like a river. I hear my soft breaths in my ears as my chest expands and contracts slowly.

This is how I relax.

Back when I was seven and I had the accident in my pool, my parents immediately got me a swim instructor who taught me how to float before anything else. She said I could get out of any pool if I rolled onto my back and let the waves take me slowly to the edge. I could float for hours on end in my pool and it in turn made me get over any anxiety that I had in the water. As soon as I got past my nerves, I became one with the water and never looked back. I was like a little fish, as my parents would call me, spending hours upon hours floating and enjoying the pool. I had overheard my father tell my mother that he was so glad they had made the investment that they did in the pool. I know Mom used to think it was a dangerous 'hole in the ground,' but Dad insisted that it would bring our family many years of fun. He was right.

My face is barely out of the water. Only my nose and mouth are exposed to the warm night air. The party noises are barely audible as I float through the pool.

Suddenly, I'm underwater, strong hands wrapped around my ankles, pulling me deeper and deeper. I start kicking, but I'm not strong enough. My lungs burn, and I wave my arms in the water, trying to gain momentum so I can reach the surface. A hand loosens from my ankle, but one still holds tight. I bend my body so I can see what's happening.

Todd Mitchell's face is all I see underwater. His eyes glow like lanterns, and his face contorts into a grisly smile. I let out the air that's crushing my chest and force all of the strength I have into kicking both of my legs, mermaid style. He lets go of me for a second, and that's all I need. I kick as fast and hard as I can toward the surface, and as soon as the warm air hits my face, I scream louder than I ever have before. "Help! Over here!" I pant and gasp for air, and I hear him surface behind me, his body pressed against me from behind.

"I was just playing with you, baby." His rough hand fondles my ass and I raise my heel, kicking him in the balls. "Ugh!" he grunts, and Brad swims up behind us with Cassie in tow.

"Is everything okay here?" Brad asks, his eyes worried.

"Sam?" Cassie asks hesitantly.

I reach the side of the pool and pull myself out in one motion, looking back at Todd as he tries to regain his monstrous composure. I know I kicked him hard, and I hope I busted at least one of his nuts, if not both. His glare causes chills to run down my spine.

"I'm fine," I say and look at the pool house. I see the large dial on the clock that hangs outside above the bar. "It's almost midnight, Cass. Your mom will be here any minute."

I look at Todd again to make sure he doesn't get out of the pool with us. I swipe my cover up and shoes and grab Cassie's things as well.

"I'm coming!" she calls after me as I head up to the house. "Brad, call me tomorrow?"

"Sure," he says, and then I hear him say, not so quietly, "Todd, what the fuck?"

Todd chuckles and another chill runs up my spine.

Cassie's mom is waiting for us, as I predicted. We wrap towels around us and ride home in silence. She's super excited about something but looks worried at the same time.

"Did you girls have a fun time tonight?"

"It was great, Mom." She giggles.

"Hey, what happened with Todd?" she whispers in my ear. "Are you okay?"

"Yeah, I'm okay." *I think.*

"What did he do to you?" she asks.

Her mother chimes in from the front seat, "What happened? Is everything alright?"

"Todd Mitchell was being a royal ass tonight. He was messing with Sam in the pool, and I think she kicked him in the nuts," Cassie announces proudly.

"Are you okay, dear?" she asks.

"Yes," I say and hope that I never see his face again.

"I can't imagine why Todd Mitchell would be at a high school party. And why isn't he at college where he's supposed to be?"

"Isn't he like twenty-five? He's in his like tenth year of college!" Cassie smirks and I cringe.

I have no idea how old Todd Mitchell is. My skin is still crawling from that menacing look in his eyes.

"I think you girls should stay away from that boy, okay? I don't think Todd is a very nice young man," Cassie's mom says, matter-of-fact.

Nope. Neither do I.

CHAPTER 13

Garrett
Past
Philadelphia, Pennsylvania
Age 19

THE CROWD ROARS as Alex's voice fills the room.

"Jaded…" he screams. "Weary…"

I stop strumming, and the room becomes silent as all eyes focus on Alex. His breaths are the only sound heard through the speakers.

The drums beat one last time, and he whispers into the mic, "Alone."

The room erupts with screams and applause and we're finished with our set.

That's always the perfect song to end with because it draws raw emotion from the fans. I look through the rows and rows of people rushing the stage, trying to find the record label executive who is supposed to be here tonight. I finally find her, seated at a small round table, feverishly writing notes in her spiral-bound book. She has a smile on her face.

Good.

Based on Dax's research, this label is the one to go with. He handles most of the business side of things, and he's confident this will be the best deal for us as a band. I trust him—I guess I have to.

Alex disappears into the crowd and I make my way to the back. Dax and Tristan are already there. I throw myself onto the couch, my fingers still vibrating from my guitar.

"That was amazing!" Tristan shouts, and I nod in agreement.

"Dax, that chick from the label was out there, and man she looked happy. I have a good feeling about this," I say, and Dax frowns.

"Don't get your hopes up, G. Who knows what they're going to offer us. I do know that part of their offer is likely to require a three-record deal. That type of deal makes me nervous. We're committing to so much. I'm not sure Alex will agree."

"What does it matter if he agrees or not?" I ask, annoyed that Dax always keeps Alex in the top of his mind.

"Because he's our songwriter. Without his words, we have nothing. He needs to be all in or we don't sign shit." Dax tosses his drumsticks onto the couch next to him and rubs his hands together. He's nervous.

"Where's Alex?" Dax asks.

"He said something about a girl and he jumped off the stage to find her in the audience." Tristan smirks.

"Dude, we don't need him getting all serious with a chick," I state. "As Dax said, he needs to be all in. We can't have his dick leading the charge."

Dax nods his head in agreement and Tristan snickers. "Man, how long have you known Alex? He's never been led by his dick." He falls over onto his side and laughs hysterically.

"I'm going to see what's up with the label exec. I'll be back in a few." Dax gets up and leaves the room.

"He's so uptight." I shrug. "That dude needs to get laid."

"Says the ladies' man." Tristan laughs again. "That reminds me, what happened with that blonde the other night. Did you bang her in the *bathroom?*"

"So what if I did." I don't know her name, but I most certainly did bang her in the bathroom. *Twice.*

"She was hot. She had her eye on you all night."

I remember spotting her in the crowd from the stage. She stared at me like I was the only one there, and she made me feel really good afterwards.

I wonder if she's here tonight.

I'm about to get up when Dax comes back into the room, excited. "She just gave me her card and told me to call her in the morning. They're working up an offer as we speak!" He can barely contain himself as he high-fives Tristan.

"That's amazing, bro!" I shout, thinking about the blonde again. "I'm going to try to find someone," I say as Alex comes rushing through the door.

He's muttering to himself, and he's not happy.

"Alex, you're never going to believe this," Dax says, and then his expression changes. "What's wrong?"

"Nothing," he mumbles and throws himself down on the couch. "What are you so happy about?" he scowls.

"The record label is working on an offer, and we should have it first thing tomorrow morning," Dax says.

"Great. Exciting." Alex isn't the least bit excited.

"Care to share why you're being a royal douchebag right now?" I ask.

"It's none of your business," he spits.

"Whatever," I say and get up. "Congrats, everyone. I'm looking forward to tomorrow, Dax. Don't worry, it's going to be a great offer."

I walk out of the room, and I hear Dax ask Alex about some girl he saw him with. The door shuts behind me before I can hear anything else.

I spot the blonde as soon as I enter the bar, and I'm ready to find another room in this place. She sees me too and makes her way across the crowded room. Just before she reaches me, my cell phone vibrates in my pocket. The only people who have this number are the guys and my mother. Since I know it's not Alex, Dax or Tristan, I realize it can only be Mom.

What could she be calling about? She called me as soon as I woke up this morning so she and Bill could sing "Happy Birthday" to me.

I swipe to answer and I hear her soft voice. "Garrett?"

It's loud in the bar area, so I hold up my finger when the blonde reaches me and I mouth, *I'll be right back.* She smiles and her full lips are so inviting. I back up into the quiet hallway behind the bar.

"Mom, can you hear me?" I ask, covering my exposed ear while I hold the phone to the other one.

"Yes, I can hear you," she says, and I can immediately tell by the tone of her voice that something is wrong.

"Is everything okay?" I ask, worried.

"No, it's not," she immediately replies. "Garrett, I'm so sorry to be calling you with this news. Especially on your birthday."

"Is Bill, I mean, Dad okay?" I ask, terrified she's about to tell me something bad happened to him.

"Yes, Bill's okay. But…" She pauses and I swallow hard.

What's going on?

"Mom?" I ask again, urging her to tell me what happened.

"But your *father*, he's—he's dead."

I close my eyes and breathe deeply. *Dead?*

"Are you okay, Mom?" I ask. I know that she's feeling this, hard. She did everything she could to save her marriage when I was a kid. She was the glue that held us together. After he left, she remained the glue and filled our house with more love than I could imagine. We didn't need that fucker in our lives.

"I don't know," she says, and I hear her sobbing through the phone.

"Tell me what to do. What can I do?" I beg her, and her sobbing just gets louder. I hear a muffled voice coming from her side, and Bill is consoling her.

"Garrett?" His voice is solid and strong.

"Bill, tell me she isn't this upset. She can't be, that asshole made her miserable. Tell her I'm okay. I'm fine." I don't want her to worry about me. I don't feel anything for him.

"There's more to it than that. John's dead, but..." He stops and I swallow hard.

"How?" I ask.

"He killed himself."

CHAPTER 14

Sam
Present
Villanova, Pennsylvania
Age 23

I WAKE WITH A SMALL JOLT OF PAIN down my neck. I feel a weight in my arms and realize I'm still holding Kai. My feet never stopped rocking us back and forth, even though I had fallen asleep. He's swaddled tightly and breathing quickly. This is a sign that he'll wake up soon. His short fits of sleep are constantly interrupted by the pain he feels throughout his body.

I've become in tune with his irregular schedule over the past month and can sense when he's about to start wailing. I get myself ready to absorb his pain, and I recline the rocker so I'm lying back. I unbutton my shirt and slide it off so I'm wearing just my sports bra, then I swiftly remove the tight swaddling from his body. He's only wearing a diaper as I press his warm body against my chest. He stiffens and begins to scream his painful cries. Each one tears through me worse than the last. I feel it all. He stiffens more and arches his back, lifting his head off of my chest. His cries become more frantic, and I reach for the warm blanket that's hanging over the side of the chair. I wrap it around my shoulders and hold him firmly against my chest as I hum softly. After about twenty minutes, he begins to slowly relax into me as I continue to melodically hum near his ear. The vibrations from my chest finally soothe him.

I close my eyes and transfer my warmth into his little body, pulling the blanket over him tighter. A sound from the corner startles me, and Garrett slowly emerges from the shadows.

"Oh my God," he says softly and walks toward me, his head hung low.

I haven't seen much of him over the past four weeks. After I attempted to give him an introductory course in caring for a drug-addicted baby, he's barely been here. He wasn't kidding when he said he had no intentions of taking care of his son. He hired me to do a job and I'm doing it, kick-ass I might add. Aunt Peggy claims to not know where he's been hiding out, and I'm sure it's been in a fancy hotel with some groupie.

"Get out," I whisper, trying not to disturb the rhythm I've created for Kai.

"Is he okay?" he asks, and I can't believe there's actual concern in his voice.

"He is for now, but he'll start screaming if you stay in here. Please leave."

He ignores my request and sinks onto the day-bed across from Kai's crib. That bed is meant for me, but I haven't slept in it yet. This chair is the only bed I've known since I moved in, and Kai has yet to see the inside of that crib.

Garrett's eyes focus on the lump of baby under the blanket. "Why aren't you wearing a shirt?" he asks. He doesn't sound all pervy, and for the first time I notice he's not trying to undress me with his eyes.

"Body warmth. It's called the Kangaroo Method. Skin-on-skin contact helps soothe him," I whisper. Kai stiffens, and I immediately hum into his ear. Once he's relaxed again, Garrett asks another question.

"Why the humming? It doesn't sound like music. It's like a pattern?"

"It causes deep reverberations in my chest and it calms him down."

He looks amused. "Kind of like when my mother says she ran the vacuum cleaner when I cried as a baby?"

I surprise myself with a smile and nod. "Yes."

"Oh," he says and continues to stare at his son. He's fixated on the thick tuft of black hair that sticks straight out in all directions. Most days, Kai looks like a mad scientist.

"Why is he in so much pain?" he asks softly. His eyes are heavy and sad.

I'm taken a little off-guard by his questions. And I'm stunned by his sudden concern for his son. He's never shown any interest in Kai, and it surprises me that he's asking these relevant questions. I'm not sure he'll be happy with the answers, but I give him the most honest responses.

"When he was in his mother's body, drugs passed into his system. He was exposed to them for a long time when she was using during her pregnancy. He needed those drugs when he was born, but they weren't there anymore. He's withdrawing, just like an adult addict would do."

He nods in understanding and leans back further on the bed.

I rock Kai silently and treasure the peace that I feel throughout his body. He's reacting differently today. Every time he hears Garrett's voice, he sinks further into my chest. *How can he know who Garrett is?*

Garrett hasn't been this close to his son since the first day

Kai came home. Maybe it's the tone of his voice that's soothing? Or the tenor?

"He's reacting to your voice," I say and lift the blanket slightly so he can see how relaxed Kai is against my chest. His tiny hands fall at my sides and his cheek is glued to my skin just above my heart. Garrett eyes his son and raises his eyebrow.

"You know you're not wearing a shirt, right?" he says, and I feel warmth spread through my entire body. I'm blushing *everywhere*. My cheeks flush. I lower the blanket over Kai so as not to wake him, at the same time covering myself. *Thank God I'm wearing my sports bra.*

I'm mortified.

"Please leave," I say, completely embarrassed.

What the hell was I thinking?

Garrett smiles and pulls a pillow out from behind him. He lies down on his side, tucking his hands underneath. The reflection from the stars on the ceiling catches his eyes just right. They're dark and soft and, for once, not angry or aloof. And for first the first time, I can't help but notice how strikingly handsome he is. His eyes are framed by the longest, thickest lashes I've ever seen on a man. His face is perfect and smooth, like he just shaved five minutes ago. His lips part slightly, and I suddenly realize he's caught me staring.

I blush again and look away from him and focus on the mobile hanging above the crib. Soft instruments dangle above the bedding. Aunt Peggy insisted on a musical theme for Kai's bedroom, for obvious reasons.

Garrett doesn't seem to be in a hurry to leave.

"How long will he be like this?" His interest appears genuine, and I want to help him understand Kai's health situation as best as I can. I guess now is as good a time as any. Tomorrow, he may go back to ignoring the fact that his son is now living under his roof.

I sigh heavily, knowing the reality I'm about to share is likely going to send Garrett running. Again. "It could be up to six months or more. I've seen babies get better sooner with early intervention."

"Like what you've been doing with Kai?" he asks.

"Yes."

His face looks drawn and worried. I realize that I may be scaring him with some of the worst-case-scenario stuff, and I try to shift the vibe in the room.

"With this type of care and comfort, I've seen symptoms gradually decline over a shorter time period." *Best case scenario.*

"So you're doing the right thing for him?"

"Absolutely," I say confidently.

"What do you think he's going to be like?"

"What do you mean?"

"When he's older? Will he need special care? Or special schools?"

"Every baby with NAS is different. Some have a really rough start and gradually get better and can function normally throughout their lives. Others need constant care and therapy. Some are in between. There's really no clear outcome." It's hard to describe the spectrum of problems that an NAS baby may have.

He looks even more drawn and says, "I don't know if I can do this."

"Do what?"

"What you're doing. I don't think I have it in me to be like you."

I'm surprised he's even thinking about taking care of Kai.

It tells me that he's contemplating his options and that maybe, just maybe, he actually cares.

"Every living person has the capacity to provide care for another; some people just have to dig deeper than others to find it."

"I respectfully disagree," he says, shaking his head.

"Then we agree to disagree," I reply.

"Why are you doing this for me?" he asks, quickly changing the subject.

"I'm doing this for Kai, not you. And because I love my aunt." I state simply.

Raindrops begin to pelt the window behind me and then they pick up speed. Garrett takes a deep breath but doesn't move. He's looking between me and his son, and a strange expression comes over his face. It's a weak smile that's a mix of contentment and worry. I can tell the questions he asked me tonight have been bothering him, and he looks like he's formulating the next one. Our silence isn't exactly uncomfortable, but something hangs in the air between us that I can't grasp.

"Your aunt is a wonderful woman. I don't know what I'd do without her." He stretches his legs out and tucks the pillow tighter under his cheek. "When I've been home, I can't think of a time when she didn't have my life in perfect order."

"Even down to a sock drawer," I say, and he immediately nods his head in agreement. I know my aunt so well. She's a perfectionist and everything has its place.

"Seriously, who knew you could fold socks that way?" he says and for the first time, I feel at ease with him, even though I wanted to pummel him when we met. His arrogance and ignorance were dumbfounding.

I suddenly feel the need to tell him. "Why were you such a jerk?"

I can tell he's taken off guard by my question, because the comfortable smile that was on his face disappears.

"I was afraid, Sam." He pauses to clear his throat. "I *am* afraid."

How can I go from contempt to caring? I was so angry with him during his absence that I prepared an epic speech, ready to chastise him and his terrible choices. I planned to eviscerate him with my words, tear him down so he could feel small and insignificant. I was so angry with him for abandoning his son. And suddenly, I empathize with him and his fear. He's as ill prepared for this as any unsuspecting bachelor would be.

"I need your help," he says.

"I am helping, Garrett. This is what I do."

"No, I mean, I need you to teach me how to do all of this." His eyes are pleading and his voice is soft. I'm shocked by his request and proud of him at the same time. *Why the sudden change of heart?*

"Of course I can teach you, but you'd be surprised how much of it you'll do naturally. Instinct takes over and you suddenly know how to parent."

He lets out a soft breath. "Again, we'll have to agree to disagree on that point. I have no instincts, and a few weeks ago, I didn't want anything to do with being a parent."

"And now you do?" I ask as I hope this is a legitimate breakthrough. "What made you suddenly decide to try?"

"My mom and dad."

"Really?"

"They told me Kai deserves a normal and healthy life. I think I want to give that to him."

I raise my eyebrow. "Yeah?"

"I haven't been around much lately because I've been staying with my parents. I had to tell them about Kai and what was going on, and I wanted to do that in person. After I came home, and met Kai for the first time, I went back to their house. I tried to hide down there. I was afraid to come back." He looks ashamed and my heart tugs. *That explains why he hasn't been around.*

"But you came back," I state.

"My mother's very convincing," he whispers.

"Garrett, if you want to do this, you have to be all in. Do you think you can do that?"

"I have to, don't I?"

I nod slowly and close my eyes. "Why don't you sleep on it and tell me in the morning if you want to begin baby boot camp."

"Sounds like a plan," he says and stretches comfortably. His eyes become heavy and he sighs deeply.

I also feel sleep pulling me deep, and I don't fight it. I take it when it comes as infrequently as that may be.

WHEN I WAKE UP, KAI IS STILL MIRACULOUSLY ASLEEP, molded into my chest. He draws from my warmth so he can recharge.

My heart sinks when I see that the day-bed is empty and Garrett is gone.

CHAPTER 15

Garrett
Present
Villanova, Pennsylvania
Age 26

I WAKE UP FULLY CLOTHED. Watching Sam sleep with my son on her chest last night was oddly soothing. I've never witnessed tenderness like that before. My mother was always loving and giving with me. But Sam has something more. *A gift.*

When I watched her with Kai as he screamed and wailed, she never looked stressed or tense. I was balling my fists, hiding in the corner of the room, wincing from the pain from Kai's agonizing cries. But Sam was an expert. She cradled him like he was her own. He fit against her chest like he belonged there and it was the safest place he could be.

A picture of Sadie fills my brain as anger fills my chest. *How could she do this to herself? To her unborn child?* I've never seen anyone experience pain like this little boy is going through. And I'm helpless, unable to do anything. I'm afraid of hurting him more than he's already hurting. I imagine the calluses on my fingertips caused by my guitar strings like daggers cutting through his skin, eliciting shrill cries.

A phone rings from my nightstand, and I answer it without looking. It's probably my mother checking in to be sure I arrived home safely. I've been spending a lot of time at my parents' home in North Carolina, mostly feeling sorry for myself and avoiding the responsibility that's right down the hall.

"Hello," I say groggily.

"Hello?" An unfamiliar male voice is on the other end. I hold the phone away from my face so I can see the Caller ID and realize I'm not holding my phone. It's in a pink case. Nope, not my phone.

"Who is this?" I ask, realizing I must have swiped Sam's phone by mistake when I left the nursery last night.

"Is this Samantha Weston's number?" he asks hesitantly.

"Yes, who's this?" I raise my voice and it surprises me.

"Tell her that Richard Jones called. I wanted to confirm our *date* for Friday night."

"Yeah, I'll tell her, *Dick*."

"Excuse me? What did you just call me?"

"Your name, it's Dick, right? Richard, Rich, *Dick?*"

"Just tell her I called." He hangs up, clearly flustered.

I hang up and instinctively erase any evidence of the call from the history. I don't want her to see evidence of a missed phone call or anything from that guy. *What's wrong with me?* I know I have absolutely no right doing this, and I don't know why I even did. I have no control over Sam. But the sound of that dude's voice annoyed me. I wonder if he's her boyfriend. *I hope not.* Again, I have no right knowing.

I'm an ass.

I roll over and feel my own phone in my front pocket. I pull it out and see that I've missed three calls from my mother.

I hit her on speed dial and press the phone against my

ear. "Garrett, I've been so worried," she says instead of saying "Hello."

"Hi to you too, Mom. I'm fine."

"We had such terrible thunderstorms that I thought your flight would be delayed."

"Nope, I made it out just in time. It was a quick, uneventful flight."

"Please don't come home again," she says sternly.

"What?" I ask as my heart leaps out of my chest. *Why would she say that?*

"Oh, I don't mean it like that. It's just, like I told you the other night, you need to focus on your son. You need to bond with him. He needs you."

When I was home, she lectured me the best way she knew how and tried to get me to see what a gift I've been given. I admitted that I've been avoiding this situation, and I do need to take responsibility, but I'm scared shitless.

"Do as you're told, Garrett." I can hear the smile in her voice.

"Yes, Mother."

"Call me on Sunday and let me know how your week has gone. Your father and I would like to come up to meet our grandson at the end of the month. Is that okay?"

"Sure," I say. I can't imagine what it'll be like when they arrive. I wonder if Kai will be better.

"Goodbye, sweetheart," she says and hangs up.

I HAD A MEETING WITH THE BAND today and our management team to discuss plans for the upcoming album. We're all dragging our feet in creating it, and the label is starting to put the pressure on. But we're all so preoccupied, most of us can't find the time. Dax has been aloof and is uncharacteristically avoiding us as much as possible. Tristan's moving into a new house that he built about twenty minutes from here and has been too busy designing his "man cave." Alex still writes for us, but he's only sent lyrics to two songs and we need at least twelve. I can't blame him; he and Tabby built a house in the same neighborhood as Tristan, and they've got two kids. The only one who's doing anything is Heath. He says he's written lyrics to a couple of songs and is anxious to get tracks laid for them.

So basically, getting us all in the same room to nail down a solid schedule is like herding cats.

I arrive home shortly after eight and the house is dark. Sam must be asleep with Kai already. I notice Peggy's car is still here and wonder if everything is okay. She's almost always gone by dinner time.

I follow a dim light through the kitchen and into the den. Peggy is reclined in the leather chair, holding Kai against her chest. Thankfully, her shirt is securely on. I couldn't imagine walking in on her with a bare chest practicing the Kangaroo Method.

"Is everything okay?" I ask.

"Hi, Garrett. Yes, everything's fine. Sam needed a break, so I'm taking over for a few hours."

I'm suddenly jealous, and I have no right to be. "Where is she?" I'm hoping she's not with Dick.

"Out there." She nods toward the backyard where the indoor pool is.

"By herself?" I ask nonchalantly as I walk to the window and see the glow from the pool.

"Of course," she answers. "Who would she be out there with?" *Good.*

I casually peer out the window to see if I can catch a glimpse of her. "I don't know, her boyfriend maybe?" *Why did I say that?*

Peggy laughs and shakes her head. "She doesn't have a boyfriend, hasn't for a long time." She furrows her brow and looks pensive. "I think it's about time she found one. She deserves a nice boy who will take good care of her. She has so much love to give. It's such a shame she doesn't open herself up to the possibilities." She smiles and rubs Kai's back. He stretches and sighs, sinking deeper into a restful slumber.

"How is he?" I ask.

"He's had a good day today. One of his best days yet. He's been able to eat four ounces of formula at a time, which is a miracle."

"Four ounces doesn't seem like a lot," I say, worried that he's not eating enough.

"Oh, it's a lot for him. His sick little tummy can't take too much food at once. It's very painful for him. In addition to his other issues, he has GERD, which triggers acid reflux as well as other painful gastrointestinal disorders. Typically, he can only drink two to three ounces at a time. But today, he graduated to four without much fuss. So it's definitely a *good* day."

"Wow, I had no idea." Every time I ask about his condition, I learn something new. It's overwhelming and I can't keep it all straight. There are so many things wrong with him, it pains me to think about it.

I look back out to the pool house and notice that the overhead lights are off, but the underwater lights are on. It looks peaceful and quiet out there, and I wonder what Sam is doing. Steam rises from the water, glowing from the dim lights in the pool.

A long, lean figure floats into view, and I see her. Her face is barely exposed to the air above, and her arms are floating weightlessly, stretched out to the side.

"Is she okay?" I ask Peggy, but I can't take my eyes off of the beauty that's emanating from my pool.

"She's fine. It's what she does to relax," Peggy responds.

"Really?" I ask as I continue to watch her drift slowly through the water. She looks completely relaxed and I'm jealous.

"I secretly think it's how she connects with her parents."

"What?" I ask, her comment piquing my interest.

"Sam almost drowned in her pool when she was seven. Her dad saved her life. Soon after, he insisted that she get proper swim lessons and he hired an instructor. She learned how to stay calm which helped her conquer her fear of the water. She learned that floating on her back will get her out of any scary situation in the water. Now she floats for therapy and relaxation."

My heart hurts for Sam, knowing that her parents were taken from her. Peggy gave me a brief history on Sam before she came to take care of Kai. I know her parents died when she was sixteen, and Peggy has raised her since.

"She's a lucky girl to have you," I say as I watch Sam get out of the pool. She's wearing a black bikini that hugs her body perfectly. Her curly hair is piled on top of her head. She grabs a towel hanging from a hook and starts to dry herself. I turn from the window, feeling like a voyeur.

"I'm the lucky one, Garrett. She saved my life."

"Oh?"

"Not literally, of course. But figuratively. When my brother was killed, I felt like I'd lost everything. He and I were so close and we only had each other. When he died, I had a renewed sense of life and purpose. I'd always helped other families.

Now I was given a chance to help my own. It broke my heart to see Sam through the rest of her teenage years, but it also strengthened it knowing what I was doing for my brother and his wife."

"You and Sam have a unique gift. Taking care of other people, the level that you both do, is astounding. Commendable." They're definitely both from the same gene pool, that's for sure.

The back door slides open and Sam enters the kitchen, wrapped in a towel. She's shivering. "I forgot dry clothes," she stammers and looks stunned to see me. Her cheeks flush pink and she pulls the towel tighter around her thin frame.

I walk past her to the closet in the hallway and remove a plush white robe and hand it to her.

"Why do you have a woman's robe in your closet?" she asks then quickly follows it up with, "Never mind, I don't want to know." She takes the robe, lets the towel drop and quickly pulls the robe on over her shaking shoulders. She does it so quickly I'm barely able to catch a glimpse of her body. But what I'm able to see is magnificent.

I'm glad she didn't press me for an answer. Several other women have worn that exact robe. The hot tub is just down the stairs on the deck, and I keep it in the hall closet for emergency use only. Every time Peggy does my laundry, she can't help herself but comment that these robes should be disposable. That explains why she's giving me a nasty look now that I've given this robe to Sam to wear. I know she doesn't approve of my extracurricular activities.

Sam walks over to Peggy and Kai. "How is he?" she asks.

Peggy gives her the same answer she gave me, and Sam squeals, quickly throwing her hands over her mouth. "He just ate four ounces?" she asks, and tears form in her eyes.

"Yes," Peggy says proudly.

"And I missed it?" She sinks into the couch and sighs.

"He'll be ready for another bottle when he wakes up in about an hour," Peggy assures her.

I sit on the couch next to Sam and my knee brushes against hers. She quickly moves over, placing a throw pillow between us. *I should have found something else for her to wear. One of my sweatshirts maybe.* It feels wrong that she's wearing a robe that other girls have worn. Girls who mean nothing to me. She doesn't deserve to wear something that groupies have touched. *I'm throwing them out tomorrow.*

"Can I try feeding him when he wakes up?" I ask without even thinking.

Sam and Peggy both gasp and look at me. "Are you serious?" Sam asks, astounded.

Shit. Now what?

"I guess?" I reply timidly.

"Alright then. Let me go get changed." She jumps off the couch and says to Peggy, "Can you bring Kai upstairs in a little while? Give me like fifteen minutes. I'll fix him a bottle and bring it with me."

Peggy nods her head and addresses me. "Are you ready?"

My body tenses up, and I realize I've made a huge mistake.

HIS SCREAMS ARE THE FIRST THING I hear when I reach the landing of the stairs. I don't want to, but I continue walking toward his nursery. My heart pumps wildly in my chest and my hands are clammy. *I can't do this.*

I can run right now. Down the stairs and out the door. Peggy left a few minutes ago, so there's nobody to stop me. I can be at the airport in less than an hour and fly anywhere I want.

But my mother's voice rings in my ears. *He needs you.*

I hesitantly walk toward the high-pitched cries and push the door open slowly. Sam is walking with Kai, holding him tight against her chest. She doesn't notice me enter at first, and I quietly observe her. How can she stay so calm and focused while Kai is obviously in excruciating pain?

She sees me and gestures that I take a seat in the rocking chair. "I don't know about this…" I say and begin to back up toward the door.

"He'll be okay in a minute. I just changed his diaper and he's a little overstimulated."

I sit in the chair and it feels uncomfortable. It's not as plush as I expected it to be, and I make a mental note to buy a new one. Sam sleeps in this chair, and it can't be comfortable for her.

Her left hand moves in a smooth circular motion as she rubs Kai's back. His crying has stopped, but she continues to walk slowly around the room. I'm tense waiting for her to bring him to me. I look down at my hands, wondering how I'm going to hold him.

She approaches me and smiles. "You okay?" she asks.

"No."

"Put your arms out and place your right elbow on the armrest." I do as she says and she bends down slowly, transferring Kai into my stiff arms. "Try to relax. He's very sensitive and will react to your rigidness." I can't relax and only stiffen my arms more. I'm surprised by the weight of him as my arms sink a little. He feels heavier than he looks. Her hands are no longer on him, and she places them on my shoulders, pressing down gently but firmly. I look up at her, surprised.

"You need to relax. Drop your shoulders and the tension will leave your arms." She slides her hands from me and sits on the ottoman that she's pulled close to us.

Kai squirms a little, and I look down at him, making eye contact for the very first time. His eyes are wide open and he's looking right at me. My heart stops when I see the innocence and light in his eyes. He's depending on me, and I'm his lifeline right now. I'm overcome with... I don't know *what*. This isn't a moment I ever envisioned happening. I'm holding a child. *My son.* This is so surreal, and I'm afraid I'm doing everything wrong. Sam places a hand on Kai's head, stroking gently. "He sees you," she says softly.

I can't take my eyes off of him. He looks so content. Relaxed. I focus on taking deep, even breaths. I don't want to jostle him, causing him to cry or become uncomfortable. Sam's presence is soothing and I begin to relax. *How does she have this power over Kai? Over me?*

"Hey, buddy," I say quietly. He blinks and purses his lips, like he's about to blow a tiny little bubble.

"He's hungry," Sam says, and she places a warm bottle into my hand.

I look up at Sam and her eyes soften. "Don't worry, I'll walk you through it."

She places her soft hand over mine and helps guide the bottle toward Kai's mouth. The tip touches his lips, and he opens his mouth so he can eat. His eyes close immediately and he begins sucking on the bottle like his life depends on it.

"See how easy it is?" Sam asks and removes her hand from mine. She looks down at Kai affectionately.

"Now what?" I ask, and my nerves start to take hold of me again. "Am I feeding him too much? Has he eaten four ounces yet?"

"Not yet. He can't eat that quickly. He's probably only taken an ounce. Let's give him another minute or two and then you'll need to burp him. You'll do that a couple of times before he finishes that bottle."

Burp him? Shit.

"I don't think I can do that."

She walks over to one of the dressers and takes out what looks like a small white towel. She places it on my shoulder and settles her hand over mine again, helping me pull the bottle out of Kai's mouth. He immediately starts to whimper, and my body stiffens along with his.

She helps guide my hands and Kai so he's positioned against my upper chest and his head on my shoulder. His whimpering starts to turn to weak cries. Sam rubs his back, patting softly. "Do what I'm doing," she instructs.

I replace her hand with mine and pat his back lightly. "You can do it a little harder. You won't hurt him. Just alternate patting and rubbing."

I continue the pattern and feel Kai stiffen under my hand. Suddenly, the loudest burp comes from his tiny mouth. I feel the vibration from the belch against my chest, and I let out a sigh of relief. It smells like sour milk and I look up at Sam. "Is that normal?" I ask.

She giggles a little and shrugs her shoulders. "The burp or the smell?"

"Both," I say nervously.

"Yes, although that one was a little loud, even for him. You'll get used to the smell."

I scrunch my nose and breathe through my mouth so I don't gag.

"Now what?" I ask. Kai begins to whimper again.

"Move him back to your arms so you can feed him some more."

I follow her directions, and he's positioned and ready to take more from the bottle. Sam hands it to me, and I place it back in his mouth. We repeat the same pattern three more times until he's finished the whole thing.

After his last burp, he becomes limp and settles comfortably against my chest. Sam brings over a crescent moon-shaped pillow. She places it under my arms gently, giving me extra support. I relax a bit more and take a deep breath.

"He's really taken to you. I can't believe how smoothly that went," Sam says, clearly surprised.

"I'm shocked," I say.

She sits on the bed across from me and folds her legs in front of her like a pretzel. "He looks like you," she says and smiles.

"Yeah?"

"You have the same exact eyes. Right down to the incredible lashes." She blushes, like she regrets telling me she's noticed my eyes.

"I don't see it," I say, pretending her comment didn't faze me.

"Should I lay him back down?" I ask.

"No, keep him like that for at least twenty minutes. Since he has GERD, he should remain upright so the acid reflux doesn't make him uncomfortable."

"Okay."

My breathing becomes slow and regular, in perfect sync with Kai's. He's out cold, and I'm thankful for that. It was amazing looking into his eyes earlier, but I worry that when he's awake, he's more likely to feel that pain that is constantly moving throughout his body.

"You're not going to leave me alone with him, are you?" I ask, terrified of her answer.

"Let's not worry about that yet, okay? Let's focus on getting you more comfortable just holding him. Like I said, everything else will come in time, and soon you'll be a natural."

I begin to rock slowly in the chair, and I'm amazed when I feel Kai relax even more. He brings his tiny hand to his mouth and begins sucking on one of his knuckles. "Is he still hungry?" I ask.

"No, that's just something he does." She smiles and watches him intently. "How do you feel?" she asks, her gaze traveling to me.

"Fucking terrified," I say, and her eyes widen. I'm terrified that I'm going to do something wrong. Terrified that I'm going to hurt Kai. Terrified of being a bad father.

"It's going to be okay," she says, and I want to believe her.

I'm tense again, and Kai starts to stir. I feel his back arch against my hand and his entire body stiffens. "What's happening?" I ask as I sit up straight.

Sam jumps from the bed and quickly swipes him from my arms. "Shh, shh, shh," she whispers in his ear. She rhythmically pats his bottom as she walks back and forth across the room. His cries subside and I'm thankful. I don't think I could listen to those piercing high-pitched screams from earlier.

I stand up and move over to the bed. I try to relax, kicking off my shoes. Sam sits in the rocking chair and cradles him in her arms.

"You don't have to stay," she says. "He's going to be asleep for a few hours. Lesson number one of baby boot camp: always sleep when your baby sleeps."

I pull the pillow from behind me and lie down on my side

like I did last night. "I'll listen to that advice and you should too."

Her eyes look heavy, and I know she wants me to leave so she can sleep.

"Thank you," she says softly.

I'm surprised and wonder why on earth she would be thanking me. "Why?"

"For trying. And for giving your son a chance to find his way into your heart." She closes her eyes and adjusts the blanket over her and Kai.

I watch them intently. She looks beautiful holding my son in her arms and so peaceful as she drifts off to sleep.

She likes my eyelashes.

Kai isn't the only one grabbing a piece of my heart.

CHAPTER 16

Sam
Past
Villanova, Pennsylvania
Age 16

"THANK YOU, MISS WESTON. We'll be in touch if we need anything else. I'm so sorry for your loss." My family's lawyer picks up the pile of papers that Aunt Peggy just signed and leaves the room.

She stands up and reaches for my hand. "Let's go home."

Home.

"My home is a pile of rubble, Aunt Peggy."

That fucker blew up my parents along with himself and the kitchen. The rest of the house burned to the ground, around their charred bodies. I can't get the image of my pregnant mother screaming for help out of my brain. My father, lying helplessly unconscious on the floor.

She's silent as she leads me from the room.

"What am I going to do, Aunt Peggy?" I ask, not really expecting an answer. I'm an orphan at sixteen.

"I'm here, Sam, and I'm not going anywhere," she promises as she pulls me against her.

"How can you promise that? How do you even know? *They're* gone, and all it took was a second…" I question her, practically accusing her of something she would never do.

"Honey, I will do my best to make sure I stay here with you. That's all I can do."

WE RIDE SILENTLY BACK TO OUR HOUSE, and I rush up to the room that used to be the guest room but is now mine. A box sits on the dresser that I've been terrified to open. It contains everything I own. Aunt Peggy went to the house and pleaded with the investigators to take what they could from what used to be my room. They sifted through charred furniture and clothes, and this box is all I have left.

There are messages taped to the top of the dresser on yellow Post-it Notes from Cassie. She's been leaving them on the front door, begging me to call her. My aunt has been moving them to my room to remind me to call my best friend.

I pick up the phone and dial blindly.

"Cassie?" I say when I hear her voice. The sobs come frequently and without prejudice. I sometimes go days without crying and other days I cry every five minutes. The loss is crushing and debilitating. I can't feel anything but immense grief and sadness.

"Hey, Sam," she says softly. "How are you?"

How can I answer that question?

I suck.

Life sucks.

My family is gone.

I'm alone.

I don't want to feel anything anymore.

"Not good, Cass," is all I say in response.

"Do you want some company?" she asks.

This grief is crippling, and I can't imagine unloading it on my best friend.

"No."

She sighs heavily and I feel bad. She wants desperately to help me through this. But nobody can. Until you feel the utter loss and destruction that I have, you just can't understand what I'm going through.

"Okay. Call me if you need anything. I love you," she says, and we hang up the phone.

I have nothing left to love.

The box sits on my dresser, and I lay my hands on it. *Am I ready to do this?* Dread fills my chest as I lift the box and carry it over to my bed. I sit down next to it tuck my feet underneath me. This small box contains the remnants of my entire life.

I pull one side open and the rest of the sides pop up. The smell of smoke and ash fills my nostrils, causing my eyes to water and my throat to burn. *Am I breathing them in? Are they a part of this ash?*

I know this is not true, because their bodies were found. Charred, unrecognizable. But they were found. We buried them next to each other.

The first thing I see is a shoe. It's burned quite a bit, but I recognize it immediately. One of my Steve Madden platform flip-flops. *Why the hell would someone even take this out of the rubble and ash?*

I hold it in my hand and turn it around, inspecting it for further damage. Without the other one, it's useless so I toss it across the room and a cloud of soot forms when it hits the floor.

Disgusted, I continue to pick through the contents of the box.

My old pink stuffed dog is in here. She's just as gray as she was before this happened, but she has a coating of fine ash and dust on her. I called her Googie because I didn't know how to say doggy when I was little. So the name stuck. My Googie.

Tears fill my eyes as I pull her to my chest. Mom told me I got her the day that I was born. I can't believe she wasn't incinerated in the fire. I place her gingerly on my pillow and know I'll be snuggling with her tonight.

There's something shiny in the box that catches my eye, and I reach in to grab it. It's my Sweet Sixteen charm bracelet. I hold it up in front of my face, dangling it from my little finger. The single charm catches light pouring in through the window. This charm bracelet was my mother's, and she gave it to me the morning of my sixteenth birthday. *The morning she died.* She was dangling it over my nose while I woke up. It's old-fashioned but retro looking. I love it, and I love that she gave me what her mother gave to her when she turned sixteen. It miraculously doesn't have a speck of ash on it. I open the lobster claw clasp and wrap it around my wrist. The coolness from the gold metal tingles on my skin, and I hold my wrist in the air so I can inspect the bracelet closely.

I love you, Mom.

I don't think I can bear to go through this box anymore. This is too painful. I stand up and prepare to close the box up again when one more thing catches my eye. I reach in and pull out the familiar blue ribbon. My First Place award from the science fair in fifth grade. I feel the threads between my forefinger and thumb and rub it gently. At one time, I felt victorious holding this between my fingers. But suddenly I feel rage.

The ribbon falls from my hand and onto my pillow, and I hurl the box from my bed. It hits the floor and another cloud of soot fills the room.

My whole life in a box.

I try to regain composure. I place my head on my pillow, next to the blue ribbon and Googie. I stare up at the ceiling and let my eyes close slowly. I imagine myself, floating in our pool, just my nose and mouth exposed to the air.

Deep breaths.

In.

Out.

I inhale and exhale as if my life depends on it. Each breath slow and deliberate.

Please tell me what to do, Dad.

Can you hear me?

I need you now more than ever.

My silent voice goes unanswered.

My breaths remain even.

I feel like I'm floating.

I wish I were floating.

CHAPTER 17

Garrett
Past
Philadelphia, Pennsylvania
Age 21

"IT'S OFFICIAL!" TRISTAN SLURS, and we all do an Alabama Slammer shot together. "You're twenty-one!"

Bob the bartender looks at me funny and shakes his head. He's been serving me for a few years, and he genuinely seems surprised that I was underage. He points to the rest of the band and demands their driver's licenses. I'm the last one to turn twenty-one, so he's in the clear.

"I could have gotten in real trouble, you assholes," he says and angrily goes to help another customer.

Dax laughs. "There's no way he didn't know."

I shrug it off and take Alex's shot from him. "Are you going to drink this?"

He waves me off and leaves the bar.

"What's up with him?" I ask. Dax ignores me and Tristan takes a call on his phone.

We're getting ready to leave on our first big tour. I gather that he and Tabby are having 'issues' and I'm not surprised. Their relationship has been a disaster since before it even started. I shrug my shoulders and drink his shot.

My phone buzzes and my mother's phone number pops up.

I pick it up and hear her and Bill singing "Happy Birthday" into the phone. I cringe when they attempt to hit the high notes and they finally stop. "Hey, honey," my mom says. "Happy Birthday."

I know she tries to make this day special for me, ever since my dad killed himself, but it's always a huge fail. I can't seem to find happiness on such an otherwise dark day.

"Promise you'll come visit us when we move," she begs. Mom and Bill are moving to North Carolina to be close to the rest of her family. They decided not to sell the house that I grew up in just in case I need a place to crash when I'm not on tour. I accept the gesture as a sign of their love for me.

"I will," I say. I see Tristan returning from the other side of the bar with several more drinks and shots. "Hey, I gotta go."

"Be safe and we love you."

I hang up as soon as he slides onto the barstool next to me. "Hey there, *mama's boy,*" he says, and I want to pummel him. He's constantly making fun of me and the dozens of times a week that she calls me.

"Shut the fuck up, douchebag."

"I can't believe we leave for tour tomorrow. It's crazy, isn't it? We're going to be huge rock stars." Tristan throws back a shot and pushes one toward me.

"Don't get ahead of yourself, dude. We're popular here, but out there, who knows." I try to ground him in reality a little bit, but he won't stay out of the clouds.

"What time do we have to meet the bus?" I ask, scanning the room for tonight's hook-up.

He groans. "Five thirty in the morning."

"Shit." I do a shot and wince. "What the hell was that?" I ask, pointing to the empty shot glass.

"I don't know. Bob made it for us."

That explains it.

He must have poured a dirty ashtray into the most god-awful booze he could find as revenge. I feel like I'm going to puke.

"Suck it up." Tristan laughs and picks up his phone. "I've got to make a call. See you tomorrow morning, birthday boy." He snatches his phone from the bar and trots to the door. He must be looking to get one last night in with Kirsten before he's on the road for a while.

I don't know how much time passes, but the place is practically empty and Bob is wiping down the bar in front of me. The house lights flick on and I squint. "Jesus, turn the lights down."

"Last call was an hour ago, G. Time for you to get going."

"What time is it?" I ask. *Did I fall asleep in here?*

"It's just after three. C'mon, we all want to go home."

How did so many hours go by and I didn't even notice? There are at least eight shot glasses turned upside down in front of me, and I have my hand wrapped around a warm beer. I must have fallen asleep sitting up.

"I'm going," I say and stand up. I walk out to the quiet city street and hail the first cab I can find. I give him an address and lean back into the seat.

"Is this it?" he asks, confused. I look out the window and see the tour bus that we'll be riding on for the next several months.

"Yup," I say and drop a twenty into his outstretched hand.

I walk up to the door and rap on it lightly. I hear rustling and heavy footsteps coming toward the front of the bus. The door opens, and a large man fills the doorway.

151

"What?" he asks, and he looks menacing.

"I'm with the band, and I'm a little early I guess."

He steps aside and lets me up the stairs. "You Garrett?" he asks.

"Yes, how did you know?"

"I'm the driver of your bus and your security team. It's my job to know."

"Oh."

"I'm Mick. Welcome aboard."

I step onto the bus and inhale deeply. It's brand new inside, and the smell of fresh leather hits my nose. "Most of your gear is stored below, and I've put some things in the back." We had to drop all of our stuff at the studio this morning so the crew could pack everything into the bus and small truck that will be traveling with us. It feels weird walking onto my home for the next several months with just my clothes on and a wallet in my pocket.

"Cool," I say and walk toward the bunks.

"I can take any one of these?" I gesture to the empty bunks on either side of the narrow hallway.

"Yes, or the room in the back," Mick responds as I push open the door.

A comfortable-looking bed is in the center of a small room. "I'll take this," I smirk and close the door behind me.

I climb into the bed and look down at my phone. Several missed calls and texts from different girls I've hooked up with over the past few months. I'm sure they're all looking to have a goodbye fuck before I leave. I wish I had the energy to entertain them all, but I'm sure this room will see a lot of action in the coming months.

I scroll through the texts and see one from my mom.

MOM: TAKE CARE OF YOURSELF AND BE GOOD I LOVE YOU SO MUCH AND I'M SO PROUD OF YOU HAPPY BIRTHDAY

I switch off my phone and tuck it under the pillow.

I close my eyes and remember a birthday party a long time ago. It must have been when I was five or six, because my birth father was there. Mom's singing and dad's blowing in a noisemaker. I'm smiling and blowing out candles. My vision turns dark and my father disappears. My mom and I are all alone. I'm crying and asking "Why?"

My mother is hugging me and telling me it's going to be okay. I remember this day when I realized my father left us for good. He deserted us and forced my mother to raise me alone.

Then he killed himself years later on this same day.

I hate this fucking day.

Sam

Present

Villanova, Pennsylvania

Age 24

"GO DOWNSTAIRS AND GET SOMETHING to eat. I've got things under control in here. Besides, you need a break. It's your birthday, sweetheart." Aunt Peggy settles into the chair with Kai sleeping in her arms.

I nod groggily and leave the room. My birthday isn't a particularly happy time for me, but my aunt has helped me get through the toughest ones. It's hard to celebrate happy times on the very day that my parents were murdered.

Garrett isn't downstairs yet, and I wonder if he's even here. He's been in and out sporadically and I can tell the situation with Kai is really rattling him. Some days, he's eager to help and try to participate in the various routines we have. Other times, he disappears for days on end. I try not to preoccupy myself with his irregular schedule, but I can't help but wonder.

His man-whore ways have been the talk of the tabloids for a while now, and I hope his bad behavior doesn't someday influence his son. Kai's going to have an uphill battle as it is with the constant worry of addiction hanging over his head. His long-term caregiver, who theoretically is going to be Garrett, will need to keep a close eye on Kai to be sure he doesn't display addictive behavior early on.

I brew a large pot of water for tea and slide onto one of the barstools. I look out the window and the sun is shining bright. What a gorgeous day. I'm suddenly jealous of all of the people enjoying their time outside. I wish I could get to the park or something, but I hesitate bringing Kai out in such bright sunlight. His eyes are very sensitive.

The doorbell rings, and I look to see if anyone is going to answer it. It rings again, and I realize that I'm the only one who can. I'm in leggings and a tank top, and I look like I just rolled out of bed.

I open the door and Cassie comes bounding in. "Happy Birthday!" she squeals and hugs me tight.

"Thanks," I say and turn back toward the sound of the water boiling in the kitchen. "Do you want some tea?" I yawn and take out two mugs from the cabinet.

"No thank you," she replies, and I slide one back in place.

"Okay."

"Good thing you're getting caffeinated because we're going out tonight!"

I shake my head. "Yeah, right." I haven't left Garrett's house in over a month. The only down time I have, I use it to swim. My aunt helps out as much as she can, but this is my job, not hers. "I can't go anywhere, Cass. I have a job to do, remember? Kai is asleep with my aunt right now, but I'm his nurse. I can't leave." I pour the hot water over two large tea bags and let them steep.

"Peggy is staying the night so you can go out and enjoy

yourself for a change!" she exclaims and claps her hands together.

"What?" Aunt Peggy didn't mention this to me, and I don't really think it's a good idea.

"Yes. I called her on Monday, and she said she couldn't think of a better way for you to celebrate your birthday than by going out with me. So drink that double-sized tea and get yourself in the shower. We're going out."

I sigh. I honestly don't have it in me to be social with anyone.

"Can't we just stay here?" I whine.

"Absolutely not."

The door opens that leads to the garage and Garrett walks in. He looks disheveled, and I wonder where he's been. *I've been wondering about him a lot lately.*

Cassie's eyes light up and she blushes. She's only met him once or twice since he's usually never here. I know she's star struck and can't help herself. "Hi, Garrett!" she exclaims. I wrap both of my hands around the hot mug and slowly sip the tea. It's black and strong with a tiny twist of lemon. *Perfect.*

"Hi, Cassie," he says, and she's twitching in her seat. I know she's thrilled that he remembered her name.

"Hey, Sam," he addresses me, and guilt sweeps across his face. "I'm sorry I wasn't around to help out last night. I had something to do. How's Kai?"

I tense a little, wondering what that 'something' was. A groupie, no doubt. I overheard a conversation the other day that Garrett was having on speakerphone in the library. The band's publicist was lecturing him on maintaining good behavior. The tabloids and local news have been very nosy around his property, trying to figure out what's been going on. After Sadie's overdose, he's been under a microscope. Miraculously, nobody has gotten wind that he has a baby. The social worker handled things discreetly, and since Sadie had no other family and few friends who knew what was going on with her, things were kept very quiet about Kai. Which is another reason I can't be seen leaving the house with him. When we take him to his doctor and therapy appointments, we're usually in one of the large SUVs with dark tinted windows. We always leave from the garage and don't get out until the doors are closed. Miraculously, no one has tried to follow us because it's Peggy who's usually driving. I think the paparazzi assume that it's just the housekeeper coming and going.

"He's good. Aunt Peggy's upstairs with him now."

"Sam's going out tonight," Cassie interrupts. "It's her birthday!"

His eyes flicker for a moment, and he walks towards me. "Happy birthday," he says genuinely and reaches out to softly touch my arm. His touch feels nice and I sigh.

Cassie looks between us and the startled look on her face is hard to miss.

"Want to come?" she asks.

Garrett smiles. "No, thank you though." He reaches into the refrigerator and takes out a large jug of Gatorade. He opens the top and starts to chug it right from the bottle. He must be hungover or something.

"You totally should come," Cassie insists, and it makes me uncomfortable.

"Sorry, I have other plans," he says and places the Gatorade back into the refrigerator.

"Of course you do," she stammers, embarrassed that she pressed him.

"So you're going out tonight?" he asks me, and I flush a little.

"I keep telling her no, but she's insisting."

He smiles. "It is your birthday, after all. You should go out and enjoy yourself. When was the last time you even left here when it wasn't a trip to the doctor or pharmacy?"

"It's been a while." I shrug.

"It's settled, then. Enjoy yourselves."

The doorbell chimes again and I answer it. This house hasn't seen this much commotion since I first arrived.

I open it and see Heath's large frame standing in front of me. This guy is so tall; it would be intimidating if you didn't know him. He's honestly one of the most down-to-earth members of Epic Fail. I've met him a couple of times, and I know he annoys Garrett when he comes by. My aunt says Heath was with Garrett the day he found out about Kai and feels connected to the little boy. It's hard not to feel a connection to Kai. I'm already in love with him.

"Hey, Heath. Garrett's in the kitchen."

"Hey, Sam."

He strides past me and addresses Garrett. "They're expecting us by four. Are you ready?"

"What time is it?" I ask Cassie without looking at the large clock on the wall.

"Three," she says while staring at Heath. Her jaw is about to hit the table.

"Wow." I completely lost track of time. I honestly thought it wasn't even lunchtime yet. Last night was a long night with Kai, and I must have really messed up my internal clock.

"I'm ready now," Garrett says and swipes his keys from the counter.

He turns back to me and says one more time, "Happy birthday, Sam."

The door shuts behind them, and Cassie says, "Oh my God. I think I'm in love. Heath is just…"

I laugh. "You say that every single time you meet a hot dude. How can you be in love with so many people?" I ask, joking.

"Easy." She shrugs and slaps me on the butt. "Get ready, we're meeting the girls for dinner, and I want to run a few errands before we go." I haven't seen Becky and Marcie since I was put on administrative leave. I admit it will be nice to see them again, but I'm mentally and physically exhausted. Full-time nursing doesn't come close to the levels of exhaustion that I feel every single day. It's like being a mom.

"I'll be down in a half hour. Make yourself comfortable." I slowly climb the staircase and tip-toe into Kai's room.

"Did you know about this?" I whisper to Peggy.

She smiles and continues rocking Kai. "You need to enjoy yourself for a change. Go out. Have a good time. Kai will be here waiting for you tomorrow morning. Happy birthday," she says and dismisses me from the room.

I take a deep breath in the hallway and duck into one of the guest rooms to shower and get ready for my date with Cassie.

I can't believe what a turn my life has taken. Never in a million years would I ever have imagined that I'd be yearning to stay home with a child that isn't even mine. I've grown so close to him and feel his every ounce of pain and suffering. I wish I could take it all away so he could be peaceful and pain-free.

I look at myself in the mirror and trace the tired lines around my eyes. I've aged more during the past few months than I have in all of my twenty-four years. *Is this what my mother looked like at my age?* She was beautiful at forty, and I doubt she looked this tired at twenty-four.

"I love you, Mom and Dad," I whisper into the mirror. *I miss them so much.*

CHAPTER 19

Garrett
Present
Villanova, Pennsylvania
Age 27

"DOES SHE KNOW TODAY'S YOUR BIRTHDAY TOO?" Heath asks as he pulls out of the gate at the end of my driveway.

"No," I respond. I'm still shaken by the fact that we share a birthday. A day where we both lost parents. My father had control over his demise, but her family did not. I wonder what goes through her mind every year on the anniversary of her parents' death. I can't help but think about all of the years I spent wondering where my father was. *Did he miss me? Did he want to see me again?*

"How long has she been with you? Four or five months?" Heath asks.

"Why?" I ask, wondering why this is a relevant question.

"You'd think you'd know by now what day her birthday is. Don't you think?"

"I don't know what you're getting at. It's not like Sam and I are… " *What are we?*

We arrive at the studio, and everyone's cars are there. Even Alex's. It doesn't seem to bother Heath too much that Alex is still involved with us and our creative process. He'll be happy if one or two of his songs make it onto the next album. Nothing really fazes Heath, and I like that about him.

Our manager and publicist are both here as well as several suits from the record label. Today is a critical day in planning for our next tour and, for the first time since Kai came to live with me, I dread having to leave him. It's been a while since I've felt the need to escape. He's growing fast, and his rough patches are starting to become less frequent. I'm conflicted about planning our tour knowing I'm going to have to leave him.

We've all filled the room and have jammed around a conference table. Our manager, Tom, shuts the door. "Okay, let's get right to it. We need to know how committed Epic Fail is to finishing this next album. From what I see, you have two tracks out of twelve complete. What's going on?"

He scans the room and tries to make eye contact with each of us. Alex is as relaxed as he could be because the pressure isn't on him at all. He has most of the lyrics written that he wants to present to us. It's up to us to create the music.

Dax speaks first, as always. "Tom, we all have competing priorities at the moment, and I think we need to lay out a flexible timeline that we can adapt to."

"We're booking stadiums for over a year from now and we need to know if you're going to have a new album to tour with," one of the record executives speaks up. I don't know his name, but I think he's been involved with planning our tours in the past.

"That's kind of hard to say," Dax responds.

My mind drifts as voices raise in the room. All I can think about is how big Kai will be this time next year. Will he be walking? Talking? Running? Will he be happy or will he still have residual issues from his drug exposure?

Will Sam still be helping us?

That's the critical question and my gut tells me no. I overheard her talking with Peggy the other day about trying to get her old job back. Apparently, the hospital administration conducted a full investigation into the death of the little boy that she was caring for. They retracted their decision to suspend her and offered to reinstate her at full pay. I don't fully understand what happened, but I think that's good news for her. But bad news for me.

"Garrett?" Tom asks, and I realize that I have no idea what everyone was just talking about.

"I'm sorry, what was the question?" I ask.

"Can you be ready to tour in six months?" Tom asks, his tone stiff.

"No way. I don't see us getting close to finishing our album and getting ourselves together that quickly," I respond and look to Dax for the assist.

"I think we can all agree that six months is way too soon." Dax jumps in, and I breathe a sigh of relief.

"How about a compromise?" Tom interjects.

Dax raises his eyebrow and leans forward. "Compromise?"

"Let's plan a small venue acoustic tour where you play your current albums and work on the new album on the road. We could potentially film it, following you as you tour various cities."

Tristan smirks. "The Foo Fighters just did something similar with Sonic Highways. Although it wasn't acoustic, it's too close to copying their last tour."

Tom shoves his hands in his pockets. "Well, I've exhausted my ideas."

Heath speaks up. "I think if we set a flexible schedule, we can get moving quicker than we all think." He looks at me. "Garrett, what about using your recording studio? Since Alex and Tristan live close to you, we can make it easy on you guys and come out there, instead of the city?"

Dax nods and seems to like this idea. Tristan would be thrilled not to have to go into the city as much as we would need to if we were recording there. My studio at home is great but could use some upgrades.

"We'll need to do a minor configuration change to the boards and add a second soundproof section of the room." I turn to Tom. "Can you get some guys out next week or the week after so we can run through specs?"

"It's going to cost money. You know this, right?" Tom replies.

Dax turns to the record executives. "If you want us on the road in twelve months, this is our deal on the table. The label handles all modifications to Garrett's studio or we push the start of our tour out indefinitely."

Tom is clearly useless in this negotiation and Dax has taken control.

The executives huddle at the end of the conference table, and by the end of their whispered discussion, they're all nodding their heads in agreement.

After a few more discussion topics, the meeting is adjourned and we all file out of the crowded conference room.

Alex approaches me and puts his hand on my shoulder. "How're you doing, bro?"

"Hanging in there," I say.

"Thanks for offering your studio."

"Well, Heath offered it up and I just agreed. I don't want to let my current situation affect the rest of these guys. I don't want to let them down, you know?"

We talk in code because the label has no idea what's going on. Our publicist advised me to keep Kai and his existence secret until he's healthy enough to share with the world. We don't need the extra stress of stalkers at my house.

"Tabby and the kids would love to come meet your little man. Just let me know when. She's been itching to get over to see him. I just don't want her getting any ideas." He laughs. "Little Noah is in his terrible two's, and trust me, this factory is closed for a while."

It's been so long since I've seen Tabby and the kids that I didn't even think Noah was walking yet. "Wow, you must have your hands full."

"You will soon." He chuckles. "Gotta run. See you in a few weeks?"

I nod and he takes off.

"Ready?" Heath says as he approaches me.

"Yeah."

"Hey, sorry about that in there. I just didn't want to see our whole deal fall apart with the label. They were squirming in their seats for a while, and I was worried they were going to force a contract restructuring or something like that."

"It's okay. I think this arrangement will work." I just hope it doesn't bother Sam. She's so used to it being quiet and somewhat peaceful at my place. I should have run this by her before I said yes. What if this disturbs Kai too much?

The drive home is short, and Heath drops me at the front door. "Want to come in for a beer?" He looks at me funny. I've never been super social with him, but somehow the two of us always wind up together.

"Nah, I'm exhausted." He looks in his rearview mirror as another car is pulling up behind him.

Cassie parks next to Heath's car and the passenger door flies open. Sam yells, "Heyyy!" and practically falls out of the car.

Holy shit, she's wasted.

Heath laughs and puts his car in reverse. "Glad to see you've got this under control, G. Happy birthday." He backs up, and I can see him laughing down my long driveway.

"I'm really sorry, Garrett. I don't know how she got like this," Cassie says and runs to help Sam into the house.

"You gave me shotsssss," she says almost incoherently.

"Only a couple. Sam, what else did you drink?"

Sam mumbles something and goes limp in Cassie's arms. "A little help?" she calls out to me, and I rush to help get Sam inside.

We bring her right upstairs to one of the guest rooms. Sam falls onto the bed, and I leave her with Cassie.

I walk down the hallway toward Kai's room. Peggy steps out into the hallway, holding him in her arms. He's sound asleep and looks content. *Good.*

"I thought I heard the girls come in. Are they here?" she whispers.

"Yeah, Sam may have had a little too much to drink," I warn her, and she smiles.

"It's been a while since she got out, and I expected she would enjoy herself a little too much." She shakes her head and turns to go back inside his room.

"You can go home tonight, if you want," I suggest. "I can take care of Kai if you need me to."

"That's okay. It's your birthday too, so you both should have the night off."

"How did you know?" I ask Peggy, curious. I don't make a habit of telling many people.

"Your mother called the house phone earlier and she mentioned it."

Cassie emerges from the guest room down the hall. "I'm so sorry, I thought I only gave her a few drinks, but wow, she's a mess." She giggles a little and walks down the stairs. "I hope you don't mind if I leave. I left our friends at the bar and I'm the designated driver."

She disappears through the front door, and Peggy says, "Why don't you get some rest? Happy birthday, Garrett."

I walk past the room where Sam is passed out, and I'm tempted to peek in. I restrain myself and head toward the other end of the floor where my room is.

I strip down to my boxers and climb into my huge bed. I sink into the mattress and immediately fall asleep.

I WAKE UP WITH A START, and I feel my covers being pulled off of me. *What the hell?* I look at my feet, and Sam is curled up at the end of the bed and she's attempting to roll herself in my comforter. She seems disoriented, and I whisper, "Sam? What are you doing?"

Startled, she sits up straight and pulls the blanket up to cover her chest.

"Where am I?" she asks, clearly confused.

"You're in my room," I state, and she gasps.

"How did I get here?"

"I have no idea."

She looks around, her eyes squinted. "Wow, I feel like shit." She holds her head, and she doesn't look so good. I glance over at the clock, and it's almost five in the morning. The blanket shifts and I see she's wearing a tight tank top.

"I guess you don't know how long you've been in here?" I ask her.

Her embarrassment is evident, and she begins to get up.

"Wait," I say to her, doing everything in my power to stop a half-naked Sam from leaving my room. "Are you okay?"

"I'm fine, just insanely hung-over." She plants her hands into the mattress, pressing downward. She seems to be trying to steady herself.

"Why don't you lie down for a second. It may help you feel better." I can't believe what I've suggested, and she does so without hesitation. She's no longer at the foot of the bed but closer to the headboard. She tucks her knees up toward her chest, and they brush up against my thigh. Her legs are bare. *Is she wearing pants?*

"So you had fun last night, huh?" I ask.

She looks mortified. "I don't even remember coming home. I didn't think I had that much to drink, but apparently I did. I'm sorry for coming in here. This must feel totally weird to you." She holds the blanket close to her face, and I see her eyes get heavy again. *It's not weird at all. It feels… good.* "I must have thought this was Kai's room."

"I hope you had a great birthday," I say.

"I think I did."

"My birthday was yesterday also." I can't believe I just told her. I didn't think that through. I never celebrate it because of what my dad did to himself on this day, but I just blurted it out without thinking.

Her eyes grow wide. "Really?"

I nod slowly and turn on my side to face her. "I don't really like to celebrate it. It doesn't elicit happy memories for me."

"Me either," she says, and her eyes glaze over. She looks exhausted. *Is she about to cry?*

"That's understandable," I say. "How do you do it, though? You seem like you have it way more together than I ever could." She's strong and confident. I'm surprised to see this moment of weakness.

"I don't know. Sometimes my birthday is really hard. Especially because it's a reminder of everything that I've lost. *My family.*" She pauses and looks pensively out the window. "I sometimes feel like I'm drowning without them, but then I remember they taught me how to *swim.*"

She's insightful and inspiring. "It seems like you've been able to find peace, in a way," I say encouragingly.

"I think I have." She holds my gaze with her sleepy eyes and says, "You should try to find peace too. You have a really big reason to do that now, you know."

I nod again and admit, "I never thought I'd be in this situation."

"Being a father isn't a situation. It's a choice."

"It wasn't my choice, Sam."

Her face hardens and her eyes fill with tears. "It's your choice *now.* It's your life *now.* That little boy depends on you to live. Stop dwelling on the events that you had no control over and start focusing on your future with Kai, because I know it's going to be wonderful."

I exhale and struggle to find my next breath. Her words are profound and tear right through me. These words come from a girl whose parents were murdered and her life forever altered.

Yet she's risen from it all and has the ability to be so positive about the rest of her life. And mine.

I reach out to push aside a thick curl that fell onto her face. She closes her eyes when my hand brushes against her cheek.

She places her hand over mine, her touch softens my soul. It transmits strength and security. Love and understanding. I don't want her to let go. She exhales softly and is sound asleep.

"Where did you come from?" I whisper.

CHAPTER 20

Sam
Past
Trenton, New Jersey
Age 20

CASSIE FALLS ONTO HER BED across from mine and lets out a sigh of relief.

"This was easily the hardest year yet. I don't think I can take clinicals anymore." She complains and rolls over, kicking off her tennis shoes. We just finished our microbiology final and we're done for the semester.

"Seriously, Cassie? You've gotten straight As so far. What are you complaining about?"

"I don't think I'm cut out for this, Sam. You'll make a better nurse than me. You're built for this. You have the *desire* to help people. Me? I'm disgusted by them. If I have to wipe another ass…" She stands up and pulls her tank top over her head. "I need a shower."

We share a one-bedroom apartment that I swear is smaller than our dorm room was on campus. She takes three steps and is already in our bathroom. The water turns on and she's still complaining. "How am I going to continue? Sure, I can do the book stuff just fine, but when you put me in front of a patient, I can't do it. You saw what happened last week when I had to find that dude's vein and draw blood. It was a mess! I should be wearing a sign that says 'Beware – Nursing Student.'"

I shrug my shoulders, knowing she's so much better than she thinks she is. Her confidence when it comes to her nursing abilities is lacking, but her skill is not. We'll just need to work on that some more.

"Hey, if it makes you feel any better, I almost vomited all over my patient right after I was told I had to give her an enema. Imagine that!" I laugh and stretch out on my bed. Googie is perched on my pillow, and I rub her like I do every day. She's as old as I am, and her stuffing is practically gone.

Cassie chuckles and I can hear the shower door close.

"Just think, this time next year, we'll be on our own in a hospital, saving lives every single day," I call out to her and wait for her response.

"Fuck that!" she says from the shower. "I need to find something else to do."

"Stop being so dramatic," I say and roll over on my side. "Always so damn dramatic."

The water turns off and she's in the room with a towel wrapped around her head and another one around her body. Drips of water trail behind her.

"Didn't you dry yourself off at all?" I scold her as she drips onto the carpet.

"You didn't listen to a word I said, Sam. Really listen. I can't do this anymore."

Her expression is serious, and I sit up on the bed. I quickly toss Googie to her and she catches her clumsily.

"Googie says you can do it, so you can. Now stop this nonsense and get your shit together."

She looks at my floppy childhood friend, and I see the smile in her eyes.

"Well, if your dog thinks I can do it, then maybe I can." She tosses Googie back to me and laughs out loud.

She slips into comfy leggings and a tank top and crawls into her own bed. Her eyes find mine and they glisten a bit. "Sam, I'm so proud of you," she says.

"Don't get sappy on me now," I respond, wondering where this conversation is going.

"Seriously, look at you. You're the star student. You do everything with ease and you have this innate desire to help people. You want to make them *all* better. Every last one of them. You have a gift and you don't even know it."

Her tone is serious, and I know she means every word that she's saying. Aunt Peggy says the same words to me all of the time.

"It's weird, Cass. I feel like I have a *purpose*, you know? I appreciate what I have and how I can help others. It scares the hell out of me that somehow I'll mess it up, but I know what I'm supposed to be doing. Don't you feel that way?" I ask her, curious.

"Hell no," she answers definitively. "I don't know what my purpose is or the reason I'm even in nursing school. I'm following your lead. Following in your footsteps. I see what makes you happy. What makes you tick. And I want to feel the same way. I want to be like you."

I snort out loud.

"No you don't. Trust me. You know me better than anyone and know everything that I've gone through. You do not want to be like me."

"Sam, what you've overcome is tremendous. I'm going to get sappy on you *again* for a second, and you have to bear with me." Her eyes are still wet, and I lie back down on my bed, staring up at the solar system poster tacked to the ceiling above me.

"Yeah, your life at sixteen was torn the fuck apart. I completely get that. But your entire outlook on life and how you function day-to-day is remarkable. Your strength is astonishing. You almost drowned when you were seven. What did you do? You got swim lessons and learned pool yoga."

I shake my head and shrug my shoulders. Her analogy is comical.

"Psycho Todd Mitchell tries to feel you up in a pool. What do you do? You nut-crunch him and then become a black belt in kickboxing."

All of this is true.

Hearing Todd's name, however, makes me cringe. A few months after the incident in Trish O'Toole's pool, Todd was arrested for multiple rapes and attempted murder. He's been in prison since he was convicted of all of his crimes. The faces of the victims are still fresh in my head. Every single one of them. The media played out the story over and over again and it made my skin crawl. I wish I could have hurt him more than I did that day he attacked me in Trish's pool. I was definitely one of the lucky ones, and I became a stronger person for it.

Cassie continues, "Your parents get killed by a deranged psycho drug addict and you vow to become a nurse to help people get better. You save people's lives every single day, Sam. You're amazing."

Hearing her describe my parents' murder sends a jolt to my heart, and I take a quick breath and hold it. What little reminders I have of them adorn my room. My bracelet dangles from a hook next to my bed. The blue ribbon is attached to the poster that I fall asleep staring at every night. My Googie sleeps next to me, reminding me of their comfort and love.

I exhale slowly and turn on my side again to look at Cassie.

"I'm done earning my badges," I say softly. "It's time for me to give back."

Her eyes light up with victory.

"Exactly my point," she says and turns off the light.

CHAPTER 21

Garrett
Past
Philadelphia, Pennsylvania
Age 25

"I CAN'T BELIEVE HE DID IT," I say, shaking my head and tossing back my sixth shot of Jameson.

"Dude, I can't even." Tristan does the same and clinks his empty shot glass against mine.

"Can't believe who did what?" Kirsten chirps as she slides onto the barstool next to Tristan.

"Alex, man. Dude got married." Tristan's eyes glaze over, and his smile freezes on his face. He's about to pass out.

Kirsten pokes him in the side, and he sits up with a jolt. "Why don't you go upstairs?" She nudges him and holds a plastic key in front of his nose. He swipes at it until it comes into focus and stands from the bar stool. "Whoa, I shouldn't have stood up so fast." He wobbles a bit on his feet and backs up toward the hotel lobby. We're in the bar after Alex and Tabby's wedding reception. It ended two hours ago, and the newlyweds are long gone.

"Where's Alex?" Tristan acts confused. And drunk.

"He's upstairs sleeping with his bride, Tristan. Exactly where you should be." Kirsten waves at him and blows him a kiss.

"Will you be up soon?" he asks, hopeful.

"Of course."

Tristan stumbles to the elevators and practically falls in. He disappears behind the doors, and I laugh.

"What an amazing wedding," Kirsten says as she flags down the bartender. She orders a glass of Pinot Noir and turns to face me. "Don't you think?"

"Sure, it was amazing." I humor her with what she wants to hear. If she starts talking about flowers and centerpieces, I'm out of here.

The bartender places a large glass of wine in front of her and says, "This is on me." He winks at her and she ignores his advances.

"I think he likes you," I joke and grab the last shot of whiskey that was lined up in front of me. I toss it back and take a large swig of my beer.

"Nah, he's just hoping for a big tip."

She sighs, raises her glass of wine and says, "Cheers."

I take another sip of beer and nod.

"There aren't two people in the world more deserving than Alex and Tabby." Kirsten is Tabby's best friend and boss. She owns a bookstore in the city and seems to be pretty successful.

"Yeah, so happy together," I muse.

"What about you, Garrett? When do you think you'll finally settle down?"

She can't be serious. Settle down? Me? I nearly choke on my words. "Let me say this in a way that you'll completely understand. Never. Ever."

"I don't believe you. Beneath that womanizer exterior is a soft and tender heart. I'm convinced of it."

"Fuck that." I finish my beer and wave my hand for another.

"What are you so afraid of?" she asks. "Have you ever been in a long-term relationship?"

I have to think about it for a second. "Nope."

"What about the sister of that girl on tour?" she asks.

"Her? No way. We were just regular fuck buddies."

She huffs and sips her wine. "I have faith, Garrett. You'll stumble into love one day and you won't even realize what's happening to you. I predict love will find you at a time and place when you least expect it." She waves her hand in the air as if she just cast a spell on me or something.

"Whatever."

She looks down at her phone and swipes through some messages. "Who are you expecting to hear from at this hour? Tristan's passed out cold right now." I look at the clock. It's almost two in the morning, and the lobby bar is still jammed with guests from the wedding reception. The party's still going strong.

"I'm compulsive about checking for messages from Tabby. She looks like she's about to give birth any second. She's bursting at the seams."

"I'm sure you'll be the first to know when she does go into labor." *Gross.* "Besides, she's just upstairs, so I think the entire hotel would know if it happened."

She raises her eyebrow when she sees the expression on my face, which I can only imagine is pure disgust.

"How many children do you want?" she asks.

"Are you kidding me? I just finished telling you I'm never settling down. Why the hell would you think I'd want kids?"

She ignores my response and continues talking. "I wanted five kids. I've always wanted so many that my husband and I would be outnumbered. The thought of the chaos excited me. The more kids I could have, the happier I'd be." The smile melts from her face. "But since I can't have kids, that dream went right out the window."

"Bummer," I say, surprised by her admission.

She raises the wine glass to her lips again. "I wonder if I'll ever find someone who will love me anyway. Even if he knows I can't give him children."

"I don't think Tristan will care either way," I say. I shift in my seat, uncomfortable with this entire conversation. My skin is getting itchy, and I think it's about time I got out of here. I didn't sign up to be Kirsten's personal therapist, and I certainly don't want to know anything about her ability or inability to have kids.

"You're so sad, Garrett. I just don't get it. What kind of family do you have that you would have such a rotten outlook on your own future?"

"My mom and stepdad are cool. My bio dad was an asshole and killed himself."

"Oh?" she looks surprised. "I'm sorry."

I shake my head. There's no need to talk about this.

"Whatever. It is what it is." I drink some more beer and pull cash from my pocket, laying it on the bar to cover the drinks.

"Goodnight." Kirsten sighs into her wine glass.

"Hey, I don't mean to bum you out, but you really have the wrong read on me, okay? I'm not the settling down type of guy, and I'm certainly not someone who wants a brood of kids. I like my life just the way it is."

She smirks at me, and I'm not sure if it's a drunk smirk or she really thinks she knows something that I don't know.

I shrug it off and walk through the bar. I scan the room to see if the hot blonde from the wedding is still here, hoping for a warm body to bring upstairs with me. I don't see her anywhere, and the remaining prospects here aren't my type. *Oh well.*

I make it to my room and strip down to my boxers. My pants get stuck around my feet, and I almost tumble to the floor. *Is the room wobbly or is it me?*

I fall to the bed and feel the plush mattress suck me in. As I'm drifting off to sleep, Kirsten's words keep ringing in my ears.

Love will find you at a time and place when you least expect it.

CHAPTER 22

Sam
Present
Villanova, Pennsylvania
Age 24

I HEAR THE BACK DOOR SLAM, and I'm startled awake. I'm sprawled out on the large couch in the den, and I crane my neck to see if Kai's still asleep. He's out cold in the pack and play in the middle of the floor.

"Sam?" Aunt Peggy says from the kitchen.

I stretch and sit up. *What time is it?* I find the clock on the wall and see it's almost five o'clock.

"I'll be right there," I say quietly and stand up.

When I get to the kitchen, Aunt Peggy is unloading groceries. "Hi," she says through a warm smile. "I'm surprised to see you up here. Isn't it time for Kai's occupational therapy?" Garrett has a home gym downstairs in the basement that we've rearranged to make into Kai's play area. We moved out all of Garrett's exercise equipment and filled the room with padded floors and climbing toys. His therapist comes to the house two times a week and today is usually one of those days. We're working on helping strengthen and tone his arm and leg muscles to counteract the tightening of his back. For many months, his frequent crying and pain caused him to overdevelop the muscles in his neck and back and neglect his arms and legs. Since developmentally, he should start crawling in a month or two, we need to make sure he stays on track.

"No, Nadia had to cancel today. She's sick." I help her empty the bags.

"Oh, that's too bad. The day after OT, Kai tends to have a great day," she says.

"That's because Nadia works him out hard," I chuckle. "He's physically exhausted after his therapy sessions."

"Is he asleep?" she asks.

I look over my shoulder to check on him. "Yes, we both passed out about an hour ago." I massage my lower back and then stretch my arms into the air. "That couch is not comfortable."

"Neither is that chair upstairs, but you sleep in it more than you do the bed," she replies and closes the refrigerator.

She looks at her watch. "Darn," she says and shakes her head.

"Is everything okay?" I ask.

"It looks like I'm going to miss my hair appointment."

"Why is that? You still have time, right?"

"I told Garrett I would make him dinner tonight."

"Really? I haven't seen you cook for him in a while. He can take care of himself," I say and slide onto the bar stool.

"Sam, that boy doesn't cook. You know better than that. I fill his refrigerator and freezer with tons of food for him to heat up. I've been doing it for years. Besides, I promised him I would make him something tonight because Heath is coming to work on some band stuff."

"I'll do it. You go and get your hair done. You deserve it," I grin, and she doesn't waste any time gathering her things. She hugs me quickly and heads toward the front door.

"Thank you! See you tomorrow," she calls out, and she's gone without even telling me what she was planning to feed them. *Crap.*

I look into the den again to make sure Kai is still asleep and begin rummaging through cabinets. I find flour and a couple of jars of sauce. *Pizza.* I can do that.

Now I need to Google how to make dough. As I'm swiping through my phone, Garrett comes in from the garage door into the kitchen. "Hey," he says, surprised to see me.

"Hi." I find the flour recipe and place my phone down on the center island.

"I hope you and Heath like pizza," I say and grab the olive oil from the cabinet.

"Uh, yeah we like pizza. Why?" he looks puzzled and tosses his keys onto the counter.

"Aunt Peggy said she was supposed to cook for you both tonight and she had to run out, so now *I'm* cooking for you."

"You don't have to cook for me, Sam," he says and walks toward me.

"What are you guys going to eat then?" I ask.

"There's been a change of plans. Heath can't make it, so I'm solo tonight." He grins and he notices the flour and oil. "You're going to make homemade pizza?" His eyes light up. "I haven't had homemade pizza in forever."

I shrug my shoulders. "Me either," I say and brush past him to find the rest of the ingredients I'll need to make the dough. "I hope you have yeast here," I say.

"What?" he asks.

"Yeast. I need yeast for the dough." I open the pantry and immediately find all of the baking supplies. You can tell my aunt is in charge of food shopping and organizing the pantry; it makes it easy to find things. "Here it is," I say and swipe the small packet from a plastic bin on the shelf.

He raises his hands in the air and says, "I'm no good here. This is *all* you. But you really don't have to make me anything. I can order something."

Everything else I need is within reach, and I have the ingredients arranged on the center island, ready for me.

"Where's Kai?" he asks.

"In there. Asleep." I motion toward the den and pick up my phone. He's watching me with amusement as I re-read the recipe. I open the flour, measure out what's needed for the dough, and dump it into the stainless steel bowl in front of me.

"How was he today?" he asks.

I look up and swipe my hand across my forehead. *I should have put my hair up.*

"His day was okay," I say and dump the rest of the ingredients into the bowl.

"Just okay?" He looks disappointed. "Where's Nadia?" he asks, and I look up again. A large curl has fallen in front of my face, partially blocking my view of him. I attempt to brush it away and at the same time get the flour mixture on myself. His smile grows and he takes a couple of steps toward me.

"She had to cancel tonight," I say and tense up as he gets closer. *Why is he looking at me like that?* "And Kai had his ups and downs."

"You've got... something on your face." He grins as he reaches out. He softly brushes the flour from my face, and I feel like I'm swaying in place.

"Th—thanks," I stammer as he tucks the nuisance curl behind my ear. His hand lingers for a moment and then he steps away.

"I think I should help," he says. "You're a bit of a mess already."

"Why don't you grate the cheese? There's a brick of mozzarella inside the top drawer in the refrigerator." I assemble the hand mixer and plug it in.

"Do I have a cheese grater?" he asks, and I try to stifle a giggle.

"You really don't spend much time in your own kitchen, do you?" I ask.

"I'm in here all the time. I just don't know where anything is. Your aunt makes sure I don't have to worry about any of that." He seems embarrassed and drops his head.

I tap the drawer next to me. "Cheese grater's in here. It's a flat, rectangular, metal thingy," I say, just in case he's never seen one before.

"I know what a cheese grater looks like, Sam. I just didn't realize I had one." He brushes past me and opens the drawer. "See." He points. "It's right there." He's standing next to me and starts his chore. I smirk as I turn on the mixer. His elbow bumps into mine as he's working, but I don't move.

"Sorry," he says, and I look over at him. Now he's grinning, and I know that I didn't really hurt his feelings. I bump my elbow into his on purpose and he smiles. He's feverishly grating the cheese, and soon a large pile is on the plate in front of him.

"Enough?" he asks, and I nod. He brushes up against my side and peeks into bowl. "That doesn't look like much dough," he says.

"That's what the yeast is for," I reply and dump the packet into the mixture. "Once this is all blended together, the dough will begin to rise. It should take about an hour and then we'll be able to make our pizza."

He raises his eyebrow. "*Our* pizza?"

"I'm not putting all of this effort into something not to get anything out of it," I say and bump my hip into his. *What am I doing?*

"Really?" he says and turns to wash his hands in the sink. "I guess that seems fair enough."

"What do you want on top?" I ask.

"What?" he chokes out.

"*Toppings?* What do you want on top of your pizza?" *Oh my God.* My cheeks are burning as I stretch plastic wrap over the bowl.

"Oh." He pauses. "I'm good with just cheese and sauce."

"Me too," I say. My hands are covered in flour, so I join him at the sink. "Can you leave the water on?"

"Sure," he says, and I place my hands under the warm stream.

"Too hot?" he asks.

"No, it's just right."

He squeezes soap into my hands, and I rub them together, building up the lather and scrubbing off the flour that's caked on. "Thanks," I say. Our shoulders are touching. He remains next to me as I finish washing up. He turns off the water and places a towel over my wet hands, his strong grip patting and squeezing my hands dry. My knees are weak, and I swear his hands are the only thing keeping me upright at the moment.

"Dry?" he asks hoarsely. I look into his eyes and nod slowly. His hands remain wrapped around mine, but I don't want to pull them away.

Suddenly Kai cries sharply from the den and I jump. Garrett drops the towel and we both rush in to calm him. Kai's lying on his back, and his arms and legs are outstretched. His screams grab me in the chest and I lift him up. "It's okay," I whisper as his body tenses against mine. I rhythmically pat his back and bounce him in my arms.

"What can I do?" Garrett asks helplessly.

"Can you fix him a bottle?"

"Yes," he says and takes off into the kitchen. Kai continues to wail and throws his head back violently.

"Hey. Shhh," I whisper against his temple, kissing him gently. I begin to hum and cradle the back of his head, gently pushing him against my shoulder. Garrett is back within a few minutes and I sit down in the recliner.

"Here." Garrett hands me the bottle and I shift Kai into a comfortable feeding position. As soon as I put the bottle to his lips, he takes it and begins to eat. But within seconds, he's screaming and arching his back again. My heart is breaking for him, and Garrett kneels down on the floor beside us. His hand replaces mine on the back of Kai's head, and he slowly massages his scalp.

Garrett looks like he's being sliced in two by his son's cries. His brows are furrowed and he's stiff and tense. *Worried.* "Keep doing that," I urge him. "I think that will help." Kai's cries slow to whimpers, and I let him calm some more before I offer the bottle again.

"How can he be so good some days and others like this?" Garrett asks softly. "I just don't understand." He looks into my eyes, hoping for answers.

"I don't know," I say. "I wish I knew."

He nods and his hand drops to my knee. "He stopped," he says.

I place the bottle against Kai's lips and he begins eating, this time uninterrupted. Garrett exhales and so do I.

Garrett's pain is tangible. I wish I could make it go away along with Kai's pain. *We'll get there, eventually.* I look down at Kai, who is now eating comfortably.

I remove the bottle and place Kai on my shoulder to burp him, which he quickly does. Garrett's warm hand remains on my knee as I begin feeding Kai again. Garrett seems to notice his contact with me and slowly pulls his hand away. "Sorry," he whispers and moves over to the couch. He sits there, helpless. Almost defeated.

"He's getting better," I encourage. "Today's just been a really rough day. His senses seem overly heightened causing everything to bother him."

Garrett nods slowly and I'm not sure he believes me.

Kai finishes his bottle and I've burped him one last time. He's sound asleep, so I place him in his bouncy seat and strap him in. Garrett's hand brushes mine as he covers Kai with the soft fleece blanket that was on the chair. I pull away and stand up.

"You okay?" I ask.

He shakes his head. "I know you keep telling me that it's going to get better. Easier. But every single time I see him like *this* I don't believe you. His pain needs to end. He can't continue to live like this."

I grab hold of his hand and squeeze. "It *will* end. I promise." His eyes glisten and he bows his head.

He lets go of my hand, and I follow him into the kitchen. I dim the lights so they don't disturb Kai's slumber.

"Time to make pizza," I say.

"Yeah," he says.

I turn on the oven and place the pizza stone inside. "Look," I say, pointing to the dough in the bowl. "The yeast did its job." The dough has expanded, almost tripled in size.

"You seem so calm, Sam. How are you not affected by what just happened in there?" he asks, his face pained.

"It's not easy, but I know soon his pain will be a thing of the past. Every time I lay my hands on him or hold him against me, I know that I'm doing something to help his suffering." I pause and his eyes lock onto mine, still searching for answers. "Every day is one more day that he doesn't have drugs coursing through his veins. The pain becomes lessened over time, and as that happens, these episodes will also begin to diminish."

He nods and I continue, "If you remember when he first came home, he would cry like that for hours on end. There were days that went by that I swear he cried for twenty-three out of twenty-four hours. Garrett, it was *really* bad." I motion toward the den. "What just happened in there was a vast improvement. And it's only the second time today. *Progress.*"

He exhales but still looks drawn and worried. I desperately want to comfort him, but I know I can't. I'm his employee. Kai's nurse.

"Now, let's make pizza," I say and remove the dough from the bowl.

"Thank you," he says weakly and touches my cheek, dropping his hand to my shoulder. "I think I believe you."

"You have to believe, Garrett. Otherwise, you have nothing."

Light flickers in his eyes and he quickly turns away. "I'm starving," he says.

"Then let's do this," I say as I begin to roll the dough out on the counter.

We prepare the pizza together in silence. I can tell he's lost in thought and in pain. I can't imagine what's going through his mind every time he sees his little boy. I know I've gone through fits of anger when I watch Kai suffer. How can someone knowingly do this to a child? Sadie made terrible choices. Choices that Kai is now paying for.

"You look mad," he says, breaking our silence. We're both seated at the kitchen island, watching the pizza cook in the oven.

I sigh. "No, just thinking."

"About?" he urges.

"I'm trying to understand what would make someone do *this* to a child. I think about it every time I hold and comfort Kai. He did nothing to deserve the pain that he's living with every day. I *do* feel anger, but I also pity her."

He clenches his fists and I tense, waiting for him to take a swing at something. He tries to regulate his breathing, and I know he's doing everything to remain calm. "I don't want to talk about her," he says.

The oven timer goes off, and I jump to my feet. I grab two oven mitts and remove the stone, placing it on top of the stove. "This needs to cool off a little," I say and turn to him.

"Sorry," he says. "I didn't mean to jump down your throat. It's just... I can't feel anything for Sadie but contempt and anger. So let's just leave it alone, okay?"

I nod. "When you're ready to put aside your anger, you'll be surprised what your heart will find." He looks at me, surprised. "Your son is a gift."

He drops his shoulders and inhales deeply. "You're right."

"Still hungry?" I ask and grab the pizza cutter from the drawer. He nods quickly and I serve the first few slices. Before I know it, the entire pizza is gone and both of our plates are empty. The air is lighter between us, and I'm thankful he's relaxed a bit.

"I've never seen a girl eat that much pizza," he jokes and pushes his plate away from him.

I blush and wipe my mouth with a napkin. "I love pizza."

"We should do this more," he says.

"Yeah?" I ask. "You mean you're going to help *cook*? I think my aunt will want to know about this."

He's unmoved by my teasing and declares, "Every Thursday is now pizza night. And next week, you'll have to show me how to make the dough." He looks around the kitchen and I notice there's flour everywhere. "You're not exactly a neat cook." He smirks.

"No, I'm not. But you have to admit, that was damn good pizza," I say, very proud of myself.

"It was amazing."

I like that we've connected tonight. I feel like I can help him open up more and become confident in his abilities to care for his son, even if he carries such anger and resentment toward Sadie. *I know I can help him.*

"Pizza Thursday," I say. "I like the sound of that."

Kai starts to stir in the other room, and we both jump up. Concern floods his face once again, and I touch his arm. "I'll take care of him. He just sounds a little fussy and probably needs a diaper change." I look around the kitchen at the mess that we made. "Why don't you clean this up and meet me upstairs in his room in a little bit?"

"Okay," he says reluctantly, and I walk past him to get Kai.

As I carry Kai up the stairs, I notice a new picture on the wall. It's a close-up of Kai, and he's smiling huge. This picture is proof of the immense progress that we've made. It took months for him to smile for the first time, and Garrett captured it perfectly in this photo.

I settle into the rocking chair with him and hold him close, his breathing even and calm. I drift off to sleep with this strong little boy pressed close to my chest. *Progress.*

I OPEN MY EYES AND SEE a familiar form on the day-bed. Garrett's awake and his eyes meet mine. "Hey," I say groggily.

He blinks slowly and says, "Hey."

"What time is it?" I ask and shift Kai gently in my arms.

"Three thirty," he says quietly and sits up. The stiffness in my neck tells me the clock must be right. I think I dozed off around ten or eleven.

"It's my turn," he says as he makes his way toward me and Kai. I nod and stand up slowly so I don't wake him.

I transfer his son into his arms as he settles himself in the chair. I stretch and feel my spine crack.

"You've got to stop sleeping in this chair," he whispers as he looks down at his son. Kai is sleeping peacefully.

I crawl into the day-bed and find the warm spot that Garrett left behind. "Soon," I say as sleep starts to take me again. "Kai's going to get better and then you won't need me."

As I drift back to sleep, I hear a soft whisper.

"We'll always need you."

CHAPTER 23

Garrett
Present
Villanova, Pennsylvania
Age 27

"OH MY GOD, THAT PIZZA WAS AMAZING," Sam says, pushing herself away from the table. It's Pizza Thursday, our third one in a row.

"Amazing," I say and wipe the crumbs from my mouth.

"If we keep eating like this every week, I'm going to need to buy new clothes." She pats her flat belly and stretches. I raise my eyebrows and quickly glance at her body. There's nothing wrong with the way she looks. In fact, she can stand to put on a few pounds. Maybe I'll institute a Pizza Friday and Saturday.

"What are you smirking at?" she asks.

"Nothing, I was just thinking that I could seriously eat pizza every night," I respond.

Her grin widens and she gets up to begin cleaning the kitchen. We've fallen into a bit of a routine and I like it. I place the dirty dishes in the dishwasher.

"Hey there." Peggy's voice fills the room. "It smells wonderful in here."

"Sorry, Aunt Peggy. We ate it all. We didn't realize you'd be stopping by." Sam finishes washing and drying her hands.

"Oh, it's okay," Peggy says. "I ate about an hour ago."

Sam turns to me. "Do you think I can get a swim in before I need to get him ready for his bath and bed?"

Before I can answer, Peggy interjects. "I'll get him ready tonight." She pulls a bag from the pharmacy from her purse. "I have a new bath wash I'd like to try. It's hypoallergenic and soothing. I'm hoping it will help with his nighttime fussiness."

"Sounds good to me," Sam says and steps into her flip-flops. "I'm going for a quick swim. Dinner was great, Garrett." She's out the door and across the backyard before I know it.

Peggy lifts Kai from his bouncy seat positioned on the floor next to the table. He sat through dinner making cute baby noises while swatting at the toys hanging over his head. A rare moment for him and allowed Sam and I to eat in peace without the threat of a nuclear meltdown. He looks so content and peaceful right now and I don't know who to thank for giving me and Sam this nice moment.

"Little dude has been having a good time tonight. I think he likes that seat," I say.

"It's a wonderful seat. It helps keep him in an upright position so he doesn't have any GERD issues. It's also restrictive, in a comfortable way. He likes to feel safe and protected, and the harness on that seat is perfect in fulfilling that need." She unsnaps him from the seat and gently lifts him to her shoulder.

"I'm going to take him upstairs to bathe him and get him ready for his last bottle and bed. Can you let Sam know she has about an hour to herself before I'm finished?" She nods toward the pool house and heads up the stairs.

"Sure," I say and walk outside. It's a beautiful night. The air is crisp and cool, but I know the temperature inside the pool house is a balmy eighty-five degrees. I enter the enclosure and Sam is already doing her laps, unaware of my presence.

I slip into the dressing room and into a pair of swim trunks. When Sam makes her turn at the close end of the pool, I dive in and join her. She's mid-stroke and lifts her head from the water briefly, then drives her arms ahead. Her strokes are powerful yet graceful. I keep pace with her as we swim thirty more laps, each one more intense than the last.

When we finally touch the wall, we emerge from the water, lungs burning, hearts pumping. Our breathing is hurried and deliberate as we try to fill our lungs with much-needed oxygen.

"Wow," I pant. "I've seen you swim before, but man." I suck in air and try to slow down my breathing. "That was intense," I finish.

She's breathing hard through her mouth and nose as her chest expands and contracts deeply. "I had no idea you were going to join me," she says.

"Your aunt sent me out here to tell you she'd be done with Kai's bath and dinner in about an hour. Then I saw you exercising and thought I should join you." I pat my belly and say, "You know, pizza and all."

She smirks. "Your six-pack thanks you." Her eyes linger a little too long on my chest and abs, and she blushes.

"It's time for my cool-down," she says and begins to lie back in the water. "Do you want to float with me?"

I suddenly feel like I'm intruding. I know this is her private time, which she uses to decompress from her day. "I should go inside. Leave you to your... thing," I say.

"You should try it, Garrett. You might enjoy it." She's on her back now, arms straight out to her sides and legs outstretched. She closes her eyes, and she allows the water to cover the majority of her body. She looks so serene. Peaceful. *Beautiful.*

I attempt to assume the same position, but my legs keep dropping to the floor of the pool. I don't know what I'm doing wrong, but I can't get as relaxed as she is. She senses my discomfort, mostly because I'm flailing around, and pops her head out of the water.

She reaches for my hand and lightly holds it. "The key is to relax. Let the water take your body whole. Breathe deeply and exhale slowly. Like this." She doesn't let go of my hand as she once again gets into her floating stance.

This time, I do as she instructs and I'm able to float. The water drowns out any external sounds and all I hear are my deep breaths mixing with hers. She releases my hand so only our fingers are touching. We drift apart and I close my eyes. I can hear my heart beating rhythmically in my chest. I'm completely relaxed.

So this is what it's like.

I don't know how long we float like this. My eyes remain closed and I'm practically comatose. I have no urgency to get out of the pool. No urgency to be away from her. We're sharing something special. Almost secret. And I don't want it to end.

I feel movement next to me, and I'm jarred from my position. "Sorry." Her soft voice echoes throughout the room. "I didn't mean to disturb you. I was just about to head up to the house and I wanted to make sure you knew I was leaving."

"Do we have to go?" I ask and suddenly feel terrible for not wanting to go inside to be with my son. *I'm selfish.*

"No, you can stay. I have to relieve my aunt in a little while," she says and makes her way through the pool to the stairs.

"Wait up," I call after her. "I'll come too."

We dry off next to each other, and I do everything in my power not to stare at her incredible body. She's half naked next to me and I want to throw her over my shoulder and take her into the dressing room.

"Good job keeping up with me," she says. "I didn't think you had it in you." Her teeth shine through her wide smile, and I can't help but laugh.

"I don't think I've swam that many laps ever," I say. "As a matter of fact, it's probably only the third or fourth time I've actually been in my own pool. And I've had it for several years."

She looks at me incredulously. "Really?" she asks.

"Yeah," I say, ashamed. "I can't believe I don't take advantage of having an indoor pool more often."

"Well, you totally should," she says. She looks up at the house, and from here it looks tremendous. I feel embarrassed again for the luxury around me and wish it was less over the top.

She wraps the towel around her shoulders and slips her flip-flops on. "Coming?"

"Yeah," I say, and we step outside.

She immediately shivers and sprints to the back door. "It's cold out here!" she calls back.

Once we're inside, it takes her a few minutes before her shivers subside. I once again restrain myself from wrapping my body around hers to keep her warm.

"We should do that more often," I say without thinking.

She smirks. "So Pizza Thursday *and* Swim Thursday?" Her grin is huge.

"Well, you said it yourself, eating pizza like that, we're going to need to work it off somehow."

She blushes again and shivers at the same time.

She fixes Kai's bottles for the night and is ready to head upstairs. "I had a nice time tonight, Garrett. Thank you," she says and walks toward the stairs.

"There's nothing to thank me for," I say. "I'll be up to relieve you in a few hours. Sound good?"

She nods. "You don't have to, you know. But I'll never turn down a few hours of sleep in a real bed."

My bed would be perfect.

"See you later," I say as I watch her walk away.

A few minutes later, Peggy comes down and finds me in the kitchen. "It was nice of you to join Sam for a swim," she says. She has a look in her eye like she knows everything that I'm thinking. It makes me uncomfortable.

She packs up her bag and grabs her keys. "See you tomorrow," she says. "Make sure you leave me a list of things you need. I'll be going shopping."

Peggy is a gift. A Godsend. She takes care of everything I could possibly need and she brought Sam into my life. I don't know what I'd be doing if she weren't here. I realize I probably would have turned Kai away and made the situation disappear. I would have thrown as much money as possible at whoever could take Kai. I wouldn't have my son, and I have Peggy to thank for that.

"Goodnight, Peggy," I say.

I close up downstairs for the night and go up to my room. After a long, hot shower, I'm dressed in sweats and a tee-shirt.

Kai's door at the end of the hallway is slightly ajar, and I quietly walk down the hall to his room. He and Sam are sound asleep in the rocking chair. Her hair is still partially wet and pulled into a high bun on the top of her head. It's a mess and beautiful at the same time. Her head is tilted to the side, and

Kai's head is burrowed into her neck, just under her chin. He has a fist in his mouth that he's sucking on, and the other is tight on her chest. Their breathing is in sync and perfect.

She looks so peaceful with my son in her arms, I can't bring myself to wake her up. I pick up an extra blanket from the day-bed and gently drape it over the two of them, momentarily resting my hands on either side of her. I'm so close to her, I can smell the oil that she uses after she swims. Her skin smells like clean and fresh linens. She exhales deeply and her warm breath touches my face. I reluctantly pull away in fear of waking them up.

The day-bed is welcoming and familiar, and I lie down facing them both. I'll be ready when she needs a break and when my son needs strong, protective hands to soothe him. But can I be strong for him? Can I be the father that he needs me to be?

Sam's words from a few weeks ago ring in my head as I close my eyes.

"You have to believe, Garrett. Otherwise you have nothing."

CHAPTER 24

Sam
Present
Villanova, Pennsylvania
Age 24

"WOULD YOU LIKE AN APPETIZER" the waiter asks as he refills my wine glass.

I'm about to shake my head when Richard interjects. "We'll have the crab dip."

The waiter nods his head and quickly walks away. *I hate crab dip.*

"I haven't eaten here in so long. It's great we've finally been able to go out. I'm so happy that Marcie insisted we get together. Too bad we couldn't get together a few months ago, but I'm glad we're out now." He's been talking incessantly since he picked me up thirty minutes ago. He must be nervous or can't handle a little silence here and there. I make a mental note to punch Marcie in the face for giving Richard my number.

"Wait until you try the crab dip," he says and reaches across the table for my hand.

I snatch it away and grab my purse. "I have to use the restroom. Excuse me."

I pull out my phone on the way and text Cassie our emergency code.

ME: GET ME OUT OF HERE CALL MY CELL IN TEN MINUTES

She doesn't respond right away, but she knows I'm out with him, and I'm sure she's on high alert. It's been months since I've been anywhere. "You can do this," I say to my reflection in the mirror. "Ten more minutes and you're done."

What was I thinking? I should be home with Kai.

I walk back to the table and sit in my seat. The crab dip is already in between us and I want to gag.

"Here, you'll love it." Richard begins to scoop some dip onto my appetizer plate.

I toss my hand over it and say, "No thanks. I'm allergic." His expression changes from joy to fear in a split second as he believes my lie.

"Oh no, I'm so sorry. Why didn't you say something before when I ordered it?"

"It's okay, the salad that's coming will be just fine as an appetizer for me. Now all of the crab dip can be for you." I feign a smile and wish I were back at Garrett's house, floating in his pool.

Peggy is at the house tonight with Kai and Garrett wasn't home when I left. I'm glad he wasn't there because I didn't want him to see me leave on this 'date.' I promised Marcie I would go, and I just want it to be over. I also don't want Garrett to think anything serious is going on with Richard. In fact, there's *nothing* going on with me and Richard. This isn't even a date, really. More like a favor for a friend.

I just want to get home and pretend I never agreed to this outing tonight. Things have been really good lately, and Garrett has been doing great with Kai. Sure, there's been a few ups and downs, but he's been so attentive and not as nervous around him as he had been.

I look up and see that Richard is shoveling the dip into his mouth and making horrid noises while he does it. I take a sip of cold water to keep my gag reflex at bay. *C'mon Cassie. Call, Goddammit.*

"Marcie never mentioned you have a brother," Richard says, catching me off guard. *Did Marcie set him up with the wrong person?*

"I don't," I state, and his expression changes again. This time he looks utterly confused.

"No? He answered your phone the very first time I tried calling you a while back."

"You must not have called the right number, because I assure you, I don't have a brother." I glance down at my phone, willing it to ring.

"Well, then some other guy answered it. He may not be your brother, but he confirmed it was your phone."

What the hell?

My cell phone vibrates loudly on the table, and I see Cassie's name pop up. "It's my aunt. She wouldn't call me if it wasn't important. She's knows I'm on a date. I'm sorry, but I have to take this."

"Hello?" I say, feigning worry.

"You're a terrible mean person. Do you know that?" Cassie scolds me.

"Hey, *Aunt Peggy*. Is everything okay?" My voice becomes uncharacteristically high, and the lie begins to flow too easily.

"I can't believe you're ditching another date. Can't you at least make it to the main course? You know, I almost didn't call you back. I almost ignored your text. But I love you too much to do that to you." I want to smile, but I bite my lip to stop myself.

"Really? He usually doesn't have a problem with that kind of formula." I continue the ruse, and I hear Cassie sigh loudly through the phone.

"Seriously, Sam. This is the last time I'm doing this. Marcie thought you'd really like this guy. He's her cousin and she swears he's the perfect catch."

That explains a lot. Marcie isn't exactly a social butterfly. She's nice and all but is very socially awkward. I look up at Richard and see a vague resemblance. *I should have known.*

"Okay, I'll leave right away. I'm sorry I left before you could run out to get his food."

"You need to get laid, Sam. If Richard isn't the one to do it, you'd better find someone soon. You're cooped up in that house with the baby all day long, and you don't have time for anything. I'm taking you out on Saturday night. We're going to find someone for you. Stat." She hangs up and I finish the fake conversation.

"I'll see you in twenty minutes. I'm so sorry. He'll be okay until I get there. I promise."

I look over to Richard, who is licking the crab dip from his fingers. He raises his eyebrows and asks, "Is everything okay? It sounded serious."

"No, it's not. The baby I'm caring for is out of formula. I thought I picked up a case from the pharmacy the other day, but that was two weeks ago. My aunt came to help out so I could go out with you tonight, and I'm afraid I left her in a bad spot. I have to leave. I'm so sorry." I gather my phone and my clutch and shift in my seat.

He puts his hand up, signaling the waiter. "No problem. Marcie says you're one of the best baby nurses around. We'll get you home right away."

We stop at the pharmacy so I can pick up the formula that I knew was waiting for me since yesterday and pull up to Garrett's house a few minutes later. I get out of the car and open the back door and take out the formula. I don't see Peggy's car, and I wonder if she pulled it into the garage.

"Thanks for everything, Richard." I smile and turn toward the door. He chases after me and follows me up the stairs. My stomach sinks. I hope he isn't expecting any physical contact. The thought of being near his crab-dip infested mouth makes my stomach churn again.

"Wait," he says and turns me around to face him. He's staring at my lips, and my body stiffens. *Shit. Shit. Shit.* He starts to lean in to kiss me, and I block him with the case of formula.

"I'm sorry, I need to get inside right away." I turn and open the door. "Bye," I say as I close it while he stands on the stoop staring.

I hear his car pull away a few minutes later, and I breathe a sigh of relief. I walk through the dark foyer into the kitchen.

"Who was that?" Garrett's voice startles me, and I drop the case onto my foot.

"Ouch! God! Owww!" I hop around and fall into his chest. His strong hands grab my arms, and he steadies me. He's warm. *So warm.*

"Are you okay?" he asks, concerned.

"Yes, I am now," I lie, and I'm flustered when he lets go of me. The faint smell of alcohol wafts in the air between us.

"Who was that?" he asks again.

"Richard," I say and wince as I try to put weight on my toe. *Shit, I hope it's not broken.*

"Are you seeing him?"

I limp past him so I can sit on the stool by the counter.

"Have you been drinking?" I ask, attempting to change the subject. I see an empty tumbler on the kitchen island.

"Kai had a rough night," he says and swipes the glass from the countertop. He puts it on the top rack of the dishwasher and turns to face me. Kai has been doing so well; it upsets me to think he's taken a step back.

"Oh?" Concern bubbles up and anger shortly follows. "So you decided to get drunk while you're home alone with him? What the hell is wrong with you?" I attempt to stand up, but pain shoots across the top of my foot where the heavy box landed a few minutes ago. "Dammit!"

"I wouldn't be alone if you were here helping me," he fires back, and my anger continues to escalate. *Where is this attitude coming from?*

"Where's my aunt?" I ask, knowing she isn't here.

"I sent her home a few hours ago. Kai drank a bottle around six and fell asleep soundly. He was content for a while, and I told Peggy I could handle things on my own. So she left." He shakes his head and leans forward, placing his elbows on the counter. "Then everything fell apart."

"Where is he now?" I ask, concerned that Garrett isn't even holding him.

"Upstairs in his crib."

Alone?

I hop off of the stool, ignoring the shooting pain in my foot, and go upstairs as quickly as I can. "I can't believe he left him alone," I mutter to myself as I reach the door to his room. I hear faint Rock-A-Bye Baby lullaby music through the closed door. I open it, and the soft glow of the universe nightlights fills my eyes. I walk over to the crib and see Kai swaddled tightly and sound asleep. There's a stuffed dog that looks like a Dalmatian perched near his head, just out of reach. *I've never seen that before.*

I'm shocked to see Kai sleeping, *in his crib.* He's never slept anywhere unsupervised. And it's extremely rare that he's sound asleep and not on top of one of us. This is a tremendous accomplishment, and I'm not sure Garrett realizes how huge it is.

I hear his soft footsteps behind me.

"I did everything wrong, didn't I?" he asks, concerned.

"No…" I can't take my eyes off of the perfectly swaddled and comfortable little boy in front of me.

I feel his warm hand graze mine causing tingles to travel up my arm.

"How did this happen?" I ask, backing up toward the hallway. My heart wants me to stand here and take this all in, but my brain tells me to leave him be so he can sleep as peacefully as possible.

Garrett follows me out and closes the door softly.

He looks at me and shrugs his shoulders. "I don't know. After Peggy left, he was sound asleep, so I brought him up here and rocked with him in the chair. After a while, we were both sleeping, until I sneezed myself awake. He woke up and started screaming like I've never heard him scream before. I think I scared him." He runs his hand through his thick black hair, and the pain on his face intensifies.

"I didn't know what to do. I tried to remember everything you've taught me over the past few weeks and I drew a complete blank. I started walking around the room with him and patting his back. I even tried singing to him. His little body was arching so much that I thought he was going to fall out of my arms."

"Oh no. I'm sorry," I say and lean against the wall.

"Then I remembered the music Peggy always plays for him and I turned it on." He shakes his head and smirks. "I still can't get used to hearing our songs playing as a lullaby."

I have to admit that I love listening to Rock-A-Bye Baby. My favorite is the Nirvana and U2 albums. I've never listed to the Epic Fail one though.

"Anyway, after I put the music on, he started to calm down a little. But he was so squirmy and kept throwing his head back. I remember you telling me that sometimes that means he has gas, so I laid him down on the changing table and did that thing with his legs that you showed me—you know when you bend his knees slowly toward his chest?" He makes a motion with his hands in the air in front of him, mimicking the movement.

I nod and he continues. "That's when I realized his diaper was full." His expression changes to disgust, and he looks like he's about to throw up. "It was really full." I can't help but laugh, and I quickly cover my mouth.

"It's not funny," he says and pulls on the front of his tee-shirt. "I'm covered in piss."

My shoulders start shaking, and now I'm full-on laughing out loud. I cover my mouth, trying to stifle the giggles. I forgot to tell him about the Pee-pee-Teepee. I try to gain my composure.

"I'm impressed, Garrett. Very impressed." I nod, and he lets go of his urine-stained shirt and wipes his hands on his jeans.

He ignores my compliment and continues the recount of tonight's adventure in babysitting. "I'm not sure I put the diaper on right, but at least he's covered." He shakes his head and leans against the wall across from me. "He started screaming and crying again with his arms and legs flailing all over the place. I wrapped him really tight in one of his blankets and carried him around the room until he fell asleep. It took about thirty minutes for him to cry this out. But once he stopped, he was out cold."

"Why did you leave him alone?" I ask, worried that Garrett had a breakdown.

"I had to go to the bathroom," he replies, embarrassed.

"Oh."

"Why didn't you call me? I would have come home sooner to help you."

"Really?" he asks and looks confused. "I thought you were looking forward to your date with Dick."

"How did you know where I was? And why did you call him that?" Anger starts to build again when I see a different side of Garrett begin to surface.

"Your aunt told me where you went." He steps away from the wall and closes the distance between us so we're toe to toe. "Who is he?" he asks, and the smell of baby pee and whiskey mix in the air in front of me, making my anger grow.

"You shouldn't have been drinking," I say firmly and stare daggers into his eyes. I feel his warm breath on my face. "If something happened to Kai—"

"I handled everything, didn't I?" He raises his voice slightly. "It's not like I drank a bottle, Sam. It was one mouthful. I needed to calm down."

"So you medicate with booze?" I snap back. "Remember his mother was an addict. You need to curb what you're doing around here so you don't model that type of behavior." He's so close to me right now I can't move. My foot is killing me, and I want to push past him, but I'm boxed in.

"Don't tell me what I can and can't do in my own home. If I want to have a shot of whiskey to calm my nerves, I'll do it a hundred fucking times over."

"Garrett, you need to calm down," I say. *What has gotten into him?*

"Do you know what day it is?" he asks.

"What? It's Thursday," I say, wondering why he's even asking me this question.

"Exactly. It's Thursday," he says, and his face softens. "It's *Thursday*, Sam."

Pizza Thursday.

Shit.

He suddenly leans closer, closing the small distance between our mouths. His lips brush against mine and I freeze in place.

"What are you doing?" I breathe.

CHAPTER 25

Garrett
Present
Villanova, Pennsylvania
Age 27

"WHAT ARE YOU DOING?" she says, and I don't give her another second to say anything else. I grab the sides of her face, tangling my fingers in her hair, and pull her lips against mine. My kiss is harsh and fast, and I feel her pushing and pulling at me with all of her strength.

I hit the wall behind me, and she takes off, limping down the hall. *What the hell just came over me? Why did I do that?*

I unclench my fists and try to calm myself down. I couldn't get the image of her with another guy out of my head all night. When Peggy told me she was out on a date, I almost lost it. I realize I have no right to feel this way, but I feel betrayed. For the past few weeks, we've spent so much time together, and she's had such a positive influence over me. She's gotten me past my fear of being alone with Kai. She's guided me on what to do when holding him and caring for him. I've been a bumbling idiot and terrified every single time I touch him, but she's talked me off the ledge and constantly reassures me that I'm doing fine.

It's Pizza Thursday. Our day.

Jealousy coursed through my veins all night, picturing her with someone else. *What's wrong with me?*

Regret sweeps through me. *I need to make this right.* I hear her downstairs in the kitchen and look for her so I can apologize.

She's assembling clean bottles and pouring formula into them for the night. She lines them up and grabs the soft cooler from under the cabinet. She puts the filled bottles into the cooler along with two bottles of water for herself. This is her nightly routine, and I don't dare interrupt her. She's limping around the kitchen, obviously in pain and flustered by what just happened.

"I'm sorry," I say.

"You should be." She snaps back at me. "Why did you kiss me? You shouldn't have done that. We shouldn't—" Her eyes are filled with guilt. The pain on her face is evident.

"Why don't you sit down. Let me get you some ice." I walk past her to the freezer and grab an ice pack.

I'm surprised by how quickly she agrees and she hops into the den, throwing herself on the couch. She's breathing heavily and squirming in pain. "I really think I broke something." She seems to forget why she was yelling at me a few seconds ago, and I sit on the couch and pull her feet onto my lap.

"Ouch. My God, it hurts bad."

I look down and see that bruising has already started on the top of her foot, spreading toward her big toe. There's some swelling, but not a lot. I place the ice gingerly on the spot that looks the worst, and she stiffens. "Cold, cold, cold," she repeats, and eventually her foot relaxes under the ice pack.

She leans back and props a pillow underneath her head. She's staring at the ceiling, I'm sure contemplating what insults to hurl my way.

"I don't know what came over me. I shouldn't have kissed you," I apologize again as I carefully hold the ice in place. I look down at her feet and admire how cute they are.

"Don't look at my feet. They're gross. I haven't had a pedicure in months, and I can't imagine what they look like right now."

"They're not bad, considering you just dropped a ten-pound box of formula on one of them."

She takes a deep breath and tries to stretch out her injured foot. "I should probably go to urgent care or something."

"Let's see if the swelling goes down with the ice on it," I suggest. I don't want her to leave. "Besides, it's your driving foot, and I'm sure you won't be able to get anywhere on your own."

She looks over at the clock on the wall, and we both notice it's after ten. "It's too late to call Peggy," she says and shifts a little on the couch.

We sit in silence for a while, and I say, "I'm an asshole."

"Yes, you are," she replies through a smirk.

"Tonight was really weird for me. After I calmed down Kai, I felt invincible. I almost convinced myself that if I had to, I could do this on my own. I stared at him in his crib, looking peaceful and calm, and it felt good. I was proud of what I could accomplish. *You* gave me that strength." Her eyes soften and she smiles.

I realize I'm rubbing her foot softly, and since she's not complaining, I keep doing it.

"Then I started to panic, thinking about everything and anything that could possibly go wrong. I pictured him screaming and crying in pain again and I felt helpless. I'm not a father. I can't be a good father. I freaked out and came downstairs to calm down. That's just before you came in. My emotions were high, and I'm sorry I grilled you about D—I mean Richard."

She tilts her head so she can look at me. There's pity on her face, and I don't like that look. "You did great tonight, Garrett. Seriously. And you did this on your own. I didn't give you anything you didn't already have inside yourself." I want to tell her how wrong she is.

She tries to shift and move her foot.

"Stay still before you hurt yourself more," I scold her and hold her foot firmly in place on my lap. "For a nurse, you sure are a difficult patient."

She nods her head. "Yes, I always have been."

We sit quietly for a few more minutes, and she speaks again.

"Richard means nothing to me, just so you know. I went out with him as a favor to Marcie. He's her cousin. She's been bugging me for months. Now who's the asshole?" She takes a deep breath and her eyes soften. "I'm sorry I missed Pizza Thursday, Garrett. I would have rather been here." She nestles into the couch further, and I continue to rub her foot.

"I'm sorry," I say again.

"Things are a bit strange here, huh?" she says, and I shrug my shoulders.

"We're thrown together like this, and it's unnatural. We've been playing house for months and spending a lot of time together. Is that why you kissed me?" she asks quietly. *There's nothing unnatural about the way I feel about her.*

"I don't know, Sam. It just felt… right. In the moment." I've wanted to claim her lips for so long.

She raises her fingers and slowly brushes her bottom lip. I

kissed her so hard they look swollen, puffy. "I'm really sorry," I say. "It won't happen again, I promise."

The look on her face confuses me. Is it regret? Disappointment? Curiosity?

"A little advice: you should warn a girl if you're going to dive in like that. I think you broke my tooth." A smile spreads across her face, and I feel the tension leave her body.

"*Next time* I promise I'll warn you." I throw my head back on the leather cushion and sigh. "I'm such an asshole."

"I'm glad you're finally admitting it," she jokes, and I pinch her good foot.

"Owww!" she screeches, and I bring my finger to my lips.

"Please don't wake him up. Let's hope he sleeps at least another hour," I say.

She smiles again and I'm captivated by her. Even in pain, she's flawless. Her curls cascade around her face, and I have a sudden urge to wrap them around my fingers. She's cast a spell on me, and I feel weak.

"I'm sorry I got mad at you," she says. "It's just, we didn't get off on the right foot when I first came here. I was so angry with you and your lack of empathy for your own child. I didn't understand why you couldn't bring yourself to love him and care for him. I've worked with critically ill babies for so long, and I don't remember ever having to convince a parent to be there for them. You confused me. And worried me."

Her instincts were right on so many levels. Kai scared me. He still scares me. "If I avoided everything, I thought it would go away."

"That's cowardice," she says.

"I know."

"When you told me about your parents' reaction to Kai, it made me happy. Your mom gave you good advice." She smiles warmly, "She seems like a great lady."

My parents were supposed to come visit Kai several weeks ago, but they changed their plans when Bill got sick. He was in bed with the flu for almost ten days, and they decided to wait a little while longer before coming up. They're worried about bringing germs with them. I FaceTimed with them last week, and they were so happy to lay eyes on a sleeping Kai. My mother had tears in her eyes when she saw him in my arms.

"She is. She's been through a lot in her life, and she got through it all with shining colors. Bill has been a great husband and father to me, and I'm grateful for that. Even though I don't show it as much as I should—or ever."

"You're lucky, Garrett. You have two parents here to love you and Kai." Her face is solemn, and I feel compelled to ask about her parents again. The last time I did, she shut it down. She's reluctant to reminisce, and I feel intrusive when I ask.

"Yeah. My gene pool isn't perfect, but I shouldn't complain about where I've come from." Now I want to change the subject because the thought of my birth father makes my skin crawl.

Her eyes are heavy, and she looks like she's about to fall asleep.

"I'll make you a deal," I say, surprising myself.

"What?" she says groggily.

"Take the rest of the night off. Completely. I'll stay with Kai in his room, and you can sleep in the guest room." For once, she'll get a good night sleep without any interruptions. *I want to do this for her.*

She raises her eyebrows and shakes her head. "I don't think that's a good idea. You haven't done a complete overnight with him ever. I'm usually an arms-length away. I don't think you know what you're agreeing to."

Neither do I, but I continue, "If I can make it through, we can talk about a schedule so I can give you back some time to yourself. You've been caring tirelessly for Kai for months, and most of the time you've done it on your own."

She nods in agreement, but she still looks worried.

"Do we have a deal?" I press, and she slowly nods again as she yawns.

"I'll sleep right here," she says. "No need for me to mess up one of the other guest rooms. Besides, I don't think I can walk upstairs again." She tenses her leg, and the ice pack slides from her foot. The swelling hasn't gone down yet, and the bruising is darker, more pronounced.

I carefully slide her foot from my lap and stand up. She looks alarmed as I stand over her and scoop her into my arms. "What are you doing?" she asks.

"Put your arms around my neck and hold on tight." I take a step forward, and she does as I say. Her arms slip around my neck and she settles into my chest.

"You don't have to carry me," she says sleepily.

"You're right, I don't." I pretend I'm going to drop her, and she squeals and tightens her grip around my neck, burrowing her head into my chest.

"Hey!" she says playfully. "Not funny."

I take my time walking up the vast staircase. I want to savor our connection as long as I can. We reach the first guest room on the left, and I open the door. A large king-sized bed is across the room in the center of the wall. Pillows are piled high, and the oversized down comforter looks so inviting.

"I don't think I've ever been in this room," she says as I carry her toward the bed.

"I'm not sure I have either." I chuckle. The house is huge, and this is one of nine bedrooms on this floor. "I'm not sure anyone has."

I know Peggy keeps all of the rooms in pristine shape, so the sheets and bedding are clean and fresh, regardless if the door has ever been opened to anyone else.

I pull back the covers with a free hand and slowly lower her onto the bed. She stares into my eyes as I reluctantly place her down. She is casting a spell on me, and I don't want to leave her. Her eyes are heavy and I know she's tired, but I don't want to let her go. I release her and lean over her to grab one of the spare pillows. I brush against her breasts and she shudders.

"You cold?" I ask, knowing she's reacting to me.

"A little," she whispers.

I gently raise her foot and place the oversized pillow under it. "Try to keep it elevated, okay?" I say and reluctantly remove my hand from her leg.

"Okay," she says and closes her eyes. I pull the covers over her, but not before I take in the beauty of her entire body. Long, lean legs. Perfectly toned. Narrow hips and soft, toned stomach. Her breasts are small but full, leading to an elegantly long neck. I lick my lips, trying not to act on my urges.

"Goodnight," I say, forcing myself to leave the room.

"Good luck," she says and turns onto her side.

I rush downstairs to grab the cooler from the counter and return to the second floor. I change my shirt before I head back into Kai's room. He's fussing in his crib but not crying.

"Hey, little dude," I say as I approach the crib. He's staring at the stuffed Dalmatian intently. He's still swaddled so tight. I'm amazed. He grunts when I pick him up and continues to squirm in my arms. After I struggle through another diaper change, we settle into his chair so I can feed him. I've only done this a few times completely on my own, and I'm suddenly terrified.

What if he cries again? Or chokes?

What if I can't handle this?

I loosen his blankets and adjust him in my arms. He takes the bottle immediately and begins sucking it down like I've never seen him do before. Before I know it, the bottle is gone and he's been burped successfully several times. He's passed out on my shoulder, and I begin rocking the chair slowly back and forth.

As I close my eyes, I relive the mistakes I made today. I vow to keep Sam at a comfortable distance so I don't scare her off. I also vow to keep the booze locked up, at least for a while. I inhale deeply and for once, I don't smell spit-up or sour milk.

Today was a good day.

SOFT SNORING WAKES ME UP and Kai is still out cold. He's warm and nestled tightly into my chest. But the snoring isn't coming from him. *Did I imagine it?*

I open my eyes further and see Sam asleep on the bed across from me. I also notice that an extra blanket is draped over me and Kai. She's curled up on her side, and her foot is resting high up on a pillow. Her mouth is open slightly and soft noises escape her perfect lips.

I could stare at her like this forever. I'm holding my son and Sam is here with us. I take a mental picture of our unconventional 'family,' and I don't want this ever to end. I don't know how we wound up here, together, but it feels right, and I will do what I can to protect this moment. Bottle it up so I can remember the peace that I feel right now. With Kai. *With Sam.*

Kirsten's words from not too long ago ring in my ears.

Love will find you at a time and place when you least expect it.

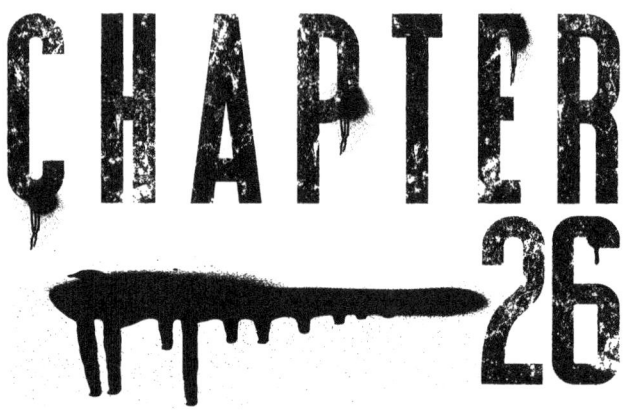

CHAPTER 26

Sam
Present
Six Weeks Later
Villanova, Pennsylvania
Age 24

"HEY, YOU HAVE YOUR FOOT BACK!" Cassie says as we walk toward the car. She drove me to the orthopedic doctor to get my final x-ray to confirm the bones in the top of my foot have healed. I had fractures in the first and second metatarsal bones, and I had to wear a large boot on my foot for six weeks. It feels great to walk without that stiff contraption on my foot. "I want to drive," I state. It's been a while since I've driven.

"Sure," she says and tosses me the keys to Garrett's SUV. My car has been at the house that I share with Aunt Peggy since I haven't been able to drive for the past six weeks. She, Garrett and Cassie have all split duties in helping chauffeur me around.

Garrett has been incredible. Since my injury, he's really taking a lead in Kai's care. In fact, he's home with Kai and the occupational therapist right now.

"Jim wants to know when you're coming back to work," Cassie says nonchalantly.

I want to go back. I really do. But I can't imagine not being here with Kai. *And Garrett.*

"I don't know, Cass."

"You've been gone for almost six months. They reversed your suspension almost three months ago. It's time, don't you think?"

"I'll think about it," I say, trying to dismiss her question.

"Sam, you know I love you, and I'm so proud of everything you're doing for Kai, but you're a *nurse,* not a nanny." She pauses and pulls something from her purse. "Maybe this will help change your mind," she says, slipping an envelope into my bag.

"What's that?" I ask, curiously.

"It's a letter… from Olivia."

My heart starts to race and I grip the steering wheel. *Ben's mother.*

"What?" I ask and start to feel faint. Thankfully, Garrett's driveway is just ahead, and I press the button to open the security gate. I slam on the brakes when we reach the top of the driveway and throw the SUV into park.

"Hey, don't stress out about it. Jim actually read it before he gave it to me. He *wants* you to read it."

I open the door and swipe my bag from the center console. "I'm going inside. Are you coming?" I ask and don't wait for her to respond before I head toward the front door.

"I can't," she calls after me. "My shift starts in an hour, and I have to go home to get my scrubs. Pink monkeys today. Jealous?" She smiles warmly, trying to make me feel better.

She walks to her own car and blows me a kiss. "Call me later?" I wave goodbye without confirming.

I enter the house, and I immediately hear giggling coming from upstairs. "Aunt Peggy?" I call out but no answer. I walk up the stairs and follow the giggles obviously coming from Kai's room.

When I open the door, I see Garrett's face close to Kai's bare belly, and he moves closer, blowing raspberries on him. Kai laughs, screeching and kicking his legs. His arms are flailing around, and he's the happiest I've ever seen him. Garrett does it again, and Kai's giggles get louder. He's barely able to catch his breath when Garrett tickles him again. "Do you like that?" Garrett asks his son, unaware of my presence.

"It sure looks like it!" I respond, and Garrett turns his head, startled.

Kai claps his hands in front of him and kicks his legs, laughing hysterically. The sight in front of me warms my heart. "Look who it is, buddy," Garrett says, picking up Kai from the table. Kai continues to giggle and clap his hands. Then he sticks his tongue out and blows raspberries into the air, causing drool to drip from his mouth.

I rush over and grab a baby wipe from the table and dab Kai's mouth and chin. He giggles and blows raspberries again, causing more drool to fall.

"I think it's a lost cause," Garrett says and places his hand over mine, taking the wipe away. Kai continues to giggle and drool, and it's beautiful. He reaches his arms out in front of him and leans toward me. "Oh, Sam's back and suddenly you want her, not me?" he teases Kai and passes him into my arms. Kai opens his mouth and places it on my cheek. It's his idea of a sloppy kiss. And I love it.

Garrett reaches out with the baby wipe and dabs it on the wet spot on my cheek.

"Has he had a nap yet?" I ask.

Our rhythm feels so much like a family right now. It's wonderful, but I know it isn't real or permanent.

"No, I was just getting ready to put him down." Garrett turns on the lullaby music and walks through the room, closing the blinds. Last week, we started putting him down in the crib awake so he can put himself to sleep. We're slowly weaning him off of his dependence on us being physically present in order to sleep. He's doing great, and it's a strong sign that his recovery is progressing positively. His fits of screaming have almost all but stopped, as his body and mind heals.

I walk over to the crib and place Kai down. He grabs his stuffed Dalmatian and puts it in his mouth immediately. I turn on the mobile above him so he can watch the instruments spin. I bend down and kiss him on his forehead. "Sweet dreams, little dude." He coos and laughs, kicking his legs in the air. He starts conversing with his stuffed animal, and Garrett and I quietly leave the room.

"You lost your boot," he observes, turning on the baby monitor and sliding it into his back pocket. We can hear Kai's baby sounds as we walk down the stairs.

"Yes, finally," I say and hop off the bottom step. Garrett winces, and I trot into the kitchen.

"Don't you think you should take it easy?" he says, following me.

"It feels great!" I look out to the backyard to the pool house. I can't wait to finally swim again.

I look over at my bag on the counter. Knowing there's a note in there from Olivia is rattling me to the core. *What could she possibly have to say to me?*

"What's wrong?" Garrett asks.

I sigh. "I have a decision to make, and I need you to help me make it."

"Oh?" He walks toward me and places his hands on my shoulders. "The answer is yes. Always yes," he says and softly squeezes.

"Jim is calling in the big guns. He sent Cassie to convince me to come back to work. Now that my foot is healed and Kai is perfect, I don't think I have any excuses not to return."

His hands fall from my shoulders. "I guess not," he says reluctantly.

"It's time, right?" I say and sit down at the counter. I rifle through my bag and find Olivia's letter. I grab it and stand up. "I'm going for a swim."

Garrett nods and walks toward the basement. "We have a recording session tonight. I'll be downstairs if you need me." He places his hand over his back pocket, confirming the baby monitor is there. "I'll get Kai if he wakes up. Enjoy your swim." He lowers his head and descends into the basement.

I know it's going to be hard on all of us when I leave, but it's really time. Kai is healthy. Garrett is able to care for him and Peggy is here if needed. I also have a list of nannies that I've been interviewing 'just in case.'

Everything's going to be just fine.

I enter the enclosed pool house and go right to the dressing room. I always keep at least one or two bathing suits and a change of clothes down here. I'm the only one who uses the pool anyway, so it's like I have my own closet here.

I slip into my suit and dive into the pool. It feels great to move freely in the water, and my foot feels incredible. *I've missed this so much.*

My muscles are tired after twenty laps, and I begin to relax in the water. I flip over and float, staring through the skylights above me. The blue sky is deep and clear. I'm still panting from the swim, and I try to slow and regulate my breathing. And then I drift.

Am I ready to go back to work?

Can I pick up where I left off?

Will parents trust me with their sick babies?

Can I leave Kai?

Can I leave Garrett?

Questions without answers swirl in my head, and I need to decide what my future holds for me. I need to get back to doing what I was born to do. I have nothing left here to fix. Kai is perfect and happy. He's on track to a healthy and normal life.

I turn in the water and swim to the edge. I see Olivia's letter on the table and pull myself out of the pool. I wrap a towel around me, paying particular attention to dry my hands and fingers. When they're dry, I open the envelope.

I tense as I unfold it, unsure of what I'm about to read.

Dear Samantha,

For months I've been at a loss for words, and now that they have finally come, I needed to contact you.

Thank you.

It must seem strange that I'm saying these words to you, but I mean them from the bottom of my heart.

Thank you.

When Benjamin was born so early, I had no hope that he would survive. He faced so many problems, and being premature was just the tip of the iceberg. His lungs were underdeveloped, his heartbeat was erratic and his brain was bleeding in more than one place. His chances were slim. Dr. Hagan was always honest with me about this. We never talked percentages, but she prepared me for the worst.

And then you arrived. You ignored the numbers. Ignored the monitors. Your care for Ben was unwavering and you did everything in your control to make sure he kept breathing for just one more day.

One more precious day.

You gave me something that I was lacking, and that was time. Every day that you cared for him, was another day that I had to see him breathe and live.

So thank you, thank you, thank you.

You allowed me to spend time with my son when he had so little of it left on this earth. It was my time with him, and you gave that gift to me.

And then it was my husband's time.

Ben wasn't meant to spend his days with me here. He was meant to be with his father, in Heaven.

I'm forever grateful to you, Samantha, and for the memories that you helped me create with my son.

Yours,

Olivia

I'm sobbing as I finish the letter. *She's thanking me? Forgiving me?*

I drop the letter onto the pavement and slide into the water, allowing it to swallow me whole. I open my eyes underwater and see clearly to the other end of the pool. I let the air out of my lungs and I scream. The water absorbs my voice and distorts it into a garbled blur of sound. I don't know how long I remain submerged, but when my lungs burn for air, I push myself up, gasping and breathing. The pool house is silent except for the sounds of the softly splashing waves made from my movement.

I don't deserve her forgiveness.

Tears mix with the chlorinated water on my face, and I swim again. My arms cut through the water like sharp knives, and the muscles in my legs burn. I don't know how many laps I do, but when I'm finished, the sun is setting. My fingertips are pruned and I'm exhausted.

I try to relax and roll onto my back, letting the water carry me through the pool.

Olivia's letter shocked me, but it also opened my eyes. I *did* give her time. I did everything in my power to keep him alive for as long as possible. When Jim initially contacted me to tell me that I was no longer suspended, he told me that a new vein in Ben's brain had started bleeding and ruptured. He was dying and we didn't even know it. He went into heart failure and cardiac arrest. The fluid in his lungs was not from the feeding tube, but from the heart failure. I felt relief and despair at the same time. Of course, I know now that I didn't actually kill him, but I hadn't recognized the fact that he was already dying.

Her words ignite my desire to get back to work. It's what I should be doing, and now I know it's something that I *have* to do. Kai no longer needs me, but many other babies do.

I continue to float. I know my parents won't answer me, but I need to ask them anyway. "Am I making the right decision?" My voice echoes in the pool house.

My heart tells me that I am.

CHAPTER 27

Garrett
Present
Villanova, Pennsylvania
Age 27

I WALK UPSTAIRS AFTER I MAKE SURE everything is ready for tonight. We have eight more songs to record for our album, and we're hoping to finish at least two or three more. Our goal may be a little out of reach, especially if Tristan can't stay focused. His ADD always brings the rest of us off the rails.

Kai's monitor stays silent, and I'm thankful that he's been sleeping better lately. Over the past two weeks, it's a rare occasion when Sam or I have to go in during the night. Although she would prefer to sleep in his room, I've convinced her to sleep in the guest room across the hall.

I look out at the pool and see Sam slumped over on the pavement. She's sobbing and holding a piece of paper in her hands. She drops the paper and slides into the pool, disappearing beneath the water. My gut tightens, and I rush toward the door, trying to get a better look at her. *Why is she crying?*

I see her emerge, and she starts furiously swimming laps. Her legs and arms are tight, and she's flying through the water like an Olympic swimmer. She looks majestic and scary at the same time. I can feel her intensity from here. I continue to watch her until she exhausts herself. She rolls onto her back and closes her eyes and floats.

I know better than to bother her during her swimming sessions. It's her private time. Her temporary escape from life. I watch her float to the stairs, and she rights herself. As she exits the pool, she looks calm. I turn away so she doesn't catch me spying on her private time.

My mind races with our discussion earlier. She decided it's time to go back to work, and I'm not ready for her to go. *We need her.*

I need her.

The back door opens and she walks in, her smile back.

"How was your swim?" I ask.

"Enlightening," she says and slides an envelope into her bag.

"What's that?" I ask, knowing I'm invading her privacy.

"A letter from Ben's mom."

She told me about the mishap with the baby she was caring for in the NICU who eventually died. His death was the reason she was suspended from work. They realized that she didn't make a mistake and asked her to come back right away. She declined because Kai was so sick then. She's ignored their requests to come back since, and officially took a leave of absence from work. I'm so thankful she did because she helped Kai and me immensely. I don't believe he'd be where he is today without her. But I feel so guilty. Sick babies need her, and she hasn't made a move to leave.

"Wow. That's unexpected, huh?" I respond, and she nods.

"She thanked me." Sam's eyes fill with tears, and now I understand why she was sobbing before.

I pull her into my chest. She wraps her arms tightly around my waist and buries her face in my neck. Tears flow onto my skin and I hug her tighter.

"Why are you crying?" I ask, my lips grazing her ear.

"I don't know," she says and sniffles. She begins to calm down, but I can't let go.

We stand toe-to-toe wrapped in each other's arms, neither of us making an attempt to move. My breathing is in tune with hers, and I don't want to let her go. "It's my turn," I whisper in her ear, letting my lips linger.

She shivers in my arms and says, "Your turn for what?"

"To thank you."

She pushes herself away a little and looks into my eyes. "You don't need to thank me."

I drop my hands so they're resting on her hips. She doesn't move. "You saved my son. You gave him a chance at life. And you saved me." I bring her close so our noses are touching. "Thank you," I say against her lips. She inhales deeply and stiffens in my arms. "I'm going to kiss you now." I promised her I'd warn her the next time I kissed her, but I still don't give her the option to back away.

I softly place my lips on hers, pulling her tighter against my body. This time, she doesn't push me away. She relaxes into me, leaning into my hips. She parts her lips and allows my tongue to intertwine with hers. Her fingers are linked behind my neck, and she moans quietly into my mouth. I lift her onto the bar stool and part her legs. I press myself against her and she moans again.

"Wait," she pants against my lips. "What are we doing?"

I ignore her words and claim her mouth once again. I want her. I need her. I want to bury myself deep inside her and make her mine.

Her hands leave my neck and lightly push on my chest. She pulls away and sighs. "Wow," she says and covers her lips with her fingers.

Her face and chest are flushed, and she looks at me with heavy eyes.

"I'm not apologizing this time. You wanted that as much as I did," I say through a huge grin. She can't help but blush, and her smile makes me rigid in my pants.

She nods and turns her head away, embarrassed. I place my hands on her thighs and swirl my thumbs on the insides of her legs. Her breath hitches and she squirms a little on the stool.

She throws her arms back around my neck, grabbing the back of my head. She pulls me toward her lips and this time she kisses me. Hard. Her breasts are pressed against me and her kiss is urgent. Needy.

Kai's monitor rumbles in my back pocket with his cries.

"Shit," she says against my lips with a smile.

"Yeah," I say, and Kai's crying continues. "He's hungry. It's time for dinner." I'm reluctant to pull away from her. I'm rock hard and ready to explode against her. "Can you get him?" I ask. I look down between us and say, "I'm not exactly decent."

She blushes again and kisses me lightly before she gets up. "Of course." She slides off the stool, and I watch her walk toward the stairs. She looks over her shoulder and smiles as she sensually saunters away. I take a deep breath and try to think of anything besides being buried deep inside her.

I open the refrigerator and take out Kai's baby food jars. I open the jar of pureed peas and inhale deeply. I gag from the smell and my hard-on deflates. *Crisis averted.*

I prepare his food and line it up on the counter near his high chair. Peas, rice cereal and formula. I make sure to grab a roll of paper towels because he's a complete slob when he eats. I should never have taught him how to blow raspberries because it's all he does with his food.

After several minutes, Sam appears with Kai, and he's giggling and talking baby nonsense. He points to me and drools. Seeing him in her arms brings me a harsh dose of reality. Soon she'll be gone, and the unconventional family that we've formed over the past six months will be no longer.

I have one goal tonight after the band leaves, and I intend to make it happen. When she moves out and goes back to work, she's going to need a reason to come back to see us.

Tonight, I plan on giving her multiple reasons.

OUR RECORDING SESSION WAS SEMI-SUCCESSFUL. We didn't get three tracks done, but we got two, so that's progress. Dax and Tristan left ten minutes ago, and Heath and I are reclined on the theater chairs in the media room.

"Your songs are awesome," I say to Heath.

"Thanks. I wasn't sure if you guys were going to like them. The lyrics are a little more subdued than what you're used to, but I think the bass and lead guitar bring them to the level our fans are used to."

"I think 'Blind Fury' is going to be a chart-topper," I say.

"You think?"

"Yeah, it has a chorus that just builds so powerfully. I think it may be one of our best songs yet. Just don't tell Alex." I smile, and he raises his beer to his lips.

"How're things?" he asks.

It's odd talking to Heath like this. Ever since everything went down with Sadie, he and I have this unusual bond. I've never really opened up to any of the guys like I have with Heath. He knows so much about my family and even my birth father. He knows more than anyone, including Sam.

"Sam's going back to work," I say and hang my head. "I'm not ready for her to leave."

"You knew this day was coming, right? She couldn't stay here forever. In fact, she should have left a month ago when Kai had his last check-up at the doctor. Remember the doctor said that all of the effects of his drug exposure have pretty much disappeared?"

He's right. Sam and I both knew then it was only a matter of time. She said she was going to find me a nanny, and even she's been dragging her feet. Kai no longer needs a live-in nurse. He just needs a father.

And a mother.

"I wonder how Kai is going to do without her here," I say, and my heart pulls.

"Dude, what are *you* going to do without her?"

"I don't know." I want to have all of the answers, but I don't. I can't picture this house without her in it. I just know that I need her here with us. With *me.*

Heath sits up straight in his chair and leans forward. "Are you in love with her?"

His words take me by surprise. "What?" *What kind of question is that?*

"You heard me, but your expression tells me. You're in love with her," he states and smirks, proud of himself.

I don't answer because I don't want to give him the satisfaction of being right. I've never been in love with anyone. Ever. How do I know what I'm feeling is *love*? Maybe it's just super lust. But my heart tells me otherwise. It's been hurting since the day I realized this arrangement was going to end.

"Whatever," I say and ignore his obvious gloating.

"Answer me this: when was the last time you got laid?" His question surprises me, but I know he already knows the answer to that too.

"I don't remember," I admit, because it really has been *that* long.

"The night before you found out about Kai," Heath answers for me, and I nod in agreement.

"Why does it matter to you?" I ask, annoyed. "Besides, I've had a lot to deal with here, don't you think?"

He shrugs and places his empty beer on the table. "Glad we got to chat, dude, but I gotta go. Same time next week?"

I stand up with him and we walk toward the stairs. "Yeah, maybe sooner if Dax can make it on Wednesday. I'll keep you posted."

"Keep your chin up, lover boy. Sam doesn't live too far from here so you can see her whenever you want." He walks out, and I lock the door behind him.

I take the stairs two at a time and rush down the hall to Kai's room, where I'm sure Sam still is. I want to see her now. Be with her now. I can't even think ahead to when she's not under my roof.

I open the door quietly and hear the familiar music playing. Sam is asleep on the bed with Kai tucked in next to her. I stand over them and see my 'family' and want to do everything in my power to keep us together. I notice a stuffed animal that I've never seen before. It's a very old stuffed dog that looks like it may have been through the washing machine several hundred times. It's gray with the faintest pink tint to it. Kai is clutching it by the ear. *I wonder where that came from.*

I lift him from the bed and place him gently in his crib. He's still grasping the dog, and I let him keep it. Then I scoop Sam into my arms. She's limp and sound asleep. I hesitate in front of her door and then walk down the hall, carrying her into my room. *This* is where I want her. I gently lay her on my bed and she rolls to her side, sighing heavily. I can't imagine how exhausted she is after her swim earlier today.

Without thinking, I strip down to my boxer briefs. I slide into bed next to her as easily as I can without disrupting her sleep. Despite what I wanted to do to her earlier, at the moment I just want her to be close. I need to feel her warmth. I drape my arm over hers and pull myself against her. She stirs slightly and then entwines her fingers with mine.

"You awake?" I whisper in her ear and she shivers in my arms.

"No," she whispers back, and I smile.

"You let me carry you all the way in here when you could have walked?"

"I think I woke up halfway here. When you bumped my foot against the door." She laughs quietly and I kiss the back of her neck.

She rolls onto her back, keeping our fingers locked together on top of her stomach, and turns her head to look at me, our noses only inches apart.

"Tell me about the stuffed dog," I demand, and she looks at me questioningly.

"You mean the Dalmatian? I have no idea where that came from."

"I gave that to him. It reminds me of one I had just like it when I was younger. The other dog, the one he's sleeping with."

"Googie," she says, and I wonder what language she's speaking.

"What?"

"It's my Googie. I got him from my parents the day I was born. When I was old enough to talk, I called him Googie because I couldn't say doggy. The name just stuck."

"Googie," I say, smiling, and kiss the tip of her nose.

She slides a little closer to me so our lips touch softly.

"Kai means everything to me, Garrett. But it's time for me to leave." Her eyes look apologetic.

"I know."

"I love him. I've never felt this way about a baby that I've cared for. I'm in love with your son." She squeezes my hand and I kiss her gently on the lips.

"You've gone above and beyond. Kai wouldn't be where he is now without you." I pause and kiss her again.

"Garrett?" she asks quietly.

"Yes?" I nuzzle into her.

"What's happening between us?" she asks.

I don't hesitate when I respond.

"Everything."

CHAPTER 28

Sam
Present
Villanova, Pennsylvania
Age 24

"EVERYTHING," HE SAYS, and I inhale deeply.

"What does that mean?" I ask.

Our fingers are still linked and he squeezes my hand. "I've never been this happy," he says, and his eyes look glassy. This tender moment is something I never thought I'd experience with Garrett.

"I'm in love with my son too," he says and blinks heavily. "I can't imagine my life without him. I see our future together and it's amazing." He smiles, and I use my free hand to wipe the tear on his cheek.

"Tell me what his future looks like," I say. I want to hear everything.

"He's going to be the starting first baseman for the New York Yankees," Garrett states as if he's seen this future already.

"The Yankees?" I ask. "You do realize you live in Pennsylvania. He'll be surrounded by Phillies fans his entire life. You're dooming his existence with constant heckling and fights."

He laughs heartily. "I'm not worried. At least he's not going to be on the Mets."

I swat him on the shoulder. "Hey, leave my Mets out of this."

"Really? A Mets fan? I should have known." He kisses me tenderly and pulls me closer against his body.

"My father's favorite team. I grew up carrying Mr. Met around with Googie." Mr. Met didn't make it through the fire, and I feel sad, remembering the day my father gave him to me.

"What else does Kai's future hold?" I ask curiously.

"That depends," he says.

"Depends on what?" I ask.

"It depends on if you'll be around to see him grow up."

His words stab through my heart and I don't understand why he's saying this.

"What?" I ask, my eyes burning with impending tears.

He kisses me deeply, and my tears spill down my cheeks. He pulls back then kisses each and every drop until my cheeks are dry.

"I realize you're leaving us to go back to work. But please don't leave for *good*. We need you. I need you."

"What do you want from me?" I ask. *What is he asking?*

"I want everything. All of you," he says and rolls so that he's on top of me, our hips pressed together. He spreads my legs apart with his knee and rests himself *there*.

I suck in a deep breath as he crushes his lips to mine. I want this. I want it all. I thrust my hips into his, and he moans against my mouth. "Sam," he whispers, and his tongue twists with mine. He absorbs every breath as I prepare to give myself to him.

"Yes," I pant, and he devours my words.

He pulls one hand over my head and laces his fingers with mine. His lips travel down to my neck as his free hand grazes the side of my breast, causing me to arch my back and press into him more aggressively. I need to feel him all over me, inside me.

His free hand caresses my cheek. My eyes open and he's hovering above me, looking contemplative. "Are you sure?" he asks, and I nod so there's no confusion about exactly what I want. What I *need*.

He doesn't hesitate further. He slides down my body, taking my leggings and panties with him. He doesn't waste his time removing his boxers. The only thing that remains between us is my tank, which he's already pushed over my breasts. He covers my nipple with his mouth, causing me to moan. He scrapes his teeth over it gently, and he moves to devour my other breast. I thrust toward him, and his hard length presses against my thigh. I feel his warm breath everywhere as his mouth nips and sucks places that haven't seen the light of day in ages.

"Garrett," I whimper.

He spreads my legs farther apart and plunges his fingers into me while his thumb swirls my most sensitive area. I thrust my hips, forcing his fingers deeper. "Look at me," he says, and I do. He stares into my eyes as he continues plunging in and out. I'm gasping for air, needing a quick release. He moves expertly, and I come apart almost immediately. My climax surprises me, but he doesn't relent. He rolls on top of me so he's once again resting *there*. So close. My hips rise and fall, and I need to feel him. All of him.

"Inside me," I pant.

He reaches for the nightstand, and I'm not surprised that there's a stash of condoms in the back. He tears one open and quickly slides it over himself.

He fills me before I can catch my breath, his lips crash into mine. We move together like we've done this a thousand times before. I open my eyes the same time he does, and he slows his rhythm and swirls his hips above mine. He lifts a hand to touch my cheek, the look in his eyes almost unsure if I'm real or not. I lift my head to kiss him softly, and he thrusts deeper into me.

We're joined. United. It's intense and powerful. In this moment, we're one, and it feels so right. My heart beats wildly and in unison with his. Our breaths mingle and feed each other. I never want this to end, and it's only just begun. He moves faster, more rhythmically, and my body responds.

"Sam," he pants and devours my mouth again.

I cry out when he thrusts deeper. "Wait," I say, and he slows down. His eyes search my face, unsure. I wrap my leg around his thigh attempting to roll us and his eyes light up. He follows my cue and wraps his arms around my back, rolling with me. It takes a little maneuvering, but now, I'm right where I want to be.

My long hair falls to the sides of my face and partially covers my breasts. He places his palm flat against my belly and slowly lifts his hips, driving further inside of me.

We move together slowly, deliberately. "Garrett," I whimper, biting my lip. He stiffens below me, and he suddenly lifts me off of him. He's shifted himself so he's sitting with his back against the headboard. We aren't separated for too long when he grabs my hips and lowers me back down on top of him, crushing his lips into mine. "You were too far away," he says frantically against my lips. I moan into his mouth and he devours me, his hands caress my face and become tangled in my hair. He continues thrusting upwards, filling me completely. I say his name again, this time incoherently as a wave of pleasure rushes through me. His mouth swallows my cries, and his last surge draws my climax in sync with his. "Sam," he says again, and I fall on top of him, the warmth between our bodies keeping us joined together.

We stay like this for as long as we can until he needs to pull out and dispose of the condom. He rolls me off of him and does so quickly. He's back in bed next to me before I know it.

He pulls me against him and nuzzles into my neck, and kisses my shoulder, letting his lips linger.

"That was incredible," he whispers against my neck. I can feel his smile.

"It was," I admit. *The best I've ever had.*

I can't help but wonder what this means for us. "Was that goodbye?" I ask hesitantly. We've both wanted this, and now that it's happened, I wonder if he'll move on to the next conquest.

His body tenses next to mine and he lifts his head so his eyes are even with mine. "Definitely *not* goodbye."

"No?" I ask and smile.

"Absolutely not."

"Then what is this?" I ask, afraid of his answer. I'm not the friends-with-benefits type, and I know he's not into long-term relationships. We're doomed even before we get started.

"I think we can figure this out together," he says and kisses me tenderly.

"I don't do booty calls," I say and push him away so he can see that I'm serious.

"I don't want that. Not with you."

"Oh," I say and turn my head away.

"Sam, look at me," he commands, and I turn back to look into his eyes. They're dark and very serious.

He takes a deep breath and exhales quickly. "I'm in love with you." His words cause me to stiffen in disbelief.

"What?"

"I love you," he says again and lowers his mouth back to mine. His kiss is slow and thorough, and I press myself into him again.

I believe him. And his words scare me. We live completely different lives. I'm not cut out to live in his world.

"Why?" I ask, and he exhales heavily.

"You gave me something I thought I'd never experience. You triggered my capacity to *love* and to give myself fully to another human being. You've consumed my heart and soul. And you helped me find the place in my heart that I never knew existed. A place reserved for my child."

His words grab my heart and I close my eyes.

"Look at me," he says gently but firmly.

My eyes pop open and he says, "I've never felt this way about anyone, Sam. You give me breath. You give me life. I'm consumed by you."

He continues, "I'm yours, Sam. All of me. I need you to tell me that you're mine."

"Yes," I say, and he smiles as he brushes his hand over my cheek.

"Thank you," he whispers against my lips. "You've given me everything I thought I'd never want or have. You *changed* me. You've made me want to erase all of the sins in my past and be worthy of you."

I can't speak. But I *feel* so much. His warmth surrounds me. Protects me. I *feel* his love. His walls have collapsed around me, and I know he's mine, and I'm his. My heart races and I pull him closer.

"Please say something," he begs. "Tell me I'm not crazy. Tell me that what I'm feeling isn't one-sided. Tell me…"

"I love you," I blurt out.

"Tell me you won't leave," he says, pleading with me.

I sigh and close my eyes.

"I have to, Garrett. Kai doesn't need me anymore, not like he did six months ago. I need to go back to work. It's time."

His eyes are heavy and he exhales. "This isn't goodbye. You're not leaving me, Sam."

I smile. "I don't intend to. I'll just be staying someplace else at night."

Relief floods his face, and he pulls me against him like he never plans to let me go.

"Good," he whispers in my ear.

"And I think that someplace else should be my bed, permanently." I feel him smile against my cheek.

"I don't think Aunt Peggy would approve," I joke, and he rolls on top of me, pinning me to the bed.

"I see I have a lot of convincing to do, don't I?" His eyes are filled with determination, and he prepares to make sure my body doesn't forget a single inch of his.

Within seconds, he's claimed me again. Our bodies move in perfect rhythm as if we were built only for each other. "Say it again," he pants as his thrusts fill me.

"I love you," I repeat over and over again.

CHAPTER 29

Garrett
Present
Villanova, Pennsylvania
Age 27

I WIPE THE FOOD FROM KAI'S FACE, and he's belly laughing.

"Did you ever think you'd see this day?" Peggy asks as she rinses Kai's bottles in the sink.

"No," I respond. "A day like today seemed almost impossible to reach."

I can still hear Kai's sharp, painful cries if I let myself remember the early days with him months ago. Days when I tried to avoid hearing his screams. I disappeared for days and weeks on end. Escaping the reality that was my life.

Looking at him now, I realize the mistake I made. I should have been here to absorb every cry of pain. Every whimper. Thank God for Sam and Peggy. They did what I couldn't do and helped Kai without hesitation.

"Thank you, Peggy," I say.

"For what?" *Your niece.*

I look at her and raise my eyebrows. "You forced me to face what I didn't want to face. And you helped me heal my son."

"You didn't need my help, Garrett. You just needed to find it in yourself to open your heart and love someone."

I love your niece, too.

"Are you ready, little man?" Peggy asks. He coos and claps his hands.

"I think he is," I say, and she lifts him out of his high chair.

"It's such a beautiful day. I'm going to take him to the park after his appointment, if that's okay with you?" Kai has a check-up today, and Peggy always insists on handling the doctor appointments. It's kind of her thing with him, and I don't complain. It's hard to see him get shots, and I know he's in good hands with her.

"We'll be back in a few hours. Enjoy the quiet while you can," Peggy says. She knows Sam is going to go back to work soon, and I'll be adjusting to a new schedule and routine on my own.

"Okay. Take your time," I say and rush up the stairs as soon as I hear the car pull away. Sam slept in today, and I plan to wake her up the best way that I know how.

I open the door to my room and am surprised to see Sam pacing, holding a pad and pencil. She's in her panties and tank top and looks so fucking hot. She's startled when I burst in and close the door behind me.

"Hey," I say and wrap my arms around her, burying my face in her neck. She smells like vanilla and sex. Two of my favorite smells.

She's tense in my arms, and I back away a little. "What's wrong?" I ask.

"I'm making a list for you to refer to when I'm gone, and I feel like I'm missing too many things."

My heart sinks when I realize she's really going to leave.

"Let's not worry about the list right now," I say and plant tiny kisses all around her lips.

She smiles and drops the pencil and pad onto the dresser. She throws herself into my arms, and we repeat last night's performance several times.

"GARRETT?" SAM ASKS AS I NUZZLE into her breasts.

"Hmm?" I respond sleepily.

"What are you going to tell Kai about me?" she asks, and I'm suddenly wide awake.

"What do you mean?"

"Well, how are you going to explain me to him when he gets older? He'll see me in pictures and will assume I was a major part of his life. I just want to know what you're going to tell him."

She's serious, and I can't think of what to say.

"Are you assuming you won't be able to tell him yourself?" I ask.

"Well, maybe?"

"You're going to tell him because I'm not letting you go. Ever." I can't picture Kai's life without Sam in it. And I can't picture my own without her next to me.

"We're family," I say to her, and she sucks in her breath.

"What do you mean?"

"Exactly what I just said. We're *family*. You're not just Kai's nurse. You helped him heal, and you love him as if he were your own. So, yeah. Family."

She smiles through happy tears and snuggles next to me.

"I want to know more about your family," she says. "Your parents are great. I want to know more. Do you have aunts, uncles, cousins?"

"My parents *are* amazing. Mom and Bill have given me a great life. They supported my dreams of becoming a musician and never once questioned my choices. They helped create a stable and loving home that was torn from me when my father left so many years ago. I didn't realize until recently how lucky I am to have them in my life." I pause and reflect once again how lucky I am to have them. "My mom's family is huge. I have four uncles and about a dozen cousins, all living in North Carolina. I'm glad they're all so close to each other down there."

"That's amazing. You're lucky to have all of them." Sam met my parents about two months ago. I could tell that my mother adored her, and she kept throwing looks my way. I think she could sense something I wasn't yet aware of. She looks a little sad, and I hope the talk of my big family doesn't upset her. I don't even know anything about hers. Maybe she has cousins out there somewhere too?

"What about your family?" I ask.

"I don't have a huge family like you. My mother was an only child, and my father's only sister is Aunt Peggy. I miss my parents so much and I hold them close to my heart. My mother gave me so many gifts, but the most important gift she gave me was to give of myself to others. I know she's looking down on me right now, thrilled that I'm a nurse. She always told me that I had a higher purpose and I never believed her until I took that oath in nursing school."

She pauses to reflect on the love she has for her mother.

"When my father saved me from drowning, he also gave me the desire and push to be brave. He gave me the gift of unconditional love and understanding. His gift allows me to open my heart to anyone, and it gives me the desire to help heal. He was a wonderful man, and Heaven is a better place with him there."

"I know you're right," I say, and realize that my father is probably in Hell.

"I'm sorry," she says. "I don't pretend my life was a fairytale when I was younger, but I have to believe in the gifts my parents gave to me in order to make sense of their deaths."

"Can you tell me about it?" I ask, expecting she'll decline.

"About their deaths?" she responds.

"Yes."

"They were murdered." She tenses next to me, and I softly run my fingers up and down her arm.

"I know. But how?" My morbid curiosity takes control as well as my sudden desire to take this awful memory from her forever.

She inhales deeply and says simply, "They were blown up in their own home by a deranged man looking for money and drugs."

My head begins to spin as the reality of what she just said sinks in. "What?" I ask, and I'm not prepared to hear anything more. I sit up in bed and place my head on my knees. Her voice becomes distant and is replaced by Bill's voice.

"He killed himself," Bill says to me solemnly through the phone.

I almost crumble in place as his words hit me in the chest. "How?" I ask again, but know I don't want to hear anything more.

"You should come home," he says, and I immediately deny his request.

"No! What good will that do? He's dead. I haven't seen him since I was seven, and he killed himself before he could see me now."

"Garrett, you don't understand. There's more that we need to tell

you," Bill pleads with me, and I can hear my mother sobbing in the background.

"What more could you possibly say? He's dead, Bill. He's been dead to me for years."

"He killed himself along with two other people. It was a murder-suicide."

"What?" I ask, barely audible to myself.

"He was in a treatment facility not too far from here when he disappeared. They called your mother the other day to see if she'd heard anything from him. She explained that she hasn't heard from him in years and had no idea he was even in this facility. They told her she was listed as his only relative and that if she should hear from him, they needed to know immediately. They explained that he was a danger to himself and others."

I can't take this all in. It's too much to comprehend.

"Who did he kill?" I ask.

"A husband and wife in Newtown on Hickory Avenue."

"How?" I ask in disbelief.

"The police believe he filled their home with gas from their stove and used a lighter. The explosion leveled the house."

I drop my phone and make a mad dash for the bathroom. I puke up everything in my stomach and more. How could my father do this? Why would he do this?

I curl up in the bathroom stall and try to drown out the noise from the bar. Animated voices joking and flirting. People who have normal lives with normal families. None of them are related to a murderer.

None of them have to look in the mirror and be forever branded with the sins of their father.

"Garrett?" Sam's voice echoes in my ears and I snap out of my daze. I flinch when she touches my shoulder.

"Oh my God, are you okay?" she asks, and her concern turns to fear.

"Sam…" I say weakly and place my hand over hers. "I'm so sorry."

"It's okay, Garrett. Even though it was difficult, I've come to terms with their deaths in the best way that I can. Please don't look at me like that. If there's one thing I hate, it's a look filled with pity." She pleads with me, and I can't help but feel worse.

I need to tell her.

"I'm sorry," I say again.

"Stop," she says, begging me not to continue. Her eyes are huge with fear.

"My father… died in a similar way. Sam, he's killed people. He died at 842 Hickory Avenue." I almost choke on the words that come out of my mouth.

Her eyes widen in disbelief, and she whimpers next to me. She begins rocking in place on the bed and shaking her head violently from side to side. "Stop. Stop talking," she screams. "This isn't true. No. No. No. NO!" she yells and starts hyperventilating. Her breathing is erratic and shallow.

I don't know how to calm her down, and the memories of the days that follow are so vivid and clear.

"June McAllister, reporting live from 842 Hickory Avenue in Newtown. The scene of an apparent murder-suicide. Benjamin and Katherine Weston, unsuspecting parents of a teenaged girl, were overtaken in their own home by John Horton. We've since learned that Mrs. Weston was several months pregnant, expecting their second child. Family of Mr. Horton was unavailable for comment, but his former wife Claire Armstrong released a statement through her representative.

"'My heart goes out to the family of Benjamin and Katherine Weston. I can't erase the pain John has caused all of you, but I can tell you I'm so incredibly sorry for your loss. I don't ask you to understand

his actions but that someday you find it in your hearts the power to forgive him. I'm so sorry.'

"John Horton's son was also unavailable for comment, and his whereabouts are unknown. John's former wife, Claire, asks that you respect her family's privacy at this time and focus on offering prayers for the Weston's orphaned teenaged daughter."

"I'm so sorry, Sam." I pull her shaking body into mine. "I don't know what else to say. I didn't know. Oh my God. I didn't know."

"Don't touch me," she screams as if I'm stabbing her repeatedly. "Get away from me!"

I release her from my grip and she bolts out of the bed.

"Sam?" I say as she pulls on her clothes and runs for the door.

"Sam!" I yell after her as I hear her running down the hall and the stairs. The front door opens and slams shut and tires squeal as she tears down the driveway.

I'm unable to move from the bed. I'm frozen in place with the vision of her family home charred and burned to the ground.

An ash-filled house of death where our families are forever entombed together.

CHAPTER 30

Sam
Present
Villanova, Pennsylvania
Age 24

I HIT SPEED DIAL OVER AND OVER again. It goes to voicemail every single time.

"Aunt Peggy," I cry into the phone. "Please pick up."

I bang my hands on the steering wheel and merge onto the interstate. I don't know where I'm going and I don't care.

How is this happening?

Garrett's father killed my family?

GARRETT'S FATHER KILLED MY FAMILY.

I press my foot to the floor and accelerate as fast as I can.

My cell phone rings and I look down at the Caller ID.

Garrett.

I send the call to voicemail and throw the phone into the back seat. I slam my foot to the floor and drive.

And then I scream.

My tears flow through my wails. It's hard to see, but I keep going. I grip the wheel; my knuckles turn white. *Is this my fault?* If Ben hadn't died, I wouldn't have ever met Garrett and Kai, and things would be normal. *Right?* This is a sick twist of fate that I don't deserve. I realize I'm being selfish, but who fucking cares. I don't deserve this. I fell in love for the first time in my life with not just one person, but two. Garrett and Kai. The reel keeps playing in my head, and I fast-forward to a future vision when Kai's a toddler, running around and playing with his father. *And me.* I have no right to envision what could have been. They aren't my family. Garrett's father took that away from me.

My sobs fill the car playing a sad, sick tune to the emptiness. Memories continue to flash through my mind as if I'm re-living every single moment. Every piercing cry from Kai's small body. Every touch and yearning look from Garrett. All of the highs and all of the lows. We spent the better part of six months forming a support structure to help protect and nurture his son. It all came crashing down today in a burning pile of ash.

I wipe my eyes and see a highway sign.

Hershey.

I've been driving for at least an hour and a half. I look down at my gas gauge and see I only have about a quarter of a tank left. And I don't have my wallet or purse with me.

Fuck.

I take the next exit and turn around. I hope I can at least make it back to my aunt's house with what's left in my tank of gas.

My cell phone starts ringing again from the back seat. I reach back and tap my hand around, trying to find it. I finally grab it and see the caller ID.

Garrett.

Again.

CHAPTER 31

Garrett
Present
Villanova, Pennsylvania
Age 27

"HERE'S DADDY." PEGGY'S CHEERFUL VOICE echoes through the kitchen where I'm pacing back and forth. I've been dialing Sam's number constantly for the past hour since she left. She won't pick up and I'm sick.

When Peggy walks into the kitchen with Kai, she freezes in her steps. "Garrett? What's going on?" she asks hesitantly, and she looks alarmed.

"Not now," I say and hit Sam's speed dial again. This time it goes right to voicemail. "Sam, it's me. Call me, please. I need to know you're okay. Please," I plead and end the call.

Peggy holds Kai close and asks again, "What's going on? Is Sam okay?"

I stop pacing and look at her. She's terrified, and Kai senses it too.

"Peggy, something happened. I can't even begin to explain it."

She kisses Kai on his forehead and says to him, "It's time for your nap. I know you're exhausted after the fun day we had." She turns to me, "I'll be down soon. Don't go anywhere."

I continue to call Sam's phone and can't get through.

Before I know it, Peggy is standing in front of me. "What's going on?"

I drop my arms down to my sides and lower my head. "Peggy, there's something you need to know. Something I just found out."

She sits tentatively on the stool in the kitchen and her eyes widen. "Is Sam alright?" she asks, worried.

I plant myself on the floor across from her and tell her everything. All that I've found out about how our families are connected. What my father did to her brother and sister-in-law, Sam's parents. As I recount the stories that I knew growing up along with what swirled around our local news stations, her eyes become more and more drawn. Tears spill down her cheeks and I feel like I'm personally responsible for them. For what my father has done. For the lives of their family that have been destroyed.

"I'm so sorry. I don't know what else to say," I say to Peggy as she stares off into space. "What can I do?" I ask.

She wipes the tears from her face and inhales deeply. Her shock is tangible.

"There's nothing to do," she says simply.

"What?" I ask in disbelief.

"*You* didn't do this, Garrett. Your father did. You have no control over what that man did with his life. You yourself told me that the last time you laid eyes on him was when you were seven. How could you possibly know or even predict that he would murder two people at the same time he took his own life? It's impossible. You can't own his crimes. You can't take the blame for his *sins*."

"But Sam…" I say, hoping that she's okay.

"Does she know?" Peggy asks, concerned.

"Yes, I figured it out an hour ago and told her. When she told me how her parents died, I realized immediately that it was my father who killed them. I had no idea, Peggy. How could I have not known?" When I found out that my father was a *murderer*, I shut out everything. I refused to watch anything on TV about what he did. The media was relentless, and the faces of her parents were everywhere. I shut everything out, including their *names*. Soon after, Epic Fail started touring and we wound up in Europe for months. Nobody knew me there and what my father had done.

She pulls me into a hug and rubs my back like my mother always did when I was younger.

"You could be asking me the same question," Peggy says. "How could *I* have not known? I've been working for you for close to six years. I followed the story when it happened to the point of obsession. I tried to trace everything about that man and what made him tick. I tried to understand what would cause a human being to take another's life from them. I did everything I could to unearth the mysteries surrounding your father."

"My last name was changed when I was a teenager. My stepdad adopted me after my mother had my father's parental rights terminated. I took the name Armstrong to make it official."

"That explains why I couldn't find his family when I was looking," she says, nodding her head.

"I'm worried about Sam."

"Me too. But one thing you need to know about her is that she rarely gets this upset. Her rational, logical mind always wins and takes over in almost all situations. She'll be back." But I don't think that Peggy believes what she's saying.

And neither do I.

CHAPTER 32

Sam
Present
Villanova, Pennsylvania
Age 24

"GOODNIGHT, DR. HAGAN," I SAY as I walk out the door of the NICU. "Take care," she says through her ever-present warm smile.

Since I've been back to work, my life has started to get back to normal. *I think.* My daily routine consists of a walk or jog, depending on my mood, a light breakfast and then an action-packed day at the hospital. So, yeah, *normal.*

My phone buzzes and I see a text message on the screen.

MAX: THANKS AGAIN FOR THE REFERRAL. KAI IS AMAZING AND THINGS ARE GOING REALLY WELL. TALK SOON.

I smile and place my phone into my backpack. I'm so relieved that Garrett hired Max. He was number one on my list to replace me, and it's working out great so far. Or at least that's what Peggy tells me.

Garrett and I haven't spoken since I left three months ago. My heart is empty, and it still hurts. *How can I possibly be with a man whose father murdered my family?* Every time he looked at me, touched me, made love to me, I would think of all that was taken away. I've heard nothing but grief from Aunt Peggy about all of this. Our conversation last night replays in my head.

"*How was work, Sam?" Aunt Peggy asks, making small-talk.*

"*It's good."* I've been welcomed back with open arms, but it still feels weird. Walking into the NICU for the first time since the incident with Ben was surreal. It was also a crazy day with four babies admitted with varying levels of issues, so I didn't have much time to lament and feel sorry for myself. I jumped right in and the days since have flown by. Everything is 'normal.'

"*Kai's crawling," she says and places a pot on the stove for tea.* My heart pulls and I bow my head. I wish I could be there to see his milestones. I miss him.

"*That's awesome!" I respond, rolling the string of the tea bag between my fingers.*

"*He's like a bullet, I swear. As soon as his knees hit the floor, he's off. Max has his hands full."*

"*I'm glad it's working out so well."*

"*It really is," she says. "Oh, I forgot to mention that his occupational therapy is also ending soon. Nadia's last day is next week."*

It's truly amazing the strides that Kai has made. He's come so far. My eyes tingle as tears threaten. I shake my head and sit up straight in the chair. "*Please give her my best, if you see her."*

The hot water comes to a boil, and she removes the pot from the stove. After she pours us each a large cup full, she pushes a spoon across the table to me. "*Sam, Garrett misses you."* She quickly realized after I left that something more was going on between the two of us. She could sense it, as much as Garrett and I tried to be discreet about the stolen kisses and longing looks. She believes that it was fate that brought us together. I don't believe her.

Another stab in my chest and I inhale deeply. "Please, don't," I say as I swirl the tea bag in the hot water.

We sit silently until she speaks again. "You need to get past this. You're acting as if Garrett killed your parents. We both know that isn't true. That poor boy had nothing to do with the actions of his estranged father."

I snap my head and glare at her. Doesn't she get it? That sick fuck's blood is running through Garrett's veins. "We're not having this conversation again." I snap and push the tea away.

I feel bad the way I left her last night, but I just can't go there right now. As much as I want to walk through his door like nothing happened, curl up next to him in his bed and wish all of this darkness to go away—I can't.

The front door opens, and I hear commotion in the foyer. "Ba-ba!" Kai's voice echoes through the halls. *He's here?*

I rush to see him and he's trying to wrangle from Aunt Peggy's arms. "Kai, please give me a minute to get into the house." She's laughing as she drops her purse and keys on the table and then places him down on the floor.

He's on all fours and at first hesitates. He hasn't been here in a long time, and he seems unsure of his surroundings. He pats his hands on the floor and then looks up, sees me and darts across the floor giggling.

"Kai!" I screech and get down on my knees, arms outstretched. Giggles and drool escape his mouth, and he's in my lap before I know it. I squeeze him tight and kiss him all over his chubby cheeks.

"What are you doing here?" I ask my aunt.

"Kai had a doctor's appointment today, and I thought I'd stop by here before taking him home." Her motives for bringing him are obvious, but I ignore them because I'm holding my favorite little man in my arms. I rub noses with him and he pats his hands on my face. He starts to squirm out of my arms and I place him back down on the floor and he once again takes off like a flash.

"We don't have a child-proof house, Aunt Peggy." I take off after him as he weaves his way through the foyer into the den. Once he's on soft carpeting, he sits up and starts clapping. Aunt Peggy hands him some toys from her bag and he bangs them together, laughing.

"We'll only be here for a few minutes," she says as she brings several other bags into the kitchen. "I needed to drop off a few things."

I sit down on the floor across the room from Kai and roll one of his balls toward him. He giggles and says, "Ba!" The ball glides toward him and he snags it, giggles and throws it up in the air. We play this game of 'catch' for several minutes, and he moves on, crawling through and exploring the den. I haven't seen him since his last well-visit, which was over a month ago. He wasn't this mobile then and it's amazing to see him so happy and active.

"Kai, buddy, it's time to go," Aunt Peggy calls out. "Your Daddy's home waiting for you." Kai giggles and tries to scamper away while saying "Da-da!" Peggy scoops him up and I stand to walk them out. I kiss him on the cheek and brush my hand across his hair. "See you, little man."

Aunt Peggy nods toward the kitchen. "There's a bag for you on the counter."

"Oh?" I ask.

She just smiles and walks out the door. "Happy Thursday."

It hurts watching Kai leave with her, and I wish there was something more I could do. I don't know when I'm going to see him again. *I love that little boy.*

There's one canvas bag left on the counter in the kitchen, and I look at it warily. *What is she up to?*

I open it and see all of the ingredients needed to make pizza, and my heart tugs in my chest. *Pizza Thursday.* There's a note sitting on top of the ingredients, and I recognize the handwriting immediately. *Garrett.*

> *Sam,*
> *Can I come over tonight and help make this?*
> *G*

My head begins to spin and my chest tightens. I crumble the note and toss it into the garbage can and then put away all of the ingredients, slamming doors and drawers as I do. *He can't be serious. This is not going to happen.*

I pick up my cell and hit Cassie's speed dial. "Hey, chick," she says, practically singing into the phone.

"I want to go out tonight," I snap and stare at the crumbled note at the top of the garbage. "I *have* to go out tonight," I state.

"What's going on?" she asks, concern in her voice.

"Nothing. I just need a night out with my bestie. Are you in or not?"

"I'm *always* in. I'm on call, but let's go out anyway. I'll pick you up in an hour." She hangs up, and I toss my phone onto the counter.

I have no intention of being here tonight.

CHAPTER 33

Garrett
Present
Villanova, Pennsylvania
Age 27

"KAI'S SOUND ASLEEP," PEGGY SAYS as she settles on the couch in the den. Max is away on vacation, and Peggy jumped at the chance to stay and help out. She's actually planning to spend the night tonight, hoping I'll be successful with our plan.

"Did you see her?" I ask. She dropped by her house earlier today with Kai so Sam could spend some time with him. It's been a while since she's seen him, and I know Peggy takes him as much as she can. I don't mind this at all and wish they would do it more often. Sam was such an integral part of the first six months of his life, and it would kill me to know that Kai didn't get to see her. I know he misses her.

"I did," Peggy responds. "She got to see Kai crawl. As soon as I put him down on the floor, he took off right into her arms. You should have seen how happy he was to see her." The vision of this hurts more than I expect. I want my son to be happy and to be with Sam. Hell, I want to be with her. Picturing him crawling and throwing himself into her arms drives deep into my chest. *It's what should be.*

"Well?" I ask, knowing I sent a note. This was all Peggy's idea, and I'm worried it's going to blow up in everyone's faces. "Did she read it?"

"Oh, I don't know. We left before she could open the bag. I'm not sure, actually." She smirks and lifts her Kindle onto her lap. "I'm sure she's read it by now," she says and begins to read.

Shit.

"I can't just show up there if she hasn't read my note," I say and start pacing around the room. "I haven't seen her in three months, Peggy. I wish you had stayed long enough for her to tell you it was okay for me to come." This was a really bad idea, and now I'm regretting even suggesting we get together.

"Relax, Garrett." She glances at the clock. "You should head over in a few minutes, otherwise you'll be cooking that pizza at midnight." She grins and looks back down at her Kindle.

I huff. "This is a mistake." I swipe my keys from the counter and head out.

When I pull up to their house, it's dark. Sam's car is in the driveway, but it looks like there's nobody home. I park my car next to hers and hesitantly get out. The front porch light isn't on, and I wonder if she's trying to tell me something.

Fuck it.

I didn't come all the way over here just to wonder 'what if.' I reach the front door and ring the bell and wait. And wait. She isn't answering. I ring again and nothing. I knock loudly and peer through the window pane. Either she's hiding in there or she's not even here.

Yes, this was a mistake.

I sink down onto the front step and kick my legs out in front of me. *What was I expecting?* That she was going to open the door and fly into my arms? Tell me how much she missed me? Declare her undying love for me? *I'm an idiot.*

I pull out my phone, about to hit her speed dial, when a car pulls into the driveway. The lights flash toward me and I lift my arm up to shield my eyes. The driver's window lowers, and Cassie's voice screeches across the yard, "Hey, Garrett! How are you?"

I can't see her because of the blinding lights. "I'm good," I say and stand up. The passenger door opens and Sam emerges.

"Sam was just telling me all about Kai's visit today. I can't believe how big he's getting," she says. "Take care!" Her window closes and she backs out of the driveway, leaving Sam standing in place.

Neither of us moves for what seems like forever. She eventually takes a step toward me then stops. "What are you doing here?" she asks, and her arms fall to her sides.

"I thought—I mean, it's Thursday, and I thought… " *Fuck.*

She walks up the sidewalk, shaking her head, and pushes past me to open the front door.

"I don't know what you thought, Garrett, but I'd rather you leave." Her voice is cold, reminding me of the very first time we spoke. How much disdain she felt for me when she thought I was a heartless prick who wanted nothing to do with my own son.

"Can we talk?" I ask weakly. *Can I hold you?*

"I don't think so," she says and walks into the house. She leaves the door open and I don't hesitate to follow her inside.

"I didn't invite you in," she says and drops her bag onto the counter. Something catches my eye at the top of the garbage can, and I see my note, crumbled.

"You got my note?" I ask, and she turns to face me.

"I did."

"You weren't here," I say and take another step toward her.

"No, and I wasn't planning on coming home this early either. I'd still be out if Cassie hadn't been called into work." Her tone is cutting through me, and I can't take much more of this. I can't stand the way she's looking at me, with disdain. *Hatred?*

"Sam, I—"

"Please, don't." She cuts me off and leans against the counter.

"Tell me what I did wrong. Because the way I see things, I didn't do anything, yet you shut me out." I'm here and I want answers. The only woman I've ever loved is standing a few feet away from me and she's staring at me like I'm a demon.

"I can't do this," she says and sighs. "Please."

I close the distance between us and I grab her hand. She immediately flinches and jerks it away. "What did I do?" I raise my voice and she brushes past me. "Sam, I didn't kill your parents!" I yell at her and she picks up her pace, darting for the stairs. "Talk to me, please!"

She takes off up the stairs and I hear a door slam. *Fuck. Fuck. Fuck.*

I take the stairs two at a time, following the sound of her soft sobs. When I reach her door, they stop. "Garrett, I need you to leave." She sniffles, and I rest my head against her door.

"I can't," I say.

"Please. Leave." Her voice shakes, and I want to bust down this door. I need to make this right. *I need her.*

Moments pass, and she's quiet and still inside her room. I place my hand on the doorknob and start to turn.

Then I stop.

I can't force my way into her room. Into her life. *Into her heart.* She wants nothing to do with me, and there's nothing

I can do about it. I release the doorknob and place my palm against the door. "I love you, Sam," I whisper and slowly back away. Down the stairs. Into my car.

I love you, Sam.

CHAPTER 34

Garrett
Present
Three Months Later
Villanova, Pennsylvania
Age 27

"I THINK WE'RE ABOUT READY to send this to the label," Dax says and pushes himself back in the chair. "It sounds amazing."

Tristan and Heath nod in agreement and they fist bump each other.

"It's one of our best albums yet," Dax interjects.

A lot of heart and pieces of each of our souls have been injected into this album. I'm not quite sure any of us will ever be the same again.

My cell phone dings, and I have another text message waiting for me. I swipe to see Kai's huge smile filling my screen.

"Your nanny documents everything that boy does." Heath grabs my phone from me so he can see him too. He scrolls through the two dozen pictures that Max sent to me since breakfast.

"You mean his *manny!*" Tristan laughs hysterically. He still can't believe that I hired a guy to watch my son, and I explain that it wasn't all my doing. Sam was the one who got the ball rolling with Max, and it worked out perfectly.

Heath tosses my phone back to me. "Another picture just came in. Dude, he's walking." I quickly look down to see a picture of Kai standing with his hands stretched out in the air. He had a huge, wide-mouthed smile that I can practically hear his happy screeches from.

"Are we done?" I ask, anxious to get upstairs to witness this huge milestone.

"We're all set," Dax says, and I don't wait for him to retract his statement.

I bound up the basement stairs and then up the back staircase that leads to the second floor. I hear belly laughs coming from his room, and I open the door.

"Da-da!" he says as soon as he sees me, and he tries to take a step toward me. He falls onto his outstretched hands and pushes himself back onto his feet. He does this again three more times before he's able to take several steps, practically leaping into my arms.

"Hey, buddy," I say as I shower him with kisses.

"Da-da!" he screeches again and Max chuckles.

"I couldn't believe it, Mr. Armstrong. He was table surfing all day today, and suddenly he let go. Once he realized he could balance, he just took off. It was amazing."

I take out my phone so I can document this with proper video. My parents are going to be amazed by this as well, and I can't wait to send it to them.

"Hey, you should get going," I say to Max, noticing the time. "Thanks for staying late today so we could finish up downstairs."

"No problem," he says and walks past us and out the door.

"Bye-bye," Kai says, and Max backs up to high-five him. Kai giggles and claps his hands.

Although Max was originally hired to be a live-in nanny, I decided that for the time being, I would do this on my own. He usually stays overnight once a week so I can do some late-night editing in the studio.

I haven't heard from Sam since Pizza Thursday almost three months ago. I haven't been able to even eat pizza since. Peggy keeps me posted on her, though. She's been pulling double shifts for months, and that tips me off that she's trying to hide away. Although Peggy says she's been enjoying her time with her friends, I don't believe her. The girl I saw that night was distant. Cold. I'm worried about her.

My heart sinks knowing that Sam isn't a daily fixture in Kai's life anymore. Or mine. She was such an important part of his life for so long and the only mother figure he's ever known. It would kill me to not allow her to see him and continue to be a part of his life.

I yearn for what the three of us finally found together. We formed a family that was destroyed by an ugly truth. A truth we found out about by accident. A truth destroyed by my father.

I need to breathe her air.

Feel her touch.

Consume her fully.

We need her back.

CHAPTER 35

Sam
Present
Long Beach Island, New Jersey
Age 24

THE CHILLY AIR SENDS A SHIVER down my spine, but I dig my bare feet into the cold sand anyway. I'm on Long Beach Island, New Jersey. Cassie gave me the key to her family's beachfront vacation home. She said I needed a break and time to *reflect*. She couldn't have been more right.

I pull the fleece blanket up to my chin and rest my head back on the beach chair. The sun is setting behind me, reflecting beautifully off of the clear water. A large, lone seagull skims along the top of the water in search of its next meal. I love it here. It's so peaceful and relaxing. Cassie and I would come out here all the time when we were in nursing school. It's only about an hour and a half from our college, and we made sure to put the house to good use. I smile as I remember some of the epic beach parties we threw. It's amazing the neighbors haven't run me off the beach by now because we sure were a nuisance back then.

Waves continue to crash, and the constant sounds of the ocean soothe me. It's weird being down here by myself; I've never been here without Cassie. Last night I slept with all of the windows open, despite the cool ocean winds. I imagined Garrett's warm arms wrapped around me as I drifted off to sleep.

Why can't I let him in?

I walked away from him months ago, and I've lived such a lonely existence since. My life is a pattern of work, sleep, repeat. I close my eyes, and the wind sweeps and swirls my long hair around my face, hiding me from the world.

A loud cracking noise startles me and I sit upright. A large group of people have joined me on the beach, and the residual smoke from a firecracker floats out over the water. They're laughing loudly as they arrange their blankets and chairs around a group of guys digging what I presume is going to become a fire pit. Watching them scamper around reminds me of the times Cassie and I would come here with our friends from college. We used to take over this whole area of the beach with our epic volleyball and whiffle ball games. *If only I could travel back in time.*

One of the girls opens a large bottle of wine, and the others hold out their glasses to be filled. Cheers and laughter continue as they clink their glasses together.

A Frisbee sails my way, landing near my feet, and one of the guys jogs over to retrieve it. "Hey," he says and smiles ear to ear. I recognize him right away; he's the son of Cassie's neighbors. He bends to pick up the Frisbee and plops himself in the sand instead. "I thought it was you, Sam." I squint, trying to remember his name. He's a twin, and I always mix up him and his brother. I'm talking to either Jake or Justin. Cassie and I spent many nights on this same beach hanging out with them.

In fact, I hooked up with Jake a few years ago at the end of a long day of swimming and drinking. He's adorable and nice, but it was just a one-time thing and we didn't let it interfere with the good times we were having. It was *uncomplicated.*

"Hi—um, Jake?" I say, hoping I'm right.

He smiles and nods his head. "That's me." He lifts his hand to shield his eyes from the sun behind me. "What are you doing out here all alone?" he asks.

"Oh, just enjoying the view and a much-needed break from life," I say.

"Where's Cassie? Is she up at the house?" He looks past me toward her back deck.

"No, I'm alone this weekend. Cassie had to work."

"Jake!" his brother calls from across the beach. Jake waves him off and tosses him the Frisbee from his seated position in the sand.

"You're here with a big crew. Are your parents down too?" I ask and look back over to his friends now huddled around a fire.

"No, they're away. A bunch of us wanted to get together, and instead of going into the city like we usually do, we decided to come down here." He peers at the waves and brushes sand off of his legs. He's wearing shorts, and I shiver thinking how cold he must be.

"That's nice," I say. "It's the perfect time of year to come down here and have this whole place to yourself."

"Yeah," he says. "So how have you been?" he asks.

How do I answer that question?

"I've been—life's been interesting."

He nods, almost as if he knows exactly what I've been through. "It's been a while since I've seen you here," he says.

"Maybe two or three years?" I can tell he's remembering the same moment that I just did when we made out under a pile of blankets almost right in the same spot that I'm in right now.

"I can't believe it's been that long. What are you doing these days?" I ask.

"I'm a third grade teacher in Spring Lake and I'm living in Belmar. I can't seem to stay away from the beach," he says.

He is a gentle soul, and it's the perfect profession for him. I bet the kids love him. "That's great," I say.

"What about you? Are you still saving lives?"

Sometimes.

"I'm a neonatal intensive care nurse in Philly," I say and don't want to talk much more about my job.

"It takes a really special person to be a nurse," he says and brushes my leg with his hand. "I don't know how you do it. Last week, one of my students puked all over his desk and I almost passed out."

I chuckle. "It's not as hard as you think."

"I beg to differ," he says. "Hey, why don't you come join us? We have lots of food and plenty to drink."

I shake my head. "Thanks, but I'm going to head up to the house in a few minutes. I leave early tomorrow and want to get to sleep soon."

He grins. "Want some company?" As tempting as that would have been a few years ago, I can't bring myself to say yes. His eyes are eager and hopeful.

I shake my head. "I don't think so."

He shrugs. "Someone probably swept you off your feet years ago. I guess I'm too late."

"Not exactly," I say and realize the only person who's ever swept me off my feet is Garrett.

"Looks like we have company." He nods to my other side and another group of people are making their way down to the beach. A little girl runs toward the water, followed by a boy about half her size. They're screeching and laughing with joy.

"Emily, Caleb! Don't go in the water," a woman, who I presume is their mother, calls after them. Several other people follow, and one of them waves toward us.

"Hi, Jake!" an older woman calls out. "Your parents here?" she asks.

"Hi, Becca. No, they're not here this weekend."

She nods and catches up with her friends. "Carly, wait up!" The group tosses blankets down.

I remember them. Becca's family owns the house on the other side of Cassie's. They're older than us by at least ten years. We used to annoy them when we threw parties at Cassie's. It almost became a sport for us to make sure our music was just a little louder than theirs. Cassie's mom told us that Becca and her friends were notorious when they were younger, so we never felt bad about annoying the older crew. "Callie! Manny! Who has the wine?" she calls out and a tall man raises his hand, holding a large bottle of red.

The two little kids run through the surf and screech again. They must be freezing. Another man scoops them out of the water and runs to the dry sand, collapsing with them on his chest. "Daddy!" They squeal and they soon forget about the cold water.

I stand up, tucking my blanket under my arms, and pick up my chair. "It's great seeing you again," I say to Jake, and he looks disappointed.

"Are you sure you're not up for some company?" he asks, persistent.

"No, not this time," I say.

He suddenly pulls me against him into a warm, tight hug. He inhales deeply and kisses my cheek. "It's really great seeing you again. You should give me a call sometime."

I don't respond as he reluctantly lets me go.

"Bye, Jake," I say and walk up to the house, waves crashing behind me.

The house is quiet and peaceful. As appealing as it was to be invited to join the party on the beach, I just don't have it in me to be social. I'm here for a solo retreat, and I intend to hold true to that. I see Jake run up to the bonfire and plop into the sand next to his brother. Justin pats him on the back and their laughter carries through the air.

How simple would it be to invite Jake in for the night? Where would that lead? A night of steamy, unattached sex? I don't think I can open my bed or my heart to anyone else.

Ever again.

Garrett ruined me.

CHAPTER 36

Garrett
Present
Villanova, Pennsylvania
Age 27

"ARE YOU READY, LITTLE MAN?" I ask Kai as I grab a bottle of water from the refrigerator.

"Da-da," he says and claps his hands. It makes me so happy that he says 'Da-da.' The other words he has in his repertoire are 'ball' and 'bye.' I remove him from his high chair, and crumbs fall from his lap into the seat. He's a mess, but he doesn't seem to care.

I carry him out the back door, down to the pool house. I've been trying to come out here at least every other day to swim. To relax me. *To connect with her.*

I place Kai in his stationary walker and make sure he has plenty of toys within reach. Now that he's walking and is so mobile, he doesn't enjoy playing in this as much as he used to. Peggy mentioned that I might want to set up a play yard in here, and I have yet to figure out exactly what that even is.

He's happy for now, so I take advantage and dive into the pool. Kai plays and watches me as I swim my laps. He screeches every time I get close to him, and I make sure I kick a little harder so he gets splashed. His giggles echo throughout the large room, and they fuel my vigorous swim. He gets quiet after a while, and I notice he's watching the large-screen television intently. Disney Junior projects through the room and just like that he's in a television coma. Peggy insists that I limit his television watching to only an hour or less a day. Max never lets him watch television, so I don't see the harm in it. The "Miles From Tomorrowland" song fills the room as I finish my last lap.

I'm breathing heavily as I roll onto my back and allow the pool to swallow me whole. I learned so much from Sam from the time that she spent with us, but the one thing I've truly come to appreciate is the art of relaxation. Floating like this slows down time for me. It allows me to reflect on things that are happening and plan for things that are coming. It clears my mind and gives me strength to live. Only my mouth and nose are outside the water, and I let the pool take me. Kai's giggles bounce around the room as he continues to watch TV.

I close my eyes and think about how far we've come. A year ago, I never would have thought I'd be home with a child. An incredible one at that. The love that fills my heart is amazing, and he's taught me so much about myself. I picture my birth father's face, drawn and sad. For the first time, I feel sorry for him. He missed out on so many years with me and my mom. He couldn't escape his demons and ended it all. He also stole the lives and future of two wonderful people. Two people who should be here today, witnessing the miracle of their daughter and the woman that she's become. My father took away his own memories and chance at a future with my son, his grandson. So, yes, I pity him. I no longer hate him, because it's not worth exhausting that kind of energy on anyone. But I pity him and the sad life that his eventually became.

I see my parents' faces, and Bill's warm smile erases my father's drawn face. Bill is the type of father that I strive to be, and every day I try to be the man that he is. I hope that Kai sees this someday and appreciates me the way I appreciate Bill.

A loud clap and a screech pull me out of my meditative state. Kai's saucer is floating in the shallow end of the pool, and my heart leaps out of my chest. He's clapping and laughing as he floats in the water, and I reach him before it's able to sink further. "Da-da!"

How did that happen? Holy shit!

I scoop him and his walker out of the pool and take him out of the seat, his diaper hanging low, filled with water. He's still laughing, and I thank God this incident wasn't worse. The play yard suddenly seems like a great idea, and I toss the stationary saucer toward the door. I need to get rid of it immediately.

After we dry off and I change his soaked diaper, I carry Kai back to the main house. I'm still shaken from what just happened. I place him on the floor after I've ensured that all of the gates have been locked throughout the downstairs. We have an entire baby gate system on the first and second floors. If the unlikely event occurs and Kai's able to breech one gate, there's always a backup that has a different locking mechanism. It's ironic that the inside of the house is so secure, yet a major catastrophe almost occurred outside in the pool house. I vow to make sure that never happens again, and I jot down a note on the pad that I share with Peggy and Max.

Play Yard
Pool Safety Class
Swim Instructions?

Peggy and Max are going to be full of questions, and I decide that I'm not going to tell them what happened today. The crisis was averted and that's what matters. I will never put Kai in harm's way again. I drop the pen next to the pad and look for my phone.

Kai is playing on the floor with some plastic cups and containers, banging them together and laughing. I sit down next to him as I swipe through my phone, reading messages from Dax. We have a busy couple of weeks ahead of us as we plan for the beginning of our upcoming tour. The management company has been easy on us and instead of scheduling one long road trip, they planned the tour in manageable trips. We'll spend less time on a bus and more time in the air as we're flown in and out of various venues and then back home again. This is going to work for me, but my heart sinks knowing there will be several days a month when I'm not home with Kai.

I lock the phone on the home screen and see the wallpaper picture. It's Kai and Sam. It's the same picture that I had enlarged and hung on his bedroom wall. He's about to kiss her, and her smile is huge. It's my favorite picture of the two of them, and it sums up the happiness and joy that she brought into our home.

"Ma-ma," Kai says next to me, and I'm startled. He's pointing to my phone and sees the picture of him and Sam.

"What did you say, little dude?" I ask him.

"Ma-ma." He tries to grab the phone and I give it to him.

"Ma-ma. Ma-ma. Ma-ma." He continues to say this as his pudgy finger presses into the screen on Sam's face.

Tears fill my eyes as I witness the joy and irony of the situation. I can't imagine where he would have learned that word because I've never referred to Sam as 'mama.' Yes, she was like a mother to Kai for so many months, but that word has never left my mouth.

I realize a sobering truth.

Sam is the only mother Kai has ever known.

CHAPTER 37

Sam
Present
Villanova, Pennsylvania
Age 24

"NO, CASSIE. DON'T BRING THIS TOPIC UP AGAIN," I say and slide across the room on my rolling chair. I'm updating medical records and need to use two different computers at the same time. I've been gliding back and forth for the past twenty minutes, and I'm starting to get dizzy.

"I refuse to back down," she says firmly. "Pick up the phone and call him for God's sake. How much longer are you going to suffer alone? Garrett didn't fill your home up with gas and flick the lighter. Why can't you see that? He didn't know, Sam."

This conversation is tiresome. I thought that by escaping to the beach a few weekends ago, she would have started to let up on this incessant banter. It happens at least once a day, if not twice. How can she not understand that I can't bring myself to be with the son of my family's killer? It's macabre. It's wrong. Garrett may not have blown up my family, but the genes in his body carry the DNA from a deranged, drug-addicted gambler.

Who's to say Garrett won't develop the same tendencies as his father?

"Do you think you have the right to see Kai without any formal arrangement with Garrett?" she asks and folds her arms across her chest.

"What?"

"Seriously. Think about it. He doesn't have to let you see his son, ever. But he does. He knows what an important part of Kai's life you've been, and he doesn't deny his visits with you. You're practically Kai's mother, Sam. Why don't you start acting like it and show some compassion for his father? Garrett's in love with you. Jesus, Sam. You're such an asshole!"

She paces through the NICU with her arms folded tightly against her chest.

"You may be trying to punish Garrett for what his father did, but you're punishing Kai worse." Her words cause my breath to whoosh from my lungs. They cut deep and it hurts.

I never thought of it that way.

"You would tell anyone listening that you moved beyond your parents' cause of death and have accepted their gifts to you of acceptance, healing and love. C'mon, Sam, stop being a fucking hypocrite."

Another punch to the gut.

Why do her words suddenly seem so true when for the past six months, I've been fighting them?

"Oh my God," I say and stop in my chair.

"Are you finally getting it?" She twists the knife a little further into my heart.

"I get it, yes." Tears prick my eyes and I hang my head.

"Good. I'm sorry I got you upset," she says, walking toward me. She bends to hug me, and I throw my arms around her neck. "But you needed to really listen to me," she says, and I nod against her chest. "Now what are you going to do about it?"

"Good morning, ladies." Dr. Hagan's peaceful voice floats through the room. Marcie and Becky trail closely behind her. We're about to change shifts and our routine begins.

I PULL INTO OUR DRIVEWAY and am surprised to see Aunt Peggy's car. She's been so busy lately now that Epic Fail has been using Garrett's house as their recording studio. She complains about it a little, but I know she's secretly happy to be able to take care of all of them. My heart sinks when I think of Kai. I miss him so much.

"Sam, you're home," she says in her sing-song voice. "You look exhausted."

"Back-to-back shifts will do that," I say and sink into the living room couch.

"Kai started walking the other day," she exclaims, and I smile from ear to ear.

"Really? That's amazing." *I can't believe I missed it.*

"Max said he was table surfing like a pro and then just let go and kept going. He falls a lot, but it doesn't stop him. No way."

"Quiet at the house today?" I ask Peggy. She gives me a sideways look and knows I'm trying to fish for information.

"Garrett's at his lawyer's office today, and Max is home with Kai." Her face lights up and she continues, "You know, Garrett will be gone for a few hours. You should go over to the house and see Kai walk. I know he'd love to see you too."

I sigh. I haven't been back to the house since that day. The day that everything between us changed.

I kick off my Danskos and curl my legs underneath me. "I haven't slept in forty-eight hours. That's my priority right now." Cassie's words ring in my head and my aunt's expression elicits guilt.

You're punishing Kai.

I stand up and slide back into my shoes before I change my mind. I hear Peggy breathe a sigh of relief when I walk toward the front door. "Give Kai a kiss for me, okay?"

"Of course," I say and shut the door.

MAX IS SURPRISED TO SEE ME when he opens the front door. "Sam, how are you?" he asks. "It's been such a long time." He steps aside and I walk past him.

I look around the foyer and see recent pictures of Kai adorning the walls. The last time I saw him was a few weeks ago when I met him and Peggy for breakfast at the diner. "Peggy says he's walking," I say and strain my neck to see if he's in the kitchen. It's quiet in the house, so I assume he's asleep.

"He's like a bull in a china shop. Thank goodness your aunt baby-proofed this entire house because everything would be on its end otherwise." He shakes his head. "Kai's a piece of work."

"I bet he is." I smile.

"Would it be okay if I go upstairs and peek in on him?" I ask hopefully.

"I don't see why not." Max smiles and walks into the kitchen, unlocking a series of gates along the way.

I slowly climb the staircase and follow the soft pings of music coming from his room. I open the door and tip-toe in. My nose fills with his baby smells, and the soft scent of powder relaxes me. I feel at home in his room, and I slide out of my shoes so I can feel the thick carpet between my toes. The aromas and sounds begin to relax me. I reach the crib and peer in. He's on his back with his head turned to the side. His Dalmatian and my Googie are clasped in either hand. His breaths are even and peaceful, and I could stand here all day taking in all of his perfections. I back away and sink into the rocking chair. This chair was my bed for months, and I close my eyes, trying to feel the weight of Kai against my chest. While those times were heart-wrenching and difficult, I try to remember the moments when we bonded. His cries would fill this room and stab through my heart.

Tears come to my eyes as I realize how incredibly far Kai's progressed. How incredibly far *Garrett* has, too. I look over at the crib and watch the instruments spin slowly above him. That's when a large picture on the wall catches my eye. It's a close-up of Kai and me, our faces pressed against each other. Our smiles are huge. Two teeth peek out from his gums, and his mouth is wet with drool. His hands are on either side of my face, and he's about to plant a wet, slobbery kiss on me. I remember the exact day that picture was taken, but it seems like a distant memory.

I pull the blanket to my nose and inhale his scent.

Why did everything have to change?

My eyes become heavy and I allow myself to drift off to sleep.

"MA-MA! MA-MA!" I HEAR, and it feels like I'm dreaming. I open my eyes, and Kai is standing in his crib, squealing. "Mama!"

Garrett steps into view and walks over to the crib. I shake my head and wonder if I'm still asleep. "Hey, little guy, what are you saying?" Garrett asks as he lifts his son out of the crib. Kai's giggles fill the room, and he squirms out of Garrett's arms. As soon as his feet hit the carpet, he's running clumsily toward me in the chair.

He reaches me quickly and throws himself into my arms.

"Hey, Kai. I've missed you," I say and pull him against me. He's squirming in my lap and says again, "Ma-ma."

Garrett says quietly, "He's been saying that for the past few days. Every time he sees your picture or hears your name." He sits down on the bed and faces us.

"Really?" I ask, and Kai plants a wet kiss on my cheek.

"Yeah, I don't know where it came from." He scratches his head and smiles as he watches Kai and me together.

"Da-da?" he says and points toward Garrett.

Garrett smiles and waves to his son.

His face becomes softer and he says to me, "How have you been?" He shifts uncomfortably on the bed, and Kai wiggles out of my lap and runs to his toy box on the other end of the room. He pulls the top open and begins digging through it, looking for toys.

"I'm good," I say and begin to fold the blanket that was covering me. "I'm sorry, I didn't mean to fall asleep in here. I hadn't slept in almost two days, and as soon as I sat down, I was out. Force of habit I guess." I shrug my shoulders, and a smile spreads across his face.

"Seeing you in here just feels right," he says and leans back on the pile of pillows.

Kai runs across the room and drops a red ball in my lap. "Ball!" he says and waits for me to acknowledge.

"Yes, it is a ball. Thank you, Kai," I say, and he runs back to the toy box.

"I can't believe he's walking," I say, shaking my head. "And talking."

"Yeah, I can't believe it either. Time has flown by. He's getting too big, too fast," he says and watches Kai dart back to me with another toy.

"Ball!" Kai says and drops a stuffed pig in my lap.

I laugh and pretend to give the pig a kiss.

"Ball is his go-to word for everything." Garrett says and reaches out to high-five Kai as he once again runs to his toys. This time, he plops down and plays on his own.

"I can see that." I smile.

"Peggy says you've been busy with work."

"Yes, it's been a crazy few weeks. Lots of babies born, and unfortunately some of them need critical care." We have six babies in the NICU this week and once again, we're at capacity.

He nods his head and begins to look uncomfortable making small talk.

He reaches into his back pocket and pulls out a large folded stack of papers. "Here, I'd like you to review these when you get a chance."

He places the papers into my hand. Our fingers brush against each other and I almost don't let go. He does reluctantly and sits back on the bed.

"What's this?" I ask, unsure of what he placed in my hand.

"I met with my lawyer today to see what I could do about formalizing documents that allow you to take Kai whenever you want. It wasn't easy to do, but he drew up a few documents that say that you're an appointed guardian in my absence. I want him to be with you when I'm on the road."

I can't believe what I'm hearing, and I slowly unfold the documents. They look legal, and they're signed and notarized with raised seals and everything. "Why would you do this?" I ask, shaking my head.

"Because, there isn't anyone on this earth that I would trust more with my son than you. He loves you, Sam."

Kai loves me?

Kai giggles from the other side of the room and says "Mama" again. He looks at me and blows kisses to me. I pretend to swipe them out of the air and press them into my heart. He laughs and continues playing.

"Garrett, I—I don't know what to say."

"There's nothing to say. I know you'll take good care of him when I'm not here."

"I have a job; you know that, right?" I say.

"I'm fully aware of that," he says and nods his head. "Peggy and Max have agreed to help you as much as you need. I can email you our travel schedule tonight when I get the final list of dates from Dax."

I sink into the chair and tears fill my eyes again. "I've missed him so much." I sob into my hands and feel Garrett next to me almost immediately. His hands cover mine, and he slowly pulls them away from my face.

"Please don't cry," he begs. "I didn't do this to make you sad. It's just—I don't want anyone else with him but you. You've been with him since the first day he came into my house when I couldn't bear to be in the same room as him. You had enough strength for two. You made him who is he and I don't want him to be without you another day."

His words take my breath away and I stare into his eyes, unable to speak.

"In addition to allowing you full guardianship while I'm on the road, I've also named you as a true legal guardian. You can come and spend time with him whenever you want. Like you're one of his parents."

I don't understand why he would do this, but I throw my arms around his neck. "Why?" I whisper against the stubble on his cheek.

"You're his mother. You always have been," he says clearly and pulls me tight against him.

"Ma-ma!" Kai yells from his pile of toys, and he giggles again.

I start to laugh, and Garrett shakes with his own fits of laughter.

I reluctantly pull away from him, trying to compose myself. I wipe away the leftover tears from my face and take a deep breath.

"Thank you," Garrett says, backing away. Kai stands up and runs to his father, wrapping his hands around his legs tightly. "Da-da!" he exclaims.

He reaches down and picks up his son, kissing him on the cheek. "What do you think, buddy? Do you want to see Sam more?"

He claps his hands and smiles, pointing at me with his little fingers.

I don't know what I just agreed to, but I feel really good. Amazing even.

There's a knock on the door and Max enters hesitantly. "Sorry to interrupt this little reunion, but Kai's lunch is ready." Garrett puts Kai onto the floor, and he runs toward Max and offers his hand to his nanny. "Let's go, dude. We're about to have a mac and cheese party."

They leave the room, and Garrett sits on the edge of the bed. His eyes don't leave mine.

"I've missed you so much," he says, and his eyes glisten.

His words tear through my heart. There isn't a night that I go to sleep when I don't think about the night we made love. The night when we spoke the words I never thought I'd say to another person before. I was in love with him and it was deep.

I am in love with him.

But time has changed us. The actions of his father destroyed the life we had together and hardened my heart.

"I don't know how to ask for your forgiveness," he says, and he places his face into his hands.

"Why would I need to forgive *you*?" I ask. I'm confused by his sadness.

"My father took everything away from you, and I just don't know how to express my sorrow and beg for your forgiveness for a sin caused by a man I hardly even knew."

His words mean more to me than any lecture I could receive from my aunt or Cassie. He had no control over his father's actions any more than I had control over my parents being at home that day. Neither of us had any power to stop the tragedy that took place. We *both* lost family that day, no matter what type of people they were. My parents left their legacy in me, and I'm the person that I am today because of them. I've realized that although I miss them so much it hurts, they're still with me in the way that I live my life. I carry their gifts with me.

I look at the large picture of Kai and me on the wall and I smile.

"Thank *you*," I say to Garrett. "I don't know what I would be doing if your son hadn't saved my life a year ago. I may have spiraled out of control after Ben's death. Kai saved me and gave me purpose. He reminded me of all of the good that my parents instilled in me. You gave me that *gift*."

He shakes his head and smiles.

"God, I love you so much, Sam."

I reach out my hand and he grabs it, squeezing tight.

"I love you too," I say quietly, and he pulls me out of the chair and onto his lap.

He buries his head in my hair and kisses my neck. He stops after he inhales deeply and pulls away from me so he can look into my eyes. He swipes his thumb across my cheek as he cradles my face.

"Thank you for coming home," he says and lightly kisses my lips.

Home.

It's true that I've felt more at home here than any other place I've lived since my parents died.

I kiss him back and press my forehead against his.

"It feels good to be home."

CHAPTER 38

Sam
Present
Villanova, Pennsylvania
Age 25

"AWESOME!" GARRETT YELLS while Kai splashes in the pool. His swim instructor is helping him learn the survival technique that I learned so many years ago. Kai is expertly floating on his back and kicking his legs when he reaches the edge of the pool. He's able to grab hold and he's smiling, truly enjoying this game that we're playing with him.

I clap and splash my feet in the water. The swim instructor takes him to do another exercise and Garrett wades over to me. He grabs hold of my bare legs and threatens to pull me into the water. He kisses my knee and looks up at me.

"You should come in with us," he says and kisses my other knee. I remain seated on the pavement and swing my legs on either side of him.

"I'm good right where I am," I say. And I truly mean it. In every possible way.

The past several months have been hectic but amazing. Kai and I have spent almost every moment together when I'm not working, and Garrett is here as much as he can be. It's like we picked up right where we left off last year. I belong here, and I should never have left.

He stands up in front of me and water cascades down his chest and abs. He's stunning perfection, perfectly chiseled and lean. He wraps his wet arms around me and soaks me completely. My face is pressed into his chest and he's laughing. "Now you have to come in," he says and swiftly pulls me into the water with him, dunking me under.

I jump out of the water and swat at him. "Don't even think about it," he says and pulls me into him for a warm kiss.

Kai is giggling and playing in the shallow end of the pool when Garrett takes my hand and lies on his back in the water. He begins to float, and I do the same. We're both on our backs, our arms outstretched.

We float quietly and peacefully, listening to Kai's happy laughter echo throughout the pool house.

"Happy birthday," Garrett says and squeezes my hand.

"Happy birthday to you too," I say in return.

Things could not be more perfect.

I'M HOLDING KAI'S HAND as we walk through the lush green grass. Garrett lifts him in the air, and he squeals with delight. He loves when we walk and swing with him between us.

"Up, up and away!" Garrett says, and Kai swings higher.

We slow our pace and find the clearing in the lawn in front of us. I approach the headstone slowly and drop a white carnation in front of the grave. Kai runs over and picks up the flower that I dropped, and he hands it to me. "Here," he says, and I smile.

"It's okay, Kai. This flower belongs next to this stone," I say and guide his hand back down to the ground.

"Flower," he says and crushes it against his nose, inhaling deeply.

Garrett stands behind us, shifting uncomfortably on his feet. He doesn't say a word, and I don't expect him to.

I touch the headstone and say softly, "Thank you."

"Welcome," Kai says, giggling from the grass. He places the flower back and puts his hand next to mine.

Sadie Moore
April 1, 1991 – August 16, 2014

I turn to see Garrett's gaze focus on her name. He barely knew her, yet she gave him a tremendous gift of a son. Despite all of her problems, she did the right thing before she died. *She found Garrett.* Even though she was an addict, she knew what she had to do. She ensured that despite her sins, her son would have a chance at life. Garrett shakes his head and shoves his hands into his pockets. He walks a little closer and leans into my side, kissing me softly on my cheek.

"Let's go, Kai," I say and lower my hand. He takes hold, and I help pull him to his feet. We turn and walk back toward the SUV. I realize Garrett isn't next to me, and I see him touching the headstone with his head bowed, as if in prayer. He mouths a few words, but I'm out of earshot. I hope he's making his peace with the troubled woman who gave us Kai.

"Are you okay?" I call out to him.

He lifts his head and smiles, the sun shining behind him.

"I'm perfect," he says and jogs to meet us. He sweeps Kai off the ground and holds him in one arm while he throws the other around me.

"I love you," he says and kisses me tenderly on the lips.

My cell phone rings and I see Cassie's name pop up. I answer it, and she immediately starts babbling.

"We're all here. Where are you?" she asks.

"We're on our way," I say and hang up.

"Let's do this."

"CONGRATULATIONS!" THE JUDGE EXCLAIMS and taps his gavel on the bench. The crowd in the small room starts to applaud, and I kiss my son on the cheek.

"Ladies and gentlemen, may I present to you the Armstrongs." Whistles and cheers fill the room and Kai claps and giggles.

Judge Henson folds the documents and slides them into a folder. "Keep these someplace safe. We'll have duplicates on file with the registrar if you ever need them."

He hands the legal documents to Sam that have her name forever tied to Kai. She officially adopted him today, and the courts finalized it with a seal.

And just twenty minutes before this ceremony, the same judge married us.

I pull my wife and the mother of my child against my side and turn to greet our friends and family who have filled the judge's chambers completely.

Nicole, Kai's social worker, is in the back of the room wiping tears that are streaming down her face. She's been involved with us as we got this ball in motion to make the adoption official. Her ties to Sadie and her desire to see Kai live a wonderful life helped fuel our quest to make this legal.

"Are you ready, Mrs. Armstrong?" I say into Sam's ear. She smiles and nods her head.

"Let's celebrate," she says.

CARS LINE THE DRIVEWAY as we pull into our wedding reception, birthday party and adoption celebration. Everyone is here, and we enter the foyer to loud cheers and hugs. My mother takes Kai from my arms and kisses him all over his face. Bill pats me on the back and pulls me into him for a huge hug. He does the same with Sam, and we make our way through the crowd that's gathered.

The day is a whirlwind of fun and music. In true form, by the end of the night, we all have an instrument in our hands, and Epic Fail performs an acoustic set in our backyard. Alex and Heath take turns singing some of our biggest hits, and the crowd loves it.

Sam is glowing today and floats throughout the crowd. She and Tabby spend a good amount of time chatting over the kids. Noah shows Kai how to do a somersault, and they're both tumbling as their mother's watch.

Sam's friends, Cassie, Becky and Marcie, are huddled outside watching the guys do shots. I can tell that at least one of them has it bad for Heath. And he knows it too.

My parents are huddled with Peggy as they toast their white wine glasses. Peggy and my mom have really hit it off working together to plan today's festivities.

Presents are piled by the fireplace in the den, and Kai begins to bang on the boxes. In lieu of wedding or birthday gifts, we asked that people shower Kai with love. We'll celebrate this day every year as not only our wedding anniversary but as Kai's Adoption Day. He's officially spoiled beyond belief. He starts pounding on the youth drum set that Dax gave him and everyone covers their ears.

Sam catches my gaze from across the room and smiles. A smile that grabs my chest every single time. She's perfect in every way, and I vow to never let her go again.

THE CROWD IS GONE, and Kai is sound asleep in his room. He fell asleep in a pile of wrapping paper in the den, and Sam just came down the stairs after putting him to bed.

She walks over to me and kisses my neck. "Happy birthday, Mr. Armstrong."

"Happy birthday, Mrs. Armstrong." I turn her to face me and kiss her tenderly. We breathe each other's breaths and melt into each other's arms.

We release each other and look into the backyard. It's filled with tables and chairs, and a large tent is still standing in the corner of the yard. "What a whirlwind of a day, huh?" I ask her, and she nods.

"It was a wonderful day. One that I'll never forget." She smiles and fixes her gaze on the pool house.

The soft glow of lights from the bottom of the pool fills the entire pool house with dim lights. Steam rises from the water, and it looks magical. Four distinct flower arrangements float in the pool and cast large shadows in the water.

"What are those for?" I ask Sam, and she wipes a tear from her cheek.

"A bit of a memorial," she says softly, and I understand fully.

The arrangements that float represent the members of our family that couldn't be here today.

Two for her parents.

One for Sadie.

And one for my father.

The flowers all float together, crossing paths and riding the small ripples they each create. Together.

"I've forgiven him, Garrett," she whispers as tears fall down her cheeks. "I've forgiven *them*," she corrects herself. "Sadie didn't intend to cause harm to her son. She just didn't know any better. And I know that if your father could have made a different choice, he would have. I forgive them," she says again and wipes her tears away. "It's time that you did too."

I reach out and wipe her tears. She leans into my hand as I sweep the curls from her face. I kiss the tip of her nose and rest my forehead against hers.

"I already have—I forgave them the day I realized we'd be together forever."

The End

COMING SOON

EPIC

BESTSELLING AUTHOR
TRUDY STILES

LIES

EPIC FAIL SERIES

Standalone
Winter/Spring - 2016

NOTE TO MY READERS

If you or someone you know is pregnant and has a drug or alcohol problem, please seek help.

For more information about how to help yourself or a loved one, please visit one of these important websites or call the toll-free hotlines.

The Watershed Addiction Treatment Programs
www.thewatershed.com
1-855-771-3970

New Directions for Women
www.newdirectionsforwomen.org
800-939-6636

National Drug Help Hotline
800-662-4357

National Alcohol and Drug Dependence Hopeline
800-622-2255

Information on Neonatal Abstinence Syndrome:
www.nlm.nih.gov/medlineplus/ency/article/007313.htm

ACKNOWLEDGEMENTS

*may contain spoilers

Okay, so I know way too much about Neonatal Abstinence Syndrome (NAS). *Way too much.* This book came from a place that I was afraid to write about for so long. A time, after we adopted our son, that I wanted to forget. But also a time that I needed to remember for the rest of my life. A time that was painful while experiencing it but is now a distant memory.

Listening to your child cry and scream in pain is a heart-wrenching and gut-ripping feeling. Something my husband and I felt for exactly nine months. *Nine long months.* Although doctors *and* textbooks *and* Google all tell you that NAS can last anywhere from one week to six months after birth, our experience lasted a bit longer than that. Nine months. You hear your child's painful pleas for help through these cries as they can't tell you exactly what hurts, but you just know that it's everything. You rarely sleep, and when you do, you're holding your child tight, close to your chest so he can feel you and derive some sort of comfort from that. To feel protected. Safe. You're terrified that your child won't thrive because eating rips apart his insides. You worry that his condition will only get worse and he'll be in pain for his entire life. You worry that all of your efforts in helping him heal will take away from your other child, a baby girl, adopted just nine months before. My husband and I know very well what Neonatal Abstinence Syndrome is because we lived through it. We *conquered* it. We won. Our healthy son is eight years old now and is known for his huge heart and infectious smile. He's perfect, and looking back, I can say whole-heartedly that I would trade places with him in a second so he would never experience that kind of pain ever again.

I realize that we are so incredibly blessed because some babies aren't as lucky as our little guy. Some don't get better. Some live with debilitating illness and developmental delays. It can remain so bad for so many of these children exposed to drugs and alcohol. Our dude is lucky, and for that we are forever grateful. Our hearts are with so many other babies and children out there who struggle with the prolonged effects of NAS.

I must acknowledge and thank the adoption agency that matched us with our son's birth family. He completed our Forever Family. He saved our family as much as we saved him. He belongs with us and we are eternally grateful.

My husband's support during those difficult months gave me the strength to be what our son needed. It was a dark time in my brain, and I cried most days along with our son. My pain was emotional while his was physical. My husband was my rock and will always be. Thanking him is easy and his son loves him so much he tells him every single day. "Dada, I love you." Hearing that never gets old. I'm also thankful that our daughter was too young to remember those hard times. She and her brother are the best of friends and our Irish Twins. The most precious gifts we have ever received.

I wouldn't have been able to write this book without my family's support. My Forever Family and my book-world family.

Amanda Maxlyn: Two years ago, we met on Facebook and became fast friends. We published our first books close together, and the support you have given me has been unwavering. It's amazing to know that in this business I can place my full trust in you. Thank you for reading this book and providing your invaluable feedback. You know the personal struggles that I went through that inspired me to write about these special characters. You're amazing and I love you with all of my heart.

Dina Littner: Your honesty and nutty ideas drive me so crazy, but I love you for it HUGE. You know how to push my buttons and to make me think about how to present a scene or scenario. All in a good way. You make me a better writer and storyteller. Shhh—don't tell anyone. I love you huge and I'm honored to have you as friend and critique partner.

My BETA girls: As my books have evolved, so has my beta process. Thank you all for being there with me through it all. I will always value your opinions and feedback above all others. You know me best and hold me to the highest of standards.

Murphy Rae: You're a saint and a miracle worker. When I came to you to help refine the Forever Family Series, you jumped in head-first. You told me things that I didn't want to hear about my first book and then you helped make it better. You helped me distinguish between voices and you breathed life into pivotal characters in these books. I'm so proud of the words that I've bled onto these pages, and your feedback and expertise have given me confidence to continue with this hobby of mine. Stay true and honest and awesome. Thank you for helping me grow as a writer.

Elaine Hudson York: I'm truly in love with the incredible interior design for Epic Sins. It literally took my breath away when I saw it. You have been a pleasure to work with and your professionalism is top notch. Thank you so much and I look forward to working with you on the rest of this series and beyond!

Sarah Hansen: Thank you for putting up with me. I know I was a pain in the ass and kept changing my mind about the look that I wanted for this book and the series. I bugged you a lot and you probably blocked my messages for a while. But what you did with this cover! What you created is just amazing. You crafted the perfect brand for the Epic Fail series, and your artistic renditions inspired me to finally finish the first book and get my butt in gear. I'm humbled and honored to call myself a client of yours. You are truly a master and produce exceptional covers. I'm thrilled to brag about you and the art that you created for me. Thank you again and I hope you take my requests in the future.

Becca Manuel: Once again, your vision of my book is stunning. The trailer you created perfectly captures the tone and feelings of Epic Sins. You work magic with your art and I'm so lucky that you connect with my stories enough to produce pure perfection. Thank you.

Julie Deaton: Thank you for your fantastic proofreading services. You are a wonderful person and a true cheerleader for me and my work. Your finishing touches on my manuscript made it perfect.

Forever Family Facebook group: Thank you for letting me pop in and share my stories with all of you. You all know how much I enjoy our interaction, and this place has been my haven to share some of the struggles I've gone through as well. Thank you for being my safe place and for always supporting me.

Bloggers: I can't narrow it down and just talk about a handful of you because you ALL are amazing. Every time I release a book or run a promotion, it astounds me how supportive you all are. It truly brings a tear to my eyes every time I see one of you supporting me in the very best way—you tell your readers and supporters to buy my books. I love you all and I hope you continue to support me as I share more stories.

Authors: My peers are some of my best friends. It's so comforting to know that I have so many of you ready to give all of yourselves to help promote me and support me. I love all of you so much!

Readers: I humbly bow down to you and thank you for each and every time you've downloaded my books and recommended them to a friend. I can't continue to write these stories without you. Thank you.

ABOUT THE AUTHOR

Trudy Stiles is a New Adult author, mom to two beautiful children, and married to the love of her life. She's the author of the bestselling Forever Family series including "Dear Emily," "Dear Tabitha," and now "Dear Juliet." She plans to write many more stories about some of the characters you've already met, and maybe a few new ones. Epic Sins is the first of three, standalone, Epic Fail series books.

Trudy is a music junkie and you'll know that she's writing when you see her plugged into her laptop with her earbuds in. Her playlist is unique and is a must for her writing sprints.

When she's not writing, she's carting her children to their various activities while avoiding any kind of laundry or housework. She also loves to run along the boardwalk of the beautiful New Jersey shore.

She celebrates Wine Wednesday almost every day.

Email:authortrudystiles@gmail.com
Facebook: www.facebook.com/authortrudystiles
Goodreads: www.goodreads.com/trudy_stiles
Twitter: @trudystiles

www.ingramcontent.com/pod-product-compliance
Lightning Source LLC
Chambersburg PA
CBHW060851250626
47159CB00008B/2689